Also by Erynn Mar

a lauren holbrook novel book 4

e r y n n m a n g u m

MATCH MADE

Chapter One

By this point, I've gotten used to the mechanics of moving to a new town. I just still haven't gotten used to the exhaustion of everything. And not even necessarily the actual act of *moving* – packing up, labeling boxes and unpacking is a cinch after all these years. It's the finding new grocery stores, getting to know neighbors, a new church…that's the real pain of moving.

My dad was in the military my entire childhood and I think I just got used to being in a new zip code every two years. We'd move to a place, I'd finally figure out the blueprint of the school I was in, maybe learn my teacher's name and then we'd be off again. About the eighth grade I gave up on ever finding a good friend who could last more than a few months as a pen pal.

It sounds bad but it isn't so bad. I'm twenty-eight years old and this is just who I am. I'm a loner. I like coffee, breadsticks and sleeping in the middle of my queen-sized bed all by myself. I like organization and knowing what is coming next and after years of leaving people who promised to write me forever behind, I'm over it.

So, this new town is likely not going to be any different.

I can hardly remember the name of it, honestly. I just know I'm back in Colorado. I think I've lived in two different cities in this state for a total of three years back when I was a kid. It's a pretty state. Lots of pine.

I put the last plate in the dishwasher, turn it on and flatten the last box. Done. I'm officially moved in. Time to celebrate with a latte or something.

I think I saw a cute little coffeehouse driving to my new apartment, so I change from my old high school ratty T-shirt and jeans into shorts and a looser, three-quarter length shirt. It's warm outside.

I climb into my Nissan and start the engine and the air conditioner. It's a good car, if not a little boring.

Sort of like myself, I guess.

I backtrack down one of the main roads in town until I see the little, wood-carved sign hanging out front. There it is.

Merson's. There's a sign in the window that says something about being voted the best coffee in town.

Considering the size of this town, it's not much of a feat,

but it's a cute little store. There are a few cars out front and I park next to one and walk in, a tiny bell dinging over the door as I come inside.

The place smells amazing. There's a whole glass-encased wall of dessert after dessert in front of my face and I'm almost getting a caffeine high just from the smell of the freshly roasted coffee beans. A menu suspends from above the counter and there are sandwiches, salads, soups and about every drink I can imagine listed.

"Hi there." A tall, lanky guy in an apron, T-shirt, jeans and a backward baseball cap is standing there, wiping his hands on a towel before tossing it over his shoulder. "Can I help you?"

My mouth is salivating. "I'll start with a latte," I tell him.

"Sure thing." He turns and starts working by the espresso machine behind him and I sit down at a counter on a barstool and look around.

It's a little shop. A few tables, most that seat four or less. There are about six barstools next to me. Soft rock is playing over the speakers. A couple is sitting at a small table in the back corner, smiling sweet, loving smiles at each other over their coffees. Three high school age kids – two girls and a guy – are sitting at another table, books and binders spread out in front of them. An older man is on his laptop next to one of the tables by the window, soaking in the afternoon sun.

"And here you go," the man says, setting a very tall glass in front of me. The smell is straight from the Pearly Gates.

I take a sip and immediately close my eyes. At one point I added up all the different places I've lived over the years and I totaled it at nineteen. I've never tasted coffee like this ever before though.

"Wow," I say once I swallow. The man smiles a friendly smile and I notice a gold wedding band on his hand. Too bad, because a latte like that would have probably had me proposing if he had been ring-less. And that's saying a lot. Until I get a job that allows me to settle down a little more, I have no plans to start dating.

Long distance doesn't work.

I know that for a fact.

"You're new around here, aren't you?" the man asks, turning to clean the espresso machine as we talk.

I nod. "Just moved here yesterday, actually."

"Nice," the man grins again. "I'm Shawn Merson."

"Thus the name of the restaurant," I nod.

"Yeah, exactly. What's your name?"

"Anne McKay." I normally don't give out my full name to strangers, but there's something about this guy that just seems genuinely nice.

Of course, they say that most serial killers seem like the nicest guy you'll ever meet when you first start talking to them.

I ask him another question, if only to get my brain to change gears. "Did you grow up here?"

He shakes his head. "No, I moved here…oh, about ten years ago or so now. My family used to drive through here all the time on our way to my grandparents' house and I always thought it just seemed like a great place to live. So, I saved up the money and bought the store a few years after college." He shrugs. "I met my wife, Hallie, here and now we're pretty much set on staying here forever."

Even the idea of staying somewhere forever just seems abnormal.

The bell dings behind me and noise immediately fills the store. Shawn looks behind me and grins at the chaos. I follow his gaze.

A sandy brunette is standing there, holding the door open with her foot, ordering a blond, curly-haired boy about three years old into the store while muscling in a baby who is screaming his heart out in an infant car seat at the same time. "Let's go, buddy. Pick up the pace," the woman says. "Your brother weighs like ninety-two pounds."

I squint at the baby and I'm guessing him to be about four or five months, so there's no way he weighs that much but based on the way the woman is sweating, red-faced and disheveled, maybe he does.

The boy takes his sweet time walking in and waves shyly at Shawn with the hand that isn't clutching a ragged stuffed dog. "Hi Mr. Shawn," he says in about the cutest boy voice I've ever heard.

"Hey Cannon, how's it going, buddy?" Shawn asks, waving at the boy. Shawn goes around the counter and takes the car seat from the woman who sighs at him.

"Thanks. My arm is about to break off. I swear that kid grows four pounds a day."

Shawn sets the car seat on a table for four and then he and the boy drag another table for four over to it along with the chairs and the boy sits at the table in front of his brother, who is still screaming. The boy starts patting the baby's foot and yelling, "IT'S OKAY, BABY CORBIN! LULLABY AND GOODNIGHT..."

Meanwhile, the woman is scurrying around, handing the boy a coloring book and crayons, grabbing a pacifier for the baby while pulling the infant out of the car seat and swinging him back and forth, back and forth while hissing a loud "SHH" sound through her teeth repeatedly.

It's sort of like watching a three-person circus.

I never knew three such small people could make so much noise. The woman is shushing, the boy is still singing to himself and the baby is finally quieting. I see his eyelids flutter and a minute or two later, he's asleep.

The woman sighs and pats her older son's head. "Your friends will be here in just a minute, sweetie." She climbs up on the barstool next to me, carefully cradling the baby in her left arm. She tiredly brushes back her hair and smiles an exhausted smile at me.

"Hi. I'm Laurie Palmer. You're new around here, aren't you?"

Right away, I like this woman, despite the craziness

surrounding her. "Just moved to town. I'm Anne."

"Hey Anne. Sorry for the mess that is my life. I need caffeine, Shawn."

Shawn, back in his place behind the counter, grins at her. "No, Laurie."

"No, I mean, *really*. I really really *really* need it."

"Really."

"*Really*," Laurie annunciates. "Cannon was up from two-thirty in the morning until five with nightmares and he fell asleep right when Corbin woke up to eat. And then Ryan had to be at work at six and I was up late last night trying to get control of the four mountains of laundry that we've named since they've been sitting in our bedroom for so long. I got through Mount George before I passed out."

"George. As in the future king of England?"

"As in Curious. Please, Shawn. I'm begging you."

"You told me that even if you begged, I still had to say no," Shawn says and I get the feeling that this isn't the first time this woman has come in here asking for coffee recently. He pours a cup from the decaf pitcher and adds sugar and cream before passing the tan-colored coffee across the counter to her.

She glowers at him before finally sighing again and just drinking the decaf. She looks at me. "Tell you what, the biggest sacrifice I've ever made as a mother was giving up caffeine."

"You can't have caffeine as a mother?"

"It passes through breast milk."

My knowledge of breast milk is basically zilch, so I just hum a little and nod, sipping my latte.

Laurie looks over her shoulder at her older son, smiles slightly at the way he is coloring totally outside the lines and then turns back at me. "So. Annie. Can I call you Annie? When did you move here? And what brought you here?"

"Um, sure," I say, though, I've never actually been called Annie before. I'm not a nickname person. I was very specifically called Anne my entire life and I've never known anyone long enough for them to resort to a nickname.

Though, granted, I've only known this woman for about three minutes and she's doing it.

"I moved here yesterday, actually. I'm a consultant," I tell her and Shawn, who is wiping down the counter in front of us.

"Oh yeah? What kind?"

"Accounting." It's about the most boring job on the planet

and no one cares to hear too much about it. My firm gets a job from a company; I get the assignment from my firm, move there, fix the company's finances and then get the next assignment.

Usually, I stay for about a year. Sometimes two years. Sometimes six months.

I never really know. So I never really get connected. My mother always told me that there is nothing worse in life than getting plugged in somewhere only to be ripped away.

Maybe that's why she and my dad eventually split and she moved back to the small Oklahoma town she came from. She remarried the math teacher at the high school. They never left town.

Whatever the case, that was a big reason I stayed off in the distance. I didn't make a lot of friends, I didn't learn a lot of names. I tried to find the biggest church in town and sit in the back every week, slipping in and out of the doors without actually saying hello to anyone.

Though one of the reasons I did that was because of a rather unfortunate event that happened at a tiny Baptist church in Topeka, Kansas. There were only about fifty people in the entire church and they made all the visitors come to the little stage and introduce themselves in front of everyone.

Despite the twelve pounds of postcards I received from those people for the next year that I lived in Topeka, I never went back.

"That's really neat, Annie. So you must be great with numbers then, right?" The woman shakes her head at me. "I'm the worst. The *worst*. I can barely add single digit numbers. And now Ryan—" She waves her hand, "He's my husband. Anyway, he has it in his head that he wants to open up his own construction company and have me do the bookkeeping."

Shawn starts laughing and Laurie nods at him. "Right? I mean, I sort of want to dig out my old algebra homework and just let him take a nice long look at it."

"You shouldn't necessarily need algebra for just basic bookkeeping," I tell her. "In fact, they make some really good software that does pretty much everything you need to do. Would he be incorporating?"

"Incorporating what?"

"The business."

Laurie shakes her head. "I don't know. I don't know anything anymore other than when it's naptime or how many times this guy has filled his diaper. I am not fit to bookkeep a company. Can I get an amen?"

"Amen," Shawn says immediately.

"Thank you."

The bell dings over the door again and a very, very pregnant, beautiful blonde woman waddles in, holding the hand of a bleach blonde girl who looks about the same age as Laurie's oldest son. The woman is wearing a black maxi-dress and flip-flops and looks like she's about to melt.

"Hey all," she says. "Look, Nat, Cannon is here. Go sit with him." She parks her daughter next to the boy and then sits on the other side of me at the counter, huffing as she pulls herself up on the barstool. "Good lands, Shawn. Did your barstools grow?"

"Nope, but you definitely did."

"Thanks." Her tone is dry and she blows her breath out, rubbing her red cheeks. "Two more months," she groans.

She still had two months to go? I'm glad I kept my mouth shut. I was about to ask if she was late.

"Hannah, this is my friend, Annie," Laurie says from the other side of me.

"Hi," Hannah says, smiling nicely at me. "I'm Hannah

Knox. It's nice to meet you."

"Annie's new here. She just moved here yesterday and she's a consultant. She does accounting," Laurie says.

"Oh that's cool! Maybe she can keep the books for Ryan because goodness only knows you shouldn't do that."

"Someone needs to tell my husband this because he doesn't listen to me."

Hannah grins. "Though he really never has, so that doesn't shock me that much."

The door dings yet again and a red-haired lady walks in, a toddler I would guess to be a little younger than the other two at the table on her hip. "Hi honey!" she waves at Shawn and he goes around the counter, giving the woman a kiss.

"That's Shawn's wife, Hallie."

"And their daughter, Rachel."

"She's pregnant too," Hannah says. "Though she's the kind that doesn't even look it until she's like about to deliver." She sighs at her friend. "I mean look at her. I looked like that when I was six weeks along."

If I squint enough, I can kind of see a little bump on Hallie's midsection. I decide it's better to just smile rather than agree with Hannah. Hell hath no fury like a pregnant woman in the heat of late summer.

So I've been told, anyway.

"So you guys have a little playgroup here?" I ask the moms while Shawn talks with his wife and tickles his daughter who giggles joyfully at her daddy.

"Playgroup," Laurie says, swiping a long strand of hair behind her ear and rolling her eyes. "Playgroup is just another name for sanity check."

"Lifesaver," Hannah nods.

"We come here, the kids play at the table or color or whatever, Shawn feeds them macaroni and us desserts and coffee and then we all go home and take naps," Laurie says.

"Well, you take naps," Hannah says. "I stopped sleeping two months ago."

"I told you to try that body pillow like twelve times. Nobody listens to me!"

I listen to the two of them banter back and forth around me and then Hallie comes over, sits on the barstool by Laurie and joins the conversation, while Shawn throws in his two cents every few minutes. There are obviously years and years of friendship in

18

this room with me.

I've never in my life been jealous of a friendship until this moment right now. Which shocks me, really. I'm a loner. I always have been. I figured I always would be. It makes me lonely just thinking about it.

Time to go.

I set a few dollars on the counter and slide off the stool.

"Hey! Where are you going, Annie?" Laurie asks.

"Oh, I've got some more unpacking to do," I lie, mostly just to have a reason to let these women have their playgroup time without me intruding.

"Unpacking," Hallie waves a hand. "Unpacking can wait. You should stay! Shawn made his famous apple crisp!"

Laurie makes a face behind her hand to me. "Go with the cheesecake," she whispers.

"No, go with the lemon cream pie," Hannah says, sighing. "Oh it's amazing. Tart, creamy, cold…"

"You never used to like tart stuff until you got pregnant," Hallie says.

"It's because this baby is already having me practice puckering up so I can just kiss him more."

"It's a boy?" I ask.

Hannah shrugs. "Or girl. We haven't found out."

"It makes me crazy," Laurie says. "It's not like you're not going to find out. Just find out earlier, for goodness' sakes."

"We don't want to."

"So, Annie," Hallie says, breaking into the argument. "Tell us where you moved from."

"Tampa," I say.

"Well, that's a slightly different place than here," Shawn says. "You adjusting to the boringness okay? Though I guess you've only been here one day."

"Hey, our town isn't boring," Laurie defends. "We even got a drive-in movie theater last month!"

"Laurie, it only plays black and white movies."

"I happen to like old movies," Laurie says.

"They aren't old movies. They're brand new releases."

"So, the projector doesn't work right." Laurie shrugs. "I actually like it in black and white. It makes you use your imagination."

Shawn shakes his head.

"I really should go," I say, trying to leave again.

"Well, you have to come on Sunday. We all go to the same church and you would love it," Laurie declares. "It starts at nine." She tells me the name and the address and makes me write it down. "Nine o'clock," she says again. "I will be watching for you."

"Stop badgering the poor woman," Shawn says.

"And we are all going to come here after church for lunch," Laurie says. "So you have to come here too. It's great. The kids sit over there, the adults sit over there and we all have a great lunch and visit. Plus then you would get to meet our husbands."

"Well, she's met mine," Hallie grins.

"I really do need to go."

"Okay, Annie. One more question before you go," Laurie says. "Do you have a boyfriend or husband or anything? I noticed you aren't wearing a ring..."

"No Laurie," Hannah warns.

"Don't answer that. Better leave now, Annie," Hallie urges.

I shake my head at Laurie. "Nope. Just me." Always has been. Likely always will be.

Laurie grins even as the other three adults around me cover their faces and groan. "It was nice to meet you, Annie. I'm one hundred percent certain we will be in touch."

I wasn't but I just nodded. Despite her orders, I doubted I went to their church on Sunday. "Nice to meet all of you. Have a good afternoon." I walk out the door, climb in my car and I'm halfway down the street before I realize I have been holding my breath since I left.

Well. That was quite the encounter. My social quota is overflowing. I might need a good week or two of no human contact to recover.

Chapter Two

I start work the next day. I kind of like starting a new job. You get to find out new problems and figure out how to fix them.

I drive to the address listed on my smart phone and stop in front of it. I was technically hired by the city for this job. The local power company needs some help with their books and hiring and I'm the one to help, apparently.

"Miss McKay, it's a pleasure to meet you." A tallish, roundish, baldish man meets me by the front desk after the nondescript secretary buzzes him into the lobby. "We've been expecting you."

I smile politely and nod. I'm carrying my briefcase, I'm wearing my black pencil skirt, purple silky button down shirt tucked in and my black heels. It's my typical first day on the job outfit. Business-like, but not so much that people get scared of me.

"Mr. Phillips," I say. "Where should I set up?"

"First let me show you around so you get the feel of the

place," Mr. Phillips says and I nod again. "We like all our employees to feel like they can call this place home."

This is usually the sign that they've gotten themselves into trouble because the boss has a soft heart and keeps hiring people he can't afford to pay.

Great. That means layoffs. Which means I'm immediately the bad guy.

He leads me down a hallway past several offices with closed doors and then into a large room filled with cubicles. People wearing headsets turn in their whirly chairs to look at me as Mr. Phillips shows me down the long hallway, pointing out conference rooms and the copier and the break room and I try my best to just smile politely as everyone stares. "This is where we field all of the four hundred plus calls we receive on a daily basis," Mr. Phillips says proudly of the cubicle room. "It's also where we do the majority of our grunt work. These employees are the backbone of this city."

At this point, the secretary from the front desk appears. "And you've already met Mrs. Stoufferson," Mr. Phillips says. "She's got an office all set up for you."

The three of us walk down another long hallway lined

with more offices and finally to a tiny room at the very end of the hall. "This is where I've cleared the space for you to work," she says in a monotone, reaching into the room and flicking on a fluorescent light.

The room is small and dank and dark, even with the flickering light. There's no window and the only workspace is an old table and a folding chair.

I can feel future migraines forming.

"Oh no," Mr. Phillips bursts. "Oh no, no, no. No. This is not an office, Mrs. Stoufferson! This is a closet! No, Miss McKay needs to be in a room with a window, at the very least. I insist on it."

I'm grateful for his kindness, even if it's likely the reason I'm here in the first place.

Mrs. Stoufferson barely hides a glower as she backtracks us down the hall and finally lands on an office that has a window, a desk and an actual chair.

"Better," Mr. Phillips nods. "Better."

Mrs. Stoufferson leaves.

"Now. Miss McKay. You be sure to let one of us know if you need anything at all. I've already had an account set up for you. You'll find all the login information here. We are looking forward to working with you." He hands me a folder, smiles and leaves and I close the door behind him.

I hate the jobs that will likely require downsizing.

I sit down at the desk, pull out my laptop and start setting up my desk. My company estimated this job would take six months, so I do my best to make this office as comfortable as I can. I set my picture that I took three years ago of the sunrise over the Florida beach on one side of the desk, I pull out my business cards and the little fancy holder I splurged on for them a few years ago and set those out and I make a note in my agenda to get a plant.

There's something nice about not being the only living thing in the office.

Except for that one time when I was at a company in Houston and we discovered the building was infested with rats.

We won't go there. It took me weeks to not immediately take a shower every time I thought of it.

I open the folder that Mr. Phillips had left me and it says "Welcome Anne!" in big, handwritten letters across the top of the front page.

I'm so going to be downsizing here. I can feel it in my

bones. And so can Mr. Phillips apparently because he is being extra friendly. It's always the extra friendly bosses who know that their hiring habits are to blame. And it's always the cold employees who know their jobs are at stake.

I flip through the pages. Wi-fi information and passwords, how to access the hard drives which held all the books, how to edit the books and a list of the personnel at this office is included in the folder. In the back, someone took the time to list out the restaurants nearby, they even included some menus and there's an invitation to a company-wide picnic next Saturday.

A week and a half away.

I log onto the company wi-fi just fine but when I go to access the hard drives, it doesn't work. All I get is a blinking cursor and a "Not Authorized" window that pops up after several minutes.

I recheck the password I entered and try again. Again, it doesn't work.

Finally, I give up and find the personnel page in the folder, using the desk phone to dial Mrs. Stoufferson at the front desk.

"Yes." Her voice is curt and unfriendly.

"Hi, Mrs. Stoufferson, it's Anne McKay."

"I can see who is calling, Miss McKay."

"Oh. Okay, well, my computer connected fine to the internet but—"

"What's the problem, Miss McKay?" she interrupts.

I don't really foresee myself going out on lunch breaks with this woman to one of those nearby restaurants.

"It's not allowing me access to the hard drives."

"Someone will come assist you."

Then there's a click and the line goes dead.

All righty then.

I spend the next several minutes checking my email, making my to-do list, trying a few more dozen times to access the hard drive and finally, after about twenty minutes, someone opens my door.

"Hi, I'm having trouble getting access to the—"

"Hard drive. I heard." The man who comes in has to be related to the secretary. He looks nothing like her, but he's completely curt and unfriendly, similar to her.

Other than the boss of this place, no one is very nice here.

It's going to be a fantastic half-year.

I sigh. "Right." I stand from my chair and the man sits in it and starts clicking around authoritatively on my computer. He's squinting at the laptop behind curly hair that is in pretty desperate need of a haircut.

Perhaps two. It's about the shaggiest cut I've seen.

Maybe the seventies are back again.

I clear my throat while he clicks around. "So. How long have you worked here?" I ask, trying to be friendly.

I'm still a little worn out socially just from the encounter yesterday at Merson's, but there's no reason to be rude to this guy because of it.

Click. Click. He doesn't look away from the screen and finally I hear him mutter something but it's more a grunt than anything.

"I'm sorry. I didn't catch that."

"Four years."

"That's a good amount of time. You must like your job then. Though, honestly, I haven't met too many tech guys who didn't like their jobs."

Another grunt.

"Did you grow up here?"

Silence and then maybe a half-grunt.

So maybe he's got a weird past like I do. But still. There was no need to be rude about it.

I finally give up and just sit in one of the chairs on the other side of the desk and stare out the window. There's a view of the parking lot outside. It's the first of September and it is ridiculously hot outside. I'm wondering when it actually becomes fall around here.

I worked in Minnesota for a year a few years back. During that one year, I would have given my right arm to be anywhere warm, even if only for a week. I never felt like I truly thawed out until about a month after I moved from there.

"Done," Mumbling Man announces, throwing my chair back and standing. He's not tall and he's not short. He's just kind of there. With his hair.

Seriously. Someone needs to tell him he really needs a haircut.

Like yesterday.

"Thanks." I will not be that person. I'm only here for six months. Though, if his hair still looks like this in six months, maybe I'll leave a parting envelope with that advice inside. I sneak a quick look at his left hand and it's bare.

Well, there were two good reasons for that. The hair and the lack of a personality.

A thought stops me with a little twinge in my esophagus and makes me squinch up my lips.

What is *my* reason for still being single?

I take a quick look down at my outfit again. I dress cute. My hair is maybe a little straggly at the moment, but I've got good plans to schedule a haircut as soon as I can find someone to recommend a stylist, and "straggly" for me means my straight hair is a little past my shoulders instead of sitting right on them. For the life of me, I can't get any curl to stay in my hair regardless of how many different and expensive gels and mousses I use. But I wear makeup. And deodorant. And I floss.

Occasionally, anyway.

Mumbling Man is just looking at me now.

"What?" I ask, frowning at him.

"You didn't answer me."

"I didn't hear a question."

He clears his throat. "I said, did you need anything else?" He says this very loudly and it reverberates around the basically empty office.

Maybe Mumbling Man wants a new nickname.

"Nope. I'm good."

"Okay then." He walks out the door and I sit back in my chair.

This could be the longest six months of my entire life.

There are two things that are always top priority for me when I move to a new location: Finding a new grocery store and finding a new church. I usually have more luck with the latter than the former. For whatever reason, I have never found a grocery store that I am completely, one hundred percent happy with.

I'm a high maintenance shopper, apparently.

There's a little supermarket right by my apartment and I stop there on my way home from work. It was a long day with very little human interaction. Which was fine. But the coffee tasted terrible, the vent in my office squeaks like the rubber elephant my aunt's toy poodle likes to gnaw on, it was about sixty-five degrees in the office and my head is now pounding.

At one point I mentioned to a man in a tie and button

down shirt in the hallway on my way to the printer that it was a little cold and he got this panicky look on his face and hissed, "Don't say that! Mrs. Stoufferson might hear you!"

Obviously she's not just unkind to me.

I'm trying to give her the benefit of the doubt. Maybe she's menopausal. I've heard the horror stories about that particular stage of life.

I make a mental note to grab a jacket on my way out the door tomorrow.

I pull a grocery cart out from the lineup of carts by the door and start walking through the store. Every single grocery store I've ever been in is laid out differently. I don't have anywhere to be tonight, so I take my time, walking up and down the aisles and getting a feel for it.

It's organized weird and it's bugging me.

I'm only here for six months. I try to remind myself of that fact while I shove the irritation about the fridge sections being split in half by the seasonal stuff they sell in every grocery store.

I mean, does anyone *really* need a garden gnome holding a sunflower? Particularly when they are likely here trying to buy a gallon of milk?

When I first graduated from college and moved out from living with my three roommates, I had this totally idealistic version of what life on my own would look like. I was going to cook all these gourmet meals for myself, I was going to portion control and freeze, I was not going to spend every dinner in front of the television. I figured I'd be on my own for like maybe a year or two before I met someone, got married and started cooking for him.

I stop in front of the frozen Lean Cuisine section and sigh at it.

It's cheaper. That's the main reason I started eating these. And it just doesn't make sense for one person to cook all that food. I get sick of it before I finish it and then I end up throwing it out because it goes bad.

Which is really sad because I really do enjoy cooking.

Way more than I enjoy working most days.

Maybe I should have thought more seriously about culinary school when I was in high school, despite the constant nagging that it wasn't a "worthwhile" degree.

I pick out six different Lean Cuisines, three packaged salad mixes, a gallon of milk, a quart of orange juice and a half-gallon of Blue Bell Homemade Vanilla ice cream.

It's the essentials, I guess.

I'm sliding my card through the card reader at the checkout when I hear her behind me.

"Annie?"

I turn and the red-haired woman from Merson's is behind me in line. I'm totally spacing on her name.

"Hi!" I say, feeling really bad that I can't for the life of me remember it. "How are you?"

"Good thanks! Do you live around here?" She's got a cart full of fresh fruits and vegetables, pastas and kid yogurts. Her adorable daughter is sitting in the front seat, a pacifier bobbing up and down in her mouth. I look at her cart and my bags and a part of me just gets very sad at the differences.

Here's the thing. I never intended for life to turn out this way.

I am happy being alone. I am happy being alone.

The statement is getting old.

I nod to her question. "Yeah, just around the corner."

"Oh that's wonderful! I live just up the road! You'll have to come over for dinner one night this week."

I nod though I have absolutely zero intentions of going to her house for dinner. Not that I don't like her – she seems like a very nice person. She seems quieter and less bossy than her friend with the two boys and not as dramatic as her largely pregnant friend, but sometimes the thing about being alone is that I don't like to be reminded too often that I am alone.

Otherwise my whole self-mantra of being okay with it starts to fall apart.

"Where do you work, Annie?"

I tell her the name of the power company and she nods. "Oh okay! I know where that is. That's not too far of a commute for you, then!"

I start gathering my plastic bags filled with premade food and the girl smiles at the cashier. "Good morning, Helen," she says.

"Hallie! How are you, honey? And good grief, little Rachel just gets more precious every day! How are you feeling?"

Hallie rubs her slightly rounded tummy and I remember that she's pregnant. "Okay. Still a little sick in the morning but okay."

I am starting to walk away when Hallie calls out. "How

about six o'clock next Tuesday night?"

I realize she's talking to me and I stop. "I'm sorry?"

"Dinner? My place? Six o'clock next Tuesday night. Shawn has to close at the shop so it will just be me and Rachel and I would really like the company. Can I get a piece of scrap paper from you, Helen?"

The cashier rips off a blank receipt and hands it to her.

"Here's my address," Hallie says and hands the paper to me. She smiles and tiredly flicks her red hair behind one ear. "See you then, Annie."

So maybe the less bossy part was wrong.

Chapter Three

A week goes by quickly. For whatever reason, my morning routine wound up being a little quicker than normal and I had a little extra time. I pick up Merson's to go on my way to work that next Tuesday morning.

I walk into the store and the smell of baking cookies hits me. The place is crowded this morning. There's only one empty table and it's crammed in the corner behind a huge group of older men who are all loudly debating something, Bibles open in front of them. A few tables with women, some college-aged kids studying and then a table or two with a single person reading the paper with their coffee make up the rest of the restaurant.

Shawn has a hopping place today. Even the counter seating is full.

"Hey there, Annie," Shawn grins at me from behind the counter as he slides a cup of coffee to a balding man sitting in the first seat by the register. Shawn is wearing jeans and flannel shirt unbuttoned over a dark gray T-shirt. And there's a towel over his shoulder again.

Maybe he uses the towel like some people use an apron.

"Hi Shawn."

"Heard you were coming over to the house for dinner tonight," Shawn grins and I nod.

"Yeah." I'm thankful he said something because I had nearly already forgotten.

"Great. Hallie is so excited."

Now I'm getting nervous. It will be just me, Hallie and her daughter to my knowledge and that's a lot of pressure to be under. What if I'm boring? What if I don't live up to whatever she's excited about?

Maybe I feel a cold coming on. Surely I will develop a sniffle before then.

"Yeah. Um. Me too," I say.

"It's good for her. I know she gets lonely on the nights when I close here. And as much as she likes the other girls, it's hard to ask them to leave their families or invite herself over there, you know?"

I nod though I have zero experience with this.

"What can I get for you this morning?"

"A latte, please. To go."

"Coming right up." He goes to the back counter and starts making my drink, whistling. He comes back with it and a pot of coffee a minute later and I hand him a five-dollar bill as he starts refilling the people's coffee that are sitting at the counter. "Hang on a second, I'll get your change."

I shrug and pop a lid on the cup. "No worries. Thanks Shawn."

"See you later, Annie."

I walk out and I realize that this is the first time in my life that I'm actually a known customer at a coffee shop. I usually go for the big name chains where the baristas change in and out like air fresheners in a high school locker room.

It's nice. And different. But mostly nice.

I get to work and wave a Mrs. Stoufferson as I walk in. "Good morning, Mrs. Stoufferson. How was your evening last night?"

My grandmother always used to tell me that you can catch more flies with honey than with vinegar. Granted, it took me most of my life before I totally understood that saying but I am going to be overly nice to Mrs. Stoufferson whether she likes it or not.

Mostly because I have beheld the power of an administrative assistant in an office environment. You don't want to mess with those people.

I go down the hallway to my office. Apparently, I am here a little early. Most of the cubicles I am passing are empty and the few people I am seeing are either staring blankly at their computers or tiredly putting their stuff away on their desks, sliding lunch boxes into their drawers and pulling on their jackets because it's again like sixty degrees in here.

It might be a slow, cold day.

I've been pounding away on my keyboard for about three hours, going over the printouts I'd done the day before with a highlighter when I hear a knock on my door as it opens.

"Annie McKay!"

I look up and it's the loud girl from Merson's the other day. Laurie. I think. I'm immediately confused, mostly because I'm at work and I also don't remember telling her where I was working.

"Uh, hi," I say, trying to instill some joy into my tone though I'm mentally going through our conversation the other day.

"Hallie told me you worked here," Lauren says, offhandedly. She walks into my office like she's been by to visit me a hundred times.

"Oh did she?" I ask, pushing back a little from my desk. I'm not sure if I should stay sitting or stand or offer to get her a chair or what I'm supposed to do.

"Yeah, so on certain days, I drop the boys at a Mom's Day Out thing at our church, so I have from eight in the morning until one in the afternoon free from kids," she says.

"That's nice," I say.

"It honestly is. I mean, here's the thing. I love those boys more than midgets love to limbo, but there are days where I just want to punch a clock and leave, you know?"

I'm nodding, though I'm more wondering if it's politically correct to say the word *midget*. I thought it was "little person" now, but I'm pretty sure all of my knowledge of this is based on TLC shows.

She nods at me. "So. I brought lunch."

All of a sudden, I notice the grease-speckled brown paper sack in her hands. I'd planned on either picking something up or just getting by on my Clif bar that was in my desk.

"Wow. That's so great of you. You definitely didn't have to—"

She shrugs and cuts me off. "I wanted to. I have a good feeling about you, Annie. I think we are going to be good friends."

Part of me hopes she's right, part of me is just overwhelmed. People don't do this kind of stuff – at least not that I've ever experienced. Apparently some of the people in this town are just extra friendly.

Those people just don't work here.

I go out in the hallway and find another desk chair in the closet that Mrs. Stoufferson originally tried to convince me was my office and roll it back to my desk. Once I get back there, Laurie's got the contents of the bag spread across the desk and it smells like greasy potatoes throughout my office.

"Burgers from Bud's," she grins. "Best and worst food for you in town."

I believe her. But I'm suddenly starving so I sit down and Laurie clutches her hands together and bows her head. "Lord, thanks for the food. May it not clog our arteries or make Corbin extra gassy tonight. May you bless Annie and her work and this new friendship. Amen."

I like how she prays. She prays exactly how she talks. Nothing fancy, no fake prayer voice like some people put on.

"So," she says, unwrapping the grease-stained paper off her burger. "How is work so far?"

I shrug. "It's fine."

"Made lots of friends?"

I shake my head. "This office is a little weird."

"You're telling me. You have to be freezing in the morning and burning up in the afternoon with the way the windows are facing."

"Well, there's that, but I meant more the *people* in this office are weird."

"It's the power company," Laurie says, shrugging and eating a fry. "They get yelled at all day by people like me whose microwaves suddenly fritz out thanks to hundred year old wiring in their homes right when their two kids are apparently dying of starvation. I wouldn't be friendly either."

I smile. "How long have you been married?"

"Almost seven years. Ryan is a patient man." She grins at me and then smushes her lips together. "Well, actually, not really but he's at least used to me by this point."

"What does he do?"

"He started off working for a construction company in town and now he's the foreman there. But he really wants to start his own business."

"Would he be able to take over at the company he's at?"

Laurie shakes her head. "I don't think so. His boss is pretty attached to it and Ryan is getting to the point where he wants to be making his own decisions about stuff."

"How old is your oldest?"

"Cannon is three and Corbin is five months." Laurie gets that lovey smile that most mothers get when they talk about their children. "Cannon was kind of a surprise. We were actually debating whether or not we even wanted kids."

"Really?"

She nods. "I'm not the world's most natural mother, you know? I mean, I like to know what's happening and I like to be able to plan things but I also like to be really spontaneous and randomly decide at ten o'clock at night that I want ice cream and a cup of coffee."

I nod though I have no idea what she is talking about. I

guess I always have the ability to go get ice cream at ten o'clock at night but then, I've more than likely gotten in my pajamas and brushed my teeth and there's no way I'm eating something after I've already brushed my teeth.

Laurie takes a bite and swallows before she keeps talking. "So, anyway, we found out we were pregnant with Cannon and all of a sudden everything changed and now I really love it and honestly, we still go get ice cream at ten o'clock, only one of us goes and gets it and brings it back while the other stays home since the kids have been in bed for like two and a half hours by then."

She finishes her burger and wads up the paper, tossing it in the big bag. "So. Tell me about yourself. Do you have a dog? Where does your family live? Where did you grow up?"

Lots of questions. "Um. Okay. No to the dog." I hate dogs, but I'm not going to tell her that. And cats too, honestly. I just am not a pet person. "My mom and her husband live in Oklahoma. My dad is in Pennsylvania." I think. I'm not totally sure, now that I think about it. I haven't talked to him in over a year. Last I heard, he was getting transferred to Pittsburgh for a two year stint and he was hoping to spend most of his weekends bumming around the historical sites up in that part of the country. He forgot my birthday again this last year but after twenty-eight years of wondering if he was going to remember, I've mostly given up.

That was my dad though. Loved our country's history but couldn't remember his family's history.

"And I pretty much just grew up in the USA," I tell her.

"No specific town?" she asks.

"Every specific town," I say. "We moved a lot."

"Wow. Military?"

I nod.

Laurie shakes her head. "That's so amazing. I mean, think of how much of this country you've seen! I've spent my entire life in this town and sometimes I would just get very travel sick to go see *something*. Ryan and I traveled a little bit before the boys came and we actually went a few places with Cannon but it's a pain in the neck to travel with babies now."

I look at the woman in front of me and realize that there really is a lot of truth to the saying about the grass being greener on the other side of the fence. Eight years ago, I was totally, one hundred percent ready and waiting to get married and jump headlong into wedding bliss.

The only problem was no one was there to marry.

I'm twenty-eight years old and I've never been in a real relationship. I've never kissed anyone, I've never had those tingly feelings about anyone and the couple of dates I've been on have been with real duds that the occasional coworker or fellow church attender has tried to set me up with.

I used to wish so bad that I had Laurie's life. Friends, family, husband, kids.

And here she is telling me she's envious of my ability to go anywhere.

"I mean..." She stops and leans forward, pushing her hair behind her ears before clasping her hands in front of her. "Here's the thing, Annie. I love my boys. *Love* them. I absolutely adore my husband and I can't imagine life without my babies." Her gray eyes get serious. "But sometimes, late at night, after the eightieth load of laundry that day and after I've gotten spit up on right after my shower and I have the *Sesame Street* theme song stuck in my head, I just find myself wishing for..."

"More," I say the word with her quietly.

"Right," Laurie says.

It's refreshing to be around someone so honest after years of surface relationships.

"Me too," I confess quietly.

"You have the *Sesame Street* theme stuck in your head now too?"

I smile. "No, but..." I wave my hands, trying to find the words. "I work all the time. I mean, *all* the time. I work at the office, I go home to my empty apartment and I have nothing else to do, so I work some more. I don't have friends because I move every six months and my family is a mess and sometimes I just feel really, really..." I sigh. "Alone."

Laurie looks at me for a long moment, eyes studying me so hard that I get the eerie feeling that she's looking straight into my soul.

Finally she nods.

"Well," she says, straightening. "I can't help the family situation, but I can help the workaholic and friendless situations."

I smile. "That's kind of you, Laurie, but in six months, I'll just be gone again." I shrug. "It stinks but it really is easier to not have to cut ties twice a year. And really, I complain, but I honestly like being by myself."

I like being alone. I like being alone.

Maybe if I repeat it enough, it will be true.

Laurie looks at me with her all-seeing eyes again. "It would be easier if that were really the truth, huh?"

Laurie leaves a few minutes later after the hamburgers have been devoured and the grease has been sopped up. I close my office door after her, sit in my chair and let out my breath.

I have dinner plans with Hallie tonight. And Sunday night, Laurie's already got me coming over for a barbecue with Hannah and her husband at Laurie's house.

"That way you can meet the better halves," she grinned as she left.

I shake my mouse to get the screen saver to leave and just stare at the numbers on the screen.

Chapter **Four**

I ring the doorbell at exactly six o'clock.

Then I immediately regret my actions and lunge for the doorbell like I could stop it but then I hit it *again*.

What if the baby is asleep?

Arg.

I'm hitting my forehead on my fist.

"Annie?"

Hallie is standing in the doorway, giving me an odd look. "Are you okay?"

"I'm so sorry, I did *not* mean to ring the doorbell. And then twice! I'm so sorry. Is your daughter sleeping? Did I wake her up?"

Hallie starts laughing. "Oh Annie, you are funny. No, she's not sleeping. And really, you could have hit the house with a bulldozer and this girl wouldn't have woken up. She sleeps deeper than an Olympic high diver can dive."

I smile at the analogy and step into the little house.

It's adorable.

"It's not much, but we call it home," Hallie says, closing the door behind me.

I'm standing in the living room and from there I can see the entire kitchen and the hallway leading to the bedrooms. The floors are a dark hardwood and the walls are all a steel gray.

Hallie's daughter – I still can't remember her name – is staring at me from a weird little seat that Hallie has up on the kitchen table, pacifier bobbing in her mouth.

"Come in, come in," Hallie says. "We're having soup and bread. Nothing super fancy." She leads me into the kitchen. She's wearing leggings and a lightweight long sleeve shirt with a super long hem and socks. If I squint, I can barely see some roundness to her midsection.

She looks as adorable as her house.

I wore a cotton skirt and a tank top because when I pulled up to her house it said ninety degrees on the dash in my car. And because I figured that a skirt can be both dressy and casual.

Not as casual as leggings and a tunic though.

I'm immediately freezing because her house is like sixty

degrees. If that.

"Soup sounds great," I say, trying to hide the shivers. I'm wondering if I still have a sweater in my car.

Hallie would get along great with Mrs. Stoufferson temperature-wise.

"How was your day?" she asks me, pulling two bowls down from one of the kitchen cabinets. Her daughter is still just staring at me.

"It was fine." Other than Laurie for lunch, I didn't speak to anyone. I told someone in the hallway hello and they barely mumbled their response, hurrying past me.

The people in this town are not overly friendly.

Except for the group I randomly ran into at Merson's.

"How was your day?" I ask her.

"Oh fine," Hallie says, offhandedly. "I didn't feel super well most of the day, so I took a nap when Rachel laid down. That seemed to help. I'm a lot more nauseous this time around than I ever was with Ray-Ray."

I smile at the nickname. "Maybe it's a boy?" I offer, though I don't have the first clue about morning sickness and it's relation to gender.

"Maybe," Hallie says with a little smile, hand on her stomach. "That would be different. We'll find out in a couple of weeks."

"Have you guys thought about names?"

She nods. "If it's a girl, I like Ashlynn but I'm still trying to get Shawn warmed up to the idea. Do me a favor and just mention it casually next time you go to the shop so he sees it's a real name. Shawn's all about the boring, non-creative names."

"Thus Rachel?"

"Exactly. With her, I was campaigning hard for Linley. Obviously you can tell who won the battle."

I smile. "And if it's a boy?"

"Shawn wants to name him Troy."

"That's cute."

She nods. "I actually like that one. It's like the only name we've ever agreed on. Cheese?" she asks, waving me over to look at the soup. "It's sort of like a potato soup."

"Sure," I say.

She sprinkles some shredded cheddar cheese on the tops of our bowls and carries them to the table. There's already a basket with a towel-wrapped blob in it in front of Rachel's weird little rubber seat, along with a tub of butter and a small container of sour cream next to it.

"Let me pray real quick," she says, sitting at the table and ducking her head. "Lord, please bless this soup and may it not make me sick and may it help our bodies to flourish. Please help Rachel to sleep tonight and please just bless my friend Annie in all she does. Amen."

I look up, touched by the word *friend*.

"So," Hallie says, reaching for the bread. "Tell me about the place you work. Do you like it?"

"Not really," I tell her honestly. "People aren't very friendly in this town, are they?"

She shrugs. "You have both types here. You have the weird small town people who just assume that everyone here is their newest best friend and leave their doors unlocked and sit out on their front porches at night...um, that would be us and then you've got the type who are just really secluded and like to keep to themselves." She shrugs. "You get used to it. Once you get plugged into a church, it's not half bad."

I nod.

"You've moved a lot though, right?"

"Constantly."

"What has been your favorite place that you've lived?"

No one has ever asked me this before. I butter a slice of bread that looks homemade and think.

"Probably the Northern California coast," I say finally. "I worked right outside of San Francisco a few years back. It was great. Every weekend I was off exploring somewhere along the coast or in the city."

Hallie smiles at me. "That sounds really nice."

"It was." I was twenty-four and life was totally open to me. I had a great paying job, so I could do whatever I wanted, I was completely happy to just be alone and do my own thing and I loved not being accountable to anyone but Jesus. Nine times out of ten, I just grabbed my Bible and a latte first thing Saturday morning and I would just drive until I found someplace that looked interesting. I'd stop and read and hike around and buy weird food from roadside shacks and it was perfect.

I wouldn't trade those years for anything.

We talk about Hallie's past for awhile, about the new baby coming and about their plans to stay here for the long haul.

"I don't know," Hallie says, putting our empty bowls in

the sink. "It just fits, you know? I mean, Shawn's shop is here, he's got a great customer base, we love our church and it's a great place to raise kids."

I nod.

"So I was craving brownies, so you are going to have to stay and help me eat some of these," she says, pulling a square Pyrex pan off the stove. She unpeels the plastic wrap off of it and the smell of chocolate immediately fills the entire kitchen. She even frosted the brownies, which totally makes or breaks a brownie for me.

"Wow," I say. "So Shawn isn't the only baker in the family, huh?"

She shrugs and smiles. "I used to work at Merson's. I learned a thing or two."

"Is that how you met?"

She grins at me. "No, actually, my friend Laurie introduced us. She kind of set us up."

I think about Laurie and nod. "I could see that."

"Oh friend," Hallie says, pulling a spatula out of a drawer and sitting back down at the table. "You have no idea."

I smile. "Well, it apparently worked. You guys seem pretty

happy."

"Oh, we're very happy. But Laurie went through a period there where every person in the world was being set up with someone or another." She grins. "I was just thankful when she married Ryan and they started remodeling their house. It gave her something else to focus on."

"So that's why you guys were all warning me to leave Merson's the day I met you all," I say.

"Exactly." Hallie cuts a very generous brownie and sets it on a napkin in front of me. "Especially if you are only going to be here for six months, it's a lot of emotional manipulation for a short term relationship." She shakes her head, setting a brownie in front of herself. "And I for one do not believe in long distance relationships."

"No?" The only people I know who say this have all had a long distance relationship end badly.

"No way. I dated a guy long distance for the first year and a half of college and it was hands down the *worst* experience of my life and I really felt like I missed out on a lot of opportunities I could have had because I was tied to the phone every night."

See. Told you.

I nod. "I've heard a lot of people say that before." Mostly from people whom I've met at different workplaces or churches who somehow feel like they can speak into my life without knowing me at all and they have told me that the reason I'm not married is because of one of the following problems:

1. I am constantly moving and if I want to be married, I'm going to have to settle down first. Like I should just plop myself into some town without knowing if there's even someone there who I could potentially be interested in.

2. My hair is too long. Men like short hair.

3. My hair is too short. Men like long hair.

4. My clothes are either not feminine enough, too overly feminine, too revealing, not revealing enough or outdated though I bought them yesterday.

5. I haven't prayed enough.

And my all-time favorite:

6. Obviously there is some sin in my life that I haven't fully confessed or haven't dealt with because why else would God be withholding this wonderful thing from me?

Part of me wants to tell these people that I really am, honest to goodness, most of the time, *very* content to be single.

And the times when I'm not, well, God and I work on that issue between the two of us.

Hallie is looking at me, chewing her brownie. "Annie," she says suddenly, interrupting my silent frustrated fit.

"Yeah?"

"I'm going to tell you something and I'm not even sure why I'm saying it but I really just feel like I need to say this to you, okay?"

I nod, bracing myself for one of the six reasons. At least I'm at Hallie's house. It's a lot easier to make an excuse and leave from someone else's house than to try and come up with reasons to kick them out of your own place.

"You've got nothing to worry about."

I look at her, trying not to let the mental body armor go, waiting for the sucker punch that's coming. But she's just calmly eating her brownie, tickling Rachel's toes and making a silly, squinty-eyed face at the baby, like she's totally finished her thought for me.

"What?" I say finally, letting only my right arm relax so I can pretend to be calmly eating my brownie as well.

She shrugs. "I just thought you needed to hear that. You

really have nothing to worry about."

"What do you mean?"

She shrugs again. "I honestly have no idea. I just really felt like I was supposed to tell you that. Though, really, how can you be worried when we are sitting here all full on soup and homemade bread eating brownies?"

She grins and her eyelashes squint up all cute and baby Rachel giggles and I lick the frosting off my thumb completely agreeing with someone's take on my life for the first time in I can't even remember how long.

Sunday morning, I wake up to my alarm clock and I turn it off, rolling over in bed and just staring at the ceiling.

Whelp.

I am always super unmotivated to try new churches.

Super. Unmotivated.

Not only do I have the lovely prospect of sitting in a completely unfamiliar church all by myself, but I also get the fun of learning brand new songs, figuring out a brand new layout and trying to see into the future on what that particular church's dress code is.

For years I struck out on that last one. I was either way underdressed or *way* overdressed. After experiencing both, I think I'd rather be underdressed than overdressed. At least you can blame the casual wear on not having a chance to take stuff to the dry cleaners, as I lied to one woman in suit-and-tie church in St. Louis.

I actually don't know if dry cleaners even still exist.

Mostly because I refuse to buy clothing if it says "Dry Clean Only" on the tag. A shirt that says that might as well say "Be Prepared To Donate Me After You Forget To Not Throw Me Into The Laundry Hamper And You Wash Me With All Your Other Clothes".

Anyway, now I have my outfit that I even call my "trying a new church" outfit. Cotton skirt, flats, tank top and a cardigan. It covers all the church bases.

I stare at the ceiling in my bed and close my eyes.

I don't want to go, Lord.

I'm so tired of spending three months finding a church I like to just move three months later. And I never get involved.

Why get involved when you are just going to leave?

I sigh at the ceiling and push myself out of bed.

Maybe if my parents had done that move a little more often, I wouldn't be in the place that I am right now.

Okay, that was a bad thought. Sorry Lord.

Obviously whatever happened with my parents happened for a reason. That's what I meant to think.

I take a shower, blow dry my hair, pull on my church outfit and go for the natural look in my makeup. It's somewhat amusing that the natural look takes me twenty minutes to complete.

I go into the kitchen, make myself a thermos of coffee and pick up my Bible off the sofa.

I finally finished getting the apartment totally done yesterday and now everything feels like it's in the right place. I hate feeling like a stranger in my own home.

I drive to the church. Find a parking space. Sit in the parking lot and grip the steering wheel while I stare out the front windshield.

It's smaller than I hoped it would be.

In order for my plan to work, I have to be in a church that

is big. But maybe this town doesn't have anything bigger. It's not a big town.

I blow my breath out, chug my coffee, find a mint in the glove compartment and step out of the car, steeling my resolve.

I've got two feet inside the door when I hear her.

"Oh Annie, you *came*?"

I look over and Laurie is pushing her way through the crowded foyer, a grin six feet across on her face. "Oh I am so glad!"

I'm already going to her house for dinner tonight. I might as well make it a day filled with the Laurie gang.

Right?

"Honey! Honey, look who came!" Laurie starts yelling, grabbing my elbow and dragging me across the packed room. People all over are staring at me.

And maybe I should have just gone to that other church down the street. My entire life goal to this point has been to sneak in and out of churches like some sort of Nondenominational Ninja. I'm the queen of sliding into the last row right as the music begins, lip-syncing the hymns so as not to call attention to my terrible voice and saying the most vague things about myself as possible during the meet-and-greet part of church that every pastor likes to make the congregation do.

"Turn to the person next to you and tell them good morning!"

One pastor at a church I tried for a few weeks had a little conversation topic for you every week. One week he told us to turn to the person around us and ask them to come up with the most creative pet's name.

I never went back after that week.

Laurie yanks me over to an especially clogged area right by a long counter filled with about a dozen huge thermoses of coffee, hot water, tea bags and stainless steel containers of cream. A few trays of cookies and donuts are out and three older women wearing plastic gloves hurriedly replace the donuts and cookies as people walk by and grab them.

I recognize the curly-haired blond boy first. He's wearing jeans and a button down shirt over a white T-shirt and he looks like a miniature version of the man he's standing next to. Jeans. Flannel shirt. White undershirt showing at the collar. Curly hair, though the man has darker hair than the boy. He's got a light stubble over his chin and he smiling nicely at me, hands full of adorable baby boy.

"Look!" Laurie says again. "She came! This is my friend Annie McKay!"

The man smiles again, brown eyes crinkling at the corners. "Nice to meet you, Annie. I've heard a lot about you. I'm Ryan Palmer."

I don't bother attempting to shake his hand since he's holding the baby. "Nice to meet you too," I nod.

"Oh, I'm so so glad you're here! Does this mean you're coming to lunch? You should *totally* come to lunch! We always go to Merson's for lunch and I just think you should definitely come. And dinner tonight, of course. Did I ask if you were allergic to anything? We're just having burgers and hot dogs, so I figured those were pretty safe." Laurie is chattering happily as she mindlessly helps her son get a donut, wipes up the crumbs with a napkin and fills a cup of coffee, handing it black to her husband and then fixing a tan-colored cup for herself.

I don't know what question to answer first.

Ryan is smiling at me. "Don't worry, you get used to her," he says quietly to me.

Someone calls Laurie's name and she turns to chat with them for a moment.

"Where does she get her energy?" I ask aloud to Ryan.

He shrugs. "For years I thought it was the vats of caffeine she drank every day but she's been on decaf for awhile now because of the boys and other than about two weeks from a region south of heaven, if you know what I mean, it hasn't really affected her that much," Ryan says, shaking his head as he looks at his wife. He gets a sweet smile on his face as he watches her. "She's very fun though." He sips his coffee, being careful to keep the cup away from the baby who is eyeing it curiously.

I stand there, feeling awkward. I never know what to say to other women's husbands. Or just men in general, I guess.

Maybe it's because I never had any brothers.

"Hey." A good-looking, dark-haired man comes up and stands next to Ryan, holding the hand of a little girl who looks familiar.

"Hi Brandon. Have you met Annie McKay?" Ryan asks.

Brandon shakes his head and then looks at me. "No, but I've heard about you. I'm Hannah's husband. I guess you met her at Merson's?"

Hannah. The beautiful, very pregnant one.

I think.

Brandon is holding his hand out to me and I shake it, nodding. "Hi."

"Hey," he says again.

Then we all just kind of stand there. I'm biting my lip, trying to think of something to say that isn't boring or pointless.

"So," Brandon says, saving me from having to come up with the topic myself. "I hear you're in finances?"

I nod. "Kind of." Now is the part of the conversation where people usually ask me to do something financially-related for them for free. The only person I've ever met who sort of related to this was a few years ago when I met a woman who was a nurse. She told me that every time someone found out what she did, they immediately wanted her to look at their sick child, ask her opinion on some new diet or get her to examine their weird mole.

Brandon nods. "That's cool. So, I don't know if the girls told you, but I own a photography studio and Ryan here is in construction."

I nod, smiling that I might not to be called on for free advice. It's lame to work on Sundays.

"I did hear that."

Laurie is back from her other conversation. "Sorry about

that, Annie. I needed to talk with Mrs. Bowden about the shower I'm helping her give for Hannah. Hey, Brandon. You haven't changed your mind about finding out the gender, have you? It would really make my job easier with this shower."

"Yeah. Sorry kid. Not happening."

Laurie sighs. "I hate neutral colors in baby showers."

"And I hate deli mustard but you don't hear me complaining," Brandon says.

"You're surprised either way," Laurie continues. "You're just delaying the inevitable!"

Brandon shrugs. "Take it up with the wife, Nutsy. My role as the husband of a pregnant woman is to agree with everything she says and then give her a backrub at the end of the day."

I wonder about the nickname, but I don't ask. Laurie gets distracted with the kids and their donut mess.

Ryan grins at Brandon. "How's that working for you?"

"We've had Raisin Bran Crunch for the last seven dinners and my hands are getting sore."

The beautiful Hannah appears then, waddling over in a yet another maxi dress. I sort of get the feeling that she doesn't wear too much else right now. She gives Brandon a look. "Really?

I'm fifty-seven weeks pregnant with your gigantic, heavy and hard-kicking child and you're complaining about your hands?" She keeps waddling past, rolling her eyes. "We're going to be late for church."

Ryan and Brandon watch her go.

"Hmm," Ryan says.

"Yep."

"About that time, isn't it?"

"Dear Lord, I hope so."

I try and fail to hide a grin. The men are funny.

The guys take the kids to the children's church and Laurie materializes beside me as I'm getting a bulletin from the overly-smiley man right outside the doors to the sanctuary.

"Good morning, good morning, good morning," he says, sounding like an old CD that keeps skipping.

"Hey Fred. Thanks," Laurie says, smiling brightly at him.

"Good morning," he smiles at her.

She leads me into the large room. The lights are somewhat dimmed, the chairs are filling up quickly and a band is taking their places on the big stage up front.

"We usually sit over here," Laurie says, pointing to a long

row near the front.

"Okay."

I follow her into the row and she starts counting spaces. "Want to sit by me?" she asks me, grinning.

"Uh, sure." I sort of feel like I'm back in the third grade. I'm half waiting for a friendship bracelet from her.

Hannah comes over slowly, one hand under her stomach, one hand on the small of her back. "I swear," she mumbles, plopping down in the seat right by the aisle. "If I pee any more times a day, I'm going to just get stuck in that position until this kid just finally comes."

"That position isn't a bad one for delivery," Laurie says off-handedly. She waves to someone behind me and I feel a slight nudge on my shoulder.

"Good morning, Annie." It's Hallie and Shawn.

"Hi," I smile.

They make their way into the row.

I sit between Hallie and Laurie. A warm feeling is building in my chest and the moment the lead guitar player strikes a chord, it blossoms until it fills my whole ribcage.

It's corny, especially considering I've spent so much of my

adult life running from this, but I really do feel for the first time in forever like I have *friends*.

The guitar guy adjusts his microphone and then leans into it, strumming his guitar. "Why don't we all stand and sing?" he asks.

"No way, Jose," Hannah mutters from the other side of Laurie.

Hallie elbows me lightly. "You'll have to stick around until after the baby's born," she whispers. "Hannah is a lot nicer when she's not pregnant."

I grin.

Laurie elbows me on the other side, harder than Hallie did. "What do you think so far?" she hisses in my ear.

"Laurie! The song hasn't even started yet!" Hallie whispers across me.

"So! The atmosphere then!"

"Shut up or there will be no chocolate mousse pie after lunch," Shawn warns in a low whisper.

Laurie is immediately quiet.

I can feel my grin growing.

The guitar guy nods to the bass player and they start

singing a hymn that's been redone to be all fast-paced and cool. I did not grow up in the church but when I first started going in college, one of the Bible studies I went to sung only hymns.

So, I'm even sort of familiar with the song.

We sing three songs and then a pastor comes up to the stage, does a couple of announcements and then we sing two more songs. Then a different pastor comes up and tells everyone to sit down.

I feel like we skipped the awkward "greet the people around you" time.

I pull my Bible onto my lap and open to the chapter he tells us to in Psalms.

I rub my hand over the pages in my Bible. I love the Psalms. You can tell because the pages look bruised since they are covered in purple and blue highlighters.

"We're in the middle of a series that is going through a few selected Psalms before we begin our new series on the book of 1 Thessalonians next month," he says.

My preference is always to go through the books of the Bible rather than doing a topical series, so it's good to hear that this is what this church does. I've been at so many churches though that honestly, as long as they are preaching Jesus, I don't really care what the style is.

The pastor talks for an hour about Psalm 91 and how God is a protection for us and what that meant to Israel and what that means for us. I find myself scribbling notes furiously in the bulletin and in the margins of my Bible.

The pastor prays and the band gets up to play again. "Let's sing another song, shall we?" the guy says.

We sing another song, pray again and then we are dismissed to have a wonderful Sunday. The church starts vibrating with the sounds of chatting, laughing and there's some background music playing softly over the speakers.

"So?" Laurie says, grinning all hopefully at me.

I smile at her. "I liked it."

"Liked? Or loved?"

"Sheesh, Laur, she's only been here once! Let the woman mull it over," Shawn says.

She rolls her eyes and then leans close to me. "Better question: What did you think of our band?" She gestures to the people milling around on stage, packing away instruments and circling up the microphone cords.

—

74

I nod. "They're really good."

"And our worship pastor is really fantastic."

"Laurie," Hallie sing-songs.

"What?" Laurie asks, gray eyes widening innocently. "He is!"

"Hey guys." A very pretty blond woman holding a coffee thermos comes down the row in front of us, a nice-looking man in a button-down shirt and tie behind her.

"Hi Lexi. Hi Nate."

"Hey Lex," Laurie says. "Hey, I have someone I want you to meet. This is Annie McKay. She's new in town."

Lexi smiles at me. "Hi Annie. I'm Laurie's older sister."

"Hi." There is no way I will ever remember everyone's name.

"Lexi, good. You're just in time to stop Laurie," Hallie says, rolling her eyes.

"What's she up to now?"

"Nothing!" Laurie insists. "I was just asking Annie if she liked the service and that is all."

Lexi shrugs and takes a sip from her thermos. "Sounds like a good question to me. What did you think of the service? Are you a Christian?"

I smile at the bluntness. I can see the family resemblance between these two. "Yes, I am. I liked it."

"Good." Lexi nods and then shrugs at Hallie. "No biggie. So what's the plan, peeps?"

"Same old, same old," Ryan says, shaking Nate's hand. "I'm going to go get the boys."

Nate is smiling sadly at Hannah.

Hannah just nods at him. "Don't ask."

"Wasn't going to."

Apparently it is common knowledge that she is a terrible pregnant person.

"Well, we're going to head that way," Shawn says, taking Hallie's hand. "You're coming to lunch, right?" He directs the question to me.

"Oh! Um, yeah...I guess so..."

"Of course she is," Laurie says. "Why would she not?"

"Laurie."

"Do you need a ride?" she asks me, ignoring Brandon.

"No, thank you, I drove here," I say.

"Okay. Well, you can follow us if you want." She looks at

Brandon and rolls her eyes. "Or not, or not," she says dramatically.

I smile.

Shawn and Hallie leave and Brandon is right after them to go get their daughter from childcare. Hannah finally pushes herself out of the chair and waddles down the aisle, pausing to talk to a few people along the way. Laurie goes to give an older woman a hug and Lexi waves at her.

"That's our stepmom," Lexi tells me, since it's suddenly just me, Lexi and her husband standing there.

I can't remember his name.

"Nate," he says loudly, holding his hand out to me.

And apparently he can read minds.

"Annie." I shake his hand and return the smile. "Do you guys do lunch at Merson's on Sundays too?"

"We don't do lunch there every week but when we do go, my whole family is there," Lexi nods. "My older sister and her family will be there too. She has five children though it will seem like about twenty. Her husband is Brandon's brother."

My brain is hurting trying to keep everyone straight. "Brandon is Hannah's husband," I clarify.

"Right." Nate nods and grins. "You'll get used to it."

It appears that I've been adopted.

I sort of like the feeling.

"Hey Nate." The lead guitar guy comes up behind Nate and Lexi and claps Nate on the shoulder.

"Hey! How's it going?" Nate's voice carries across the room. Lexi grins at the man.

"Hey Zach."

Come to think of it, Lexi's voice is a little louder than normal too.

These two are quite the pair. I shouldn't judge. Maybe they are both slightly hard of hearing.

"Have you met Annie McKay?" Nate asks, turning slightly so as to include me in the conversation right as I was about to do the polite wave thing and leave.

"No." The man's face splits in a friendly smile as he reaches for my hand. "Hi Annie. It's nice to meet you. Are you new here?"

"First time is today," I nod.

"Wow. Well, it's really great to meet you!" He is bursting with happy friendliness like he belongs on a PBS Kids' show.

"Likewise," I nod. Too many people, too many names.

I need some strong coffee when I get to Merson's.

"Hi Zach!" Laurie suddenly materializes beside me and grins cheekily at the music pastor. "How are you? Did you meet Annie? Do you have lunch plans?" She doesn't allow him time to answer.

"Well, I—"

"Great!" Laurie declares. "We're all going to Merson's."

"Well, that's—"

"We'll just see you over there in a few minutes."

"Okay but I—"

"See you then!" Laurie waves and heads out the doors.

Nate, Lexi and I all look at each other and then at Zach who nods.

"Well. It appears I will be joining you all for lunch."

"So it seems," Lexi says, sipping her coffee. "So it seems."

Chapter Five

I pull into the Merson's parking lot a few minutes later and take a deep breath, hanging onto the steering wheel.

I wouldn't necessarily call myself an introvert but at things like this, I always leave fairly convinced that I am.

I get out of the car, straighten my skirt and walk up the front door.

There are already about twenty people here. And the only people I recognize are Lexi, Nate, Hallie and Shawn.

"Hi Annie," Shawn grins at me, walking past with a tray full of bowls of macaroni and cheese. "I thought you might have chickened out and gone home."

"The thought crossed my mind," I confess.

"You might should have listened to it." He's got a backwards baseball cap over his hair and his sleeves are rolled up, his dishtowel in place. "Here we go guys!" he hollers to a table full of loud kids of all ages. "Round one is up!"

An older couple comes up and introduces themselves to me as Laurie's parents right as a dark blond woman and a tall man come over and told me they were Laurie's oldest sister and brother-in-law. They point out their children but I can't keep them straight. Especially since there are two sets of twins.

Brandon and Hannah show up with their daughter. Another couple who I think were named Nick and Ruby show up with three kids, ranging from about three to probably seven years old. Laurie and Ryan come with their two boys, the baby is bawling at the top of his lungs. Two of the boys at one of the tables, who look identical and about nine or so, are arguing over which superhero is the best, two smaller children are singing loudly as they color in coloring books, a young teen girl is somehow reading at the table in the middle of the chaos.

This is just one family?

Lexi comes over and stands next to me, holding a huge mug of steaming coffee. "You look a little like a deer in the headlights," she tells me, taking a sip.

I watch everyone trying to corral their children, the grandparents assisting, the men bantering as the women chatter with each other and just shake my head. "You guys have a big family."

"We tend to add people as we go, which doesn't help," Lexi nods. "Caffeine is a good assistant in times like these." She holds up her cup.

"Are any of these kids yours?"

She sips her coffee and then smiles one of those smiles that isn't really a smile, sadness touching her eyes. "No," she says, drawing the word out as she takes a breath. "We tried for about six years to have a baby and just were never able to."

Oh.

I don't know what to say. It's one thing to want a family when you don't have the means to the family – like a husband, for example. It's another thing to want a family and have all the building blocks for it and nothing happens.

"I'm really sorry."

She nods. "Thank you. It was six years of frustration, sadness and honestly, being really mad at the Lord but we've spent the last year letting go of a lot of dreams and actually, we just submitted our application to the state to be foster parents." She shrugs like it's no big deal but I can see the excitement in her eyes. "We'll see what happens."

I barely know this woman yet I know her enough to say what I say next. "You and Nate would be amazing foster parents."

"Thanks Annie. We'll see."

The older man starts clapping his hands really loud, trying to get everyone's attention and finally Lexi lets off a piercing whistle that leaves a ringing sound in my left ear.

Everyone quiets down.

"Let's pray," the man says over the ringing in my ear. "Lord, thanks for bringing us here today, thank you for Shawn's cooking and the family and friends. Jesus, we pray for our safety against the germs in this room and especially the diseases outside and we just pray your protection over the dear ones we love. Amen."

I get the feeling that Mr. Holbrook might be something of a germaphobe.

Feeling is exchanged for fact. He goes around the room, squirting a huge glob of antibacterial hand sanitizer in everyone's hands.

I rub the gel in and look at Lexi, who waves her hands to dry them and then picks her cup back off the table she set it on like her dad does this every time she sees him.

And likely, he does.

"So I think Shawn is making French dip," she says.

My mouth starts watering. "That sounds amazing."

"Yeah. We have a good thing going with him. He usually will try out new menu items on us on Sunday lunch day." She sips her coffee. "We all kind of pitch in for ingredients but Shawn is the master chef. Don't tell Adam I said that. He thinks he's the king of the grill, but he burns my hamburgers every time. Word of the wise, if you want yours with a little pink tonight, you need to tell Adam that you want it mooing."

The door opens behind us and Zach walks in. He surveys the insanity and turns to me and Lexi.

"What did you guys do? Invite the block?"

"Yep," Lexi nods. "You know it."

Zach grins.

"Zach!" Laurie yells, coming over, baby on her hip. "You made it!"

"It didn't sound like I had much of a choice," he says. He starts rolling up the sleeves on his arms to his elbows.

I wish all men knew how much women like it when they roll their sleeves up to their elbows.

Laurie grins. "I guess that's true. Hey, we saved you guys seats."

"Great," Lexi says. "I always get stuck at the kid table and I'm sick and tired of telling Jess that Spider-Man is obviously the best."

"He is not!"

The kid has to have superhero hearing to have heard his aunt over the noise level in here.

Laurie rolls her eyes. "Not you, Lexi. Zach and Annie. I've got seats saved for the new people. You're always here. Find your own seat."

Lexi sighs. "Here we go again. Dude," she says loudly, spreading her hands to her nephew. "The guy could shoot *webs* out of his *arms*. I mean, if that doesn't automatically launch you to the top of the pack, I don't know what does."

She leaves and sits beside her nephews and I sort of get the feeling that as much as she complains, Lexi would much prefer to sit at the kid table anyway. The boys are flipping over each other to get her attention and she is laughing and knuckling their blond heads.

She really is going to be a great foster mom.

Laurie leads Zach and I over to a bunch of tables that have all been pushed together to make one big table. "Why don't you guys sit there?" she says, pointing to a couple of seats near one end.

We sit obediently.

Shawn is rushing around, setting out food and drinks and making trips back and forth with the coffee pot. Somehow I get a big cup of coffee poured in front of me and Hallie comes around with Rachel in a front pack, setting out napkins and utensils and coffee fixings.

"This is craziness," Zach mutters.

Somehow I catch what he says. "Amen."

He grins at me. "So. How did you…"

It's hard to hear him over the noise, so I have to duck my head a little closer. "I'm sorry what?"

"I said, how did you get dragged into this chaos?" He's basically yelling in my ear and my ear immediately goes back to ringing.

I wince.

He grimaces. "Sorry about that."

"It's really loud in here."

Zach waves at Shawn as he comes back with the coffee.

"Need a refill?" Shawn yells happily over the din.

"How much longer for the food, Shawn?"

"Mm...ten minutes? Fifteen?"

"Great." Zach stands and motions for me to follow him. We walk outside totally unnoticed by the crowd.

The second the door closes and the silence of the outdoors surrounds us, we both exhale.

I grin. "Hi. I'm Annie McKay. I'm an only child and I don't have any extended family. And I live alone."

He shakes my outstretched hand. "I'm Zach Murphy. I have one older sister who is a librarian. And my parents raised us to be seen and not heard. I always got in trouble for breaking that rule, but at least we had the rule in place."

I smile.

Both of us just stand quietly for a minute and while there are times that silence can be awkward, it's actually a wonderful break. The sun is shining, there are birds twittering in a tree nearby and the slightest possible coolness is in the air, promising that fall is coming soon.

I take a deep breath.

This really is a pretty little town.

I will be sad to leave it.

Best to not focus on that right now.

Zach smiles at me. "So Annie. I heard you are working at the power company."

I nod. "It's a temporary assignment. I work for a company who hires me out to fix the finances if a company is in financial trouble."

"Wow. That's a big job."

I nod, rubbing my cheek. "And it usually involves some not fun moments with some of the staff." I hate the assignments that require downsizing the company.

"Yeah. That sounds rough."

"You're the music pastor?"

He nods. "Going on three years."

"What did you do before that?"

"I lived in Austin. I worked part time at a church as the music leader and part time at Starbucks." He shrugs. "I was ready to use my seminary degree and have a full time job and an actual home. You know, with benefits and a dishwasher and all those grown up things." He smiles at me. "So, I saw the listing for the job, interviewed and moved here."

"This weather is a lot better than the weather in Austin."

He nods. "It's definitely a lot cooler."

The noise level goes up. "There you guys are." Lexi pokes her head out the door. "Shawn's serving lunch. If you want any, you'd better come in." She closes the door again.

I look at Zach and we both take a deep breath. "Well. Let's do it," I tell him.

"Ready for it?" Zach grins at me.

"I hope so." I open the door.

Most everyone is sitting now, full plates with shredded beef sandwiches and little dishes of beef juice to dip them in front of them. On the counter, Shawn has all the serving dishes lined up. Beef, potato salad and some fruit.

It's a feast considering most of my meals are out of a packaged salad bag. I look at all the work Shawn did and how exhausted he looks as he hands me a plate and I smile nicely.

"This looks amazing. Thank you for letting me come."

He smiles back. "You're welcome."

"If you ever need any help cooking, please let me know," I say, pulling a bun out of the package.

"Like to cook?" Shawn asks me, handing Zach a plate.

I nod. "I don't do it often. There's not a lot of reason to cook for just one person."

He grins. "That's why I opened a restaurant."

I fill my plate and go sit in the spot Laurie had picked out for me. The table conversation is overflowing with good-hearted banter, movie quotes and political debates. I watch everything quietly, eating my food and noticing the personalities at play.

Laurie and Lexi, who is back from the kid table for the discussion, are the loudest, arguing passionately for whatever they are currently talking about and they also, despite the passion, seem to have the least stake in the conversation. Nate is a close second.

I remember one of the secretaries at a job I worked a few years ago telling me that the boss could argue over how quickly ice melted and it seems like this family has a lot of those people in it.

The older couple seem content to just listen, smile at each other, hold the babies and play with the kids. Every so often, the grandfather will frown at something one of his daughters said and offer his two worried cents, but he mostly stays out of it.

Brandon and Ryan are sitting beside each other and they spend most of lunch muttering sarcastic comments back and forth to each other and then grinning at their wives. Hannah looks miserable and does a lot of complaining. Laurie's oldest sister is the voice of reason. Nick and Ruby offer bits of advice and a few dashes of argument here and there between taking care of their kids.

And Zach joins in like he's with this family every day.

"I just don't see what the big deal is," he says cheerfully, stabbing his potato salad with his plastic fork.

It's like he knows this is going to cause an explosion.

And it does.

"Seriously?" Lexi yelps.

"You have *got* to be kidding," Laurie says, rolling her eyes. "It's a huge deal!"

"Huge," Lexi nods.

"Why?" Zach says, goading them. "Tell me why *Pride and Prejudice* is such a big deal that we have to have thirteen different film adaptations of it."

"Dangerous territory, dude," Brandon says, shaking his head.

"First of all," Laurie says, taking a deep breath. "There aren't thirteen different movies."

"Maybe ten," Lexi says.

"Maybe nine," Hallie says, joining in on the conversation.

"And second of all, it's a huge deal because obviously it's like the greatest love story in the whole history of the modern world," Laurie says.

"Way better than anything else," Lexi nods.

Hallie shrugs. "Except for maybe *Emma*."

Zach rolls his eyes. "It's only popular because it is about the British and they have cool accents and they wear interesting clothes because of the time period. That's it. There are so many better, more interesting, more well-written books out there that should have had ten different movies made from them."

"Getting on thin ice there, man," Ryan says, warning lacing his tone.

"Like what?" I ask Zach.

"What?"

"What book should have had more adaptations?"

"I don't know. *Tom Sawyer*."

"*Tom Sawyer*?!" Laurie bursts. "Seriously? Over *Pride and*

Prejudice? Have you even read *Pride and Prejudice?*"

"Yes."

"It's only the great love story. *Ever,*" Laurie says, slapping her hand on the table for emphasis which then wakes up her youngest son who was somehow sleeping through this debate in his daddy's arms.

The baby starts crying and Laurie takes him, shushing him while gently patting his bottom. "Sorry, baby boy. Mommy got caught up talking to the dumb man."

"Hey!" Zach says. "I'm not the one watching the same story in fifteen different versions and getting all worked up for every single one!"

"And there's the crack in the ice," Ryan sighs.

All of the women at the table flip out.

"And down he goes," Brandon mutters.

Ryan nods. "Into the deep, dark abyss."

"Where there is only darkness, more darkness and those creepy, bloated looking fish with the weird noses," Brandon says.

Ryan starts laughing.

Laurie finally finds her voice. "I mean, I don't even know what else you could want in quality literature," she says. "It's got a great plot, fantastic characters…"

"A great setting," Lexi adds.

"Danger."

"Intrigue."

"Lots of humor."

"A crazy mom."

"Mr. Darcy."

"Mr. Darcy." Lexi, her stepmother and Hannah all sigh.

"Am I right or am I right?" Laurie looks at me, still lightly patting her son's bottom. "What do you think, Annie?"

I shrug. "I don't know, guys."

"Ah-ha!" Zach yells, pumping his fist in the air. "A supporter!"

"I definitely do not think we need ten movies about Tom Sawyer," I tell him, silencing his seated victory dance.

"So let the new friend talk," Shawn says, finally getting to sit down and relax at the table. "What is your favorite film adaptation?"

Thirteen pairs of eyes turn to look at me.

I shrug, feeling my cheeks flame a little to suddenly be the center of attention. "I don't know," I stutter. "Probably *Anne of*

Green Gables."

"*Anne!*" All of the women at the table start nodding, agreeing, murmuring and sighing.

"Gilbert," Hannah says, smiling for the first time since I've seen her today. "Ah, sweet Gilbert."

"Dear goodness, here we go again," Brandon says, rubbing his temples.

"Good going, Annie. This train won't stop until we all leave," Nate says but he grins at me.

"Did you like it because of your name?" Hallie asks me.

"What do you mean?"

"You have the same name. Anne and Anne."

I shrug again. "Maybe that's part of it. I really just liked the characterization. You sort of feel like you know the people when you're done reading the books and the movies did a good job of keeping to that."

Hannah is nodding. "Plus. There's Gilbert."

"Gilbert." Everyone is sighing again over the hero of *Anne.*

"I do love him so," Hallie nods.

"What is it about these guys that make women so crazy over them?" Zach asks, shaking his head.

"You can tell he's single," Brandon says to Ryan. "I stopped asking that question on my second week of marriage."

Ryan laughs.

Laurie's stepmom starts in. She has a soft, sweet voice and she weaves her fingers together on the table as she speaks. The whole atmosphere of the room changes when she talks. Her presence is just very calming.

I don't know what happened to Laurie's biological mother, but this woman is quite possibly the perfect mom for this crazy family.

"Zachary," she says and everyone quiets to listen to her, even the baby who was still making noise. "If I may?"

"Of course, Joan," Zach nods.

Joan. That was her name!

Joan nods at him. "I think that the best way to describe the fascination that the women in this room have with these characters is to think of the way you feel about your favorite sports team."

"The Yankees?"

"Exactly," she nods again. "To us, the Yankees are just that. A baseball team and, likely, nothing else but that. But to you, they are a source of entertainment, they bring many moments of joy and interesting ideas to your life and you probably feel that your life is enriched more for quote-unquote 'knowing' this baseball team. Am I right?"

He shrugs, seeing where she's going with this, and smiles. "I guess so."

"It's the same thing with the literary characters we are discussing. I remember as a young girl laying on my bed reading *Pride and Prejudice* and *Anne of Green Gables* and feeling like the characters therein where some of my dearest friends when I closed the book."

I smile at Joan. "Exactly."

"And for me, it was precisely that," she continues. "I didn't have the childhood that most of you at this table had. I moved quite often and because of that, I spent a good amount of time being either schooled at home or going to a new school and meeting new people very frequently. The books were my one source of constant friends."

Laurie's dad takes Joan's hand and smiles at her.

Everyone else, still under the calming vibe of Joan's voice are all nodding.

I am immediately wanting to pull her aside to talk to her

about her childhood since it sounds so much like mine.

Zach grins. "All right. You win."

Joan smiles cheekily at him. "Oh, I know I did, dear."

He laughs.

Chapter Six

We clear the table of lunch plates and the parents of the smaller kids pack up to head home for naps. Everyone else exchanged goodbyes since it will be a whole four hours until they see each other again at Laurie's house for the barbecue.

Seriously. These people spend longer saying goodbye to each other for an afternoon than my own mother says to me when she likely won't see me for over a year, if not more.

It sounds like some of them weren't going to make it tonight. I'm fervently hoping it's the people whose names I remember who are coming.

I wave at everyone and assure Laurie that I really am coming tonight before ducking into my car and driving the couple of minutes to my apartment. I park in my assigned parking, walk up the cement steps, unlock the front door, close and lock the door behind me and then collapse on the couch.

Wow.

I have not had this much social interaction in years.

Decades.

Maybe ever.

I roll to my back and look up at the ceiling. Everyone was so nice today. I never felt left out or like an outsider even though all of the people at lunch had obviously been friends for years and years.

And it was starting over again tonight.

By the time I go to work tomorrow, I will have spent more time with these people than with ninety percent of the people I've worked with over the years.

Including the people who actually employ me.

I push myself up to a sitting position and grab my laptop. Time to check the email. And maybe do a couple of things to make tomorrow not such a long Monday.

I log into my work email and think again about the way Laurie's family interacts.

They genuinely love each other. Even though they obviously have differing opinions on things, even though the kids fight and the guys have some good natured kidding going on. No one got hurt, everyone left happy and I could just tell that they all really enjoyed being around each other. The grandparents and aunts and uncles doted on the kids, the adults all cared for each other.

It was nice.

It was so different than my family.

I rub my cheek. I honestly try kind of hard to just not think about my family, if at all possible.

Time to work.

By five o'clock, the sunshiny, summer day we'd been enjoying has turned into an overcast, chilly, full-fledged fall evening. I look out the apartment window and just shake my head.

The weather in this town is just so weird.

I change out of my short skirt and into jeans, a tank top and a lightweight cardigan. Might as well look like it's fall.

I'm hoping the barbecue isn't really taking place outside. Especially since I open my door and a very cold breeze blows straight into the apartment and right through my jeans.

Hadn't I just needed the air conditioner in the car

yesterday? What happened?

I hurry down the steps and climb into my car. Laurie's house is right on the edge of town. I follow the directions I scribbled on the back of an envelope at lunch.

This area is nice. Lots of grass, lots of huge, old trees. I squint for the house numbers as I crawl along the street and finally see a bunch of cars parked out front of a small, white house. There is a white picket fence running all around a gigantic grass lot and trees shade the majority of the field and the house.

There's a big front porch and I can hear people laughing and talking in the back.

I knock lightly on the door before I see the sticky note covering the doorbell.

Come on in! We're out back!

I open the door, holding the big plate of caprese bites I'd put together for today. If there is going to be the same amount of people here tonight that were at lunch, I definitely didn't bring enough.

The house is adorable.

It's small but definitely big enough for four people. The kitchen has obviously been recently redone. Wood floors are throughout the house. A cozy little family room is decked out in pictures of Laurie and Ryan and their adorable boys. Hand-knit blankets and fluffy pillows are scattered on the couch and loveseat, which face a small fireplace and TV.

It looks like a great house to snuggle up in on a cold day.

A coffeemaker is gurgling in the kitchen, which shouldn't surprise me, given what I know of Laurie. An odd assortment of mugs sit on the counter and I decide I like it even better that she doesn't have matching coffee mugs for everyone.

I walk through the big screen door and there's an obviously new porch out back. People are gathered around a big table in the center of it, sitting on a few wooden benches or milling around by the smoking grill. There are a bunch of little kids playing in the grass and an old, multi-colored dog is wagging his tail, nosing around everyone. A big playhouse that I would bet money Ryan built is off to the side of the yard, their oldest son is racing up the steps to it, a red superhero cape flying out behind him.

"Annie! Hi!" Laurie says, waving from the table where she's seated. She's got a blanket over one shoulder and I can see the baby's legs sticking out from under it. She grins at me. "I'll have to give you a welcome to our home hug in a few minutes."

I smile. "Your house is beautiful."

"Thanks! We've done a lot of work to it."

Hannah is sitting at the table beside Laurie, Hallie is across the table. Hallie stands, takes the plate from me after oo-ing and ahh-ing over it, hugs me and then points to the empty chair next to her. "Please! Sit! How was the rest of your afternoon?"

I shrug. "Uneventful. I worked on a few things."

Hallie nods and pulls a ball of yarn and the beginnings of what looks like a tiny hat into her lap. "Sounds like the rest of us."

"You've really got to teach me how to do that," Hannah says to Hallie. We're all a little mesmerized I think by the way her hand deftly moves the crochet hook around and around the yarn.

"Oh my gosh, it's so easy. I can totally teach you."

"I don't know why you need her to teach you, though," Laurie says, grinning at her friends. "Hallie already keeps our kids' heads warm all winter."

"True." Hannah nods.

Hallie smiles. "I love to do this," she tells me. "I didn't grow up with a mom who was crafty so I swore to myself that the minute I found out I was expecting, I was going to learn every type of craft I could."

"And did you?" I ask her.

"Well. I learned how to crochet." She grins at me. "I just sort of fell in love with it and that's pretty much what I stick to. We all have our little hobbies now. Hannah loves to do interior design stuff. You need to see her kids' rooms. And Laurie is our photographer."

That explains the family room and the dozens of pictures on the wall.

Laurie nods at me. "What about you, Annie?"

"I like to cook," I tell them.

"Like actual cooking? Or like baking?" Hannah asks.

I shrug. "Both I guess. I really just enjoy trying new recipes. I don't do it too much though. It's hard to get motivated to destroy the kitchen to cook for just me."

Laurie grins sideways at me. "Oh we'll fix that," she says. Or at least, that's what I think she says since she kind of mutters it under her breath.

"What?"

She ignores me and pulls the baby out from under the blanket, sitting him in her lap and lightly patting his back. "So

Annie," she says and I get the feeling she's changing the subject. "Tell us more about you."

I'm pretty sure I've told them everything that needs to be said. So I lightly shrug it off.

As much as I like my new – dare I even say it? – friends, I'm not really one for divulging all personal history. Particularly if it's not nearly as pleasant of history as these women apparently have.

Ryan is standing by the grill drinking a Coke and talking with Shawn. Brandon is out in the yard with the kids.

Brandon comes up to the porch, huffing.

"Out of shape?" Ryan grins at him.

"You try being the bad pirate with one leg for thirty minutes." Brandon sighs and takes the Coke Ryan offers him. "Thanks." He looks at the table and whistles. "Who brought these?" he asks, lifting off the plastic wrap from my caprese bites.

"Annie did," Laurie tells him.

"Wow, these look great." He takes a bite and closes his eyes. "Wow, these *are* great!"

"It's just cheese and tomatoes and basil on a toothpick," I say, waving away the compliment.

"But there's like a sauce or something on here too!"

"Balsamic vinegar."

"Wow."

I smile. Hannah looks at me. "I'm apparently going to need the recipe," she says.

"Dinner is about ready," Ryan says, checking the grill again.

Laurie hands the baby to me and goes inside and I suddenly freeze for fear of dropping him and him shattering into a million pieces on the porch.

He's squinting up at me in the clouded over sunlight, chunky cheeks puffing out as he studies my face. I do my best to look as competent as possible.

"Hello," I say and I sound like I'm entering a job interview.

He squints at me again and I guess I pass inspection because he moves on to hitting himself over and over again on the leg.

Hannah is leaning back in her chair, hands rubbing her huge stomach. "Oh girls. I'm officially full term."

Hallie smiles at her friend. "Why do you think I'm over

here crocheting baby hats like crazy?"

"Think it's a boy or a girl?"

Brandon looks at his wife. "Boy. Definitely boy."

"Why?"

"Brandon Michael Knox Jr. I just know it's him."

Hannah rolls her eyes. "We've been over this. Even if it's a boy, it's not going to be Brandon Jr. The poor kid would be called Junior his entire life and I'm not going to do that to him."

"I'm on Hannah's side for this," Hallie declares.

Brandon looks at me.

"Oh no," I say, shaking my head. "I'm new here. You can't pull me into this debate."

He grins.

Laurie's son is now grabbing anything he can find and shoving it directly into his drooly mouth, including my hair and the edge of my cardigan. I awkwardly shift him around so he's facing out. He sort of slumps over and I straighten him back up.

Babies are hard.

"What are the other name options?" Hallie asks, continuing to crochet at lightning fast speed.

"I like Olivia," Hannah says immediately.

"What about for a boy?" Hallie asks.

"Mm. I really, really love Hamilton," Hannah says.

Hallie hums. "I remember you mentioning that a long time ago."

"And I think it's terrible," Brandon says.

"Why?"

"Hamilton? *Hamilton?* I mean, first off all, it just sounds kind of snobbish, but second, what are the kids in second grade going to call him?"

"Hamilton," Hannah says.

"No, they're likely going to call him Ham. Or Hammie or Hambone or something much worse like Porky."

I am actually siding with Brandon on this but there's no way I'm going to voice that to Hannah.

"I can see his point," Hallie says.

Hannah sighs, rubbing her red cheeks and fanning her face.

Meanwhile, I'm over here freezing and concerned that Laurie's baby is not nearly dressed warm enough in a long-sleeve shirt and pants. I can't for the life of me remember his name.

"What about using your middle name instead?" I ask. "I

like the name Michael."

"So did my brother and sister-in-law," Brandon says.

"Oh."

"Dinner's ready!" Ryan declares, coming out of the house with Laurie, holding an empty plate. He goes to the grill and starts stacking delicious looking chicken and sausages on the plate. Laurie is holding a huge bowl of cut up watermelon and cantaloupe mixed together and a basket filled with forks, knives, paper plates and napkins. Hallie tucks her yarn and half-finished hat into a bag and goes into the house and comes back out holding a piping hot casserole dish full of homemade macaroni and cheese.

It's like these people bleed food. I haven't had this much to eat in one day since I can't even remember when.

Maybe ever.

Ryan prays a quick prayer and then all the moms line up and fix plates for the little kids who are suddenly swarming the deck. I'm terrified to move with the baby, so I sit in the chair and the two of us just people watch.

Soon, all the little kids are sitting at a miniature picnic table in the yard. Laurie comes and takes the baby and commands me to fill up my own plate. "Eat a lot, we have a ton of food," she tells me.

I will gain weight being friends with these people.

We all sit at the table on the porch and the carefree banter of years of friendship begins. It's fun to be around. They ask me a lot of questions about my work, I listen to stories about their lives before they all got married and I stifle a laugh when Laurie's oldest son somehow ends up with a bowl full of watermelon upside down on his head thanks to one of the girls.

"Oh well," Ryan says after doing his best to clean the poor kid up with a paper towel. "You need a bath tonight anyway."

I leave at nine as everyone else is hauling tired kids into their car seats and Laurie, Hannah and Hallie all give me hugs and ask when I'm free throughout the week.

I smile the whole way home.

Chapter Seven

Monday morning and the day dawns in full-fledged fall weather. I dig out my cold weather clothes from the back of the closet and end up picking out a short, straight skirt, thick stockings, heels and a sweater over a button down shirt.

I look ready for winter.

Which is exactly what the office feels like. It has to be like fifty degrees. I step inside and my nose immediately starts to run.

It's like Mrs. Stoufferson wants all of us to go home sick every day. I feel like I work with Elsa from *Frozen*.

A few people nod to me as I walk past to my office, but again, no one says hello or good morning, even though I try my best to greet everyone cheerfully.

I sit down at my computer desk, plug in my laptop and load up the documents I was working on.

Or, I *attempt* to load the documents. After watching the loading circle spin for almost five minutes, a window finally pops up.

No network detected.

I can't help the growl.

I pick up the phone and push the button, rubbing my forehead with my other hand.

"Yes."

"Good morning, Mrs. Stoufferson."

"What do you need?"

Just such a charming lady.

"My computer isn't connecting to the network again. Could you please send the tech people here?" I ask meekly.

There's a click and so I'm going to assume that either yes, she's sending someone or no, I'll just be here struggling for awhile.

I click around on my computer but nothing ever starts working. Someone once told me that using a computer was like baking from a recipe – you just needed to follow directions and it was easy.

Well, they were wrong. I distinctly remember everything that the mumbling guy did last time and it isn't working today.

The door opens suddenly and it's the mumbling man again. He looks at me and just shakes his head.

"Yep. Sorry." I stand out of my chair and let him sit there.

He sits and starts clicking around.

"So. How was your weekend?" I ask.

The guy flicks his head up to look at me and his hair waves around like a peacock with his feathers open on a windy day.

Seriously. The guy needs a haircut so badly it's ridiculous.

"Good," he says. "How was yours?"

It's the very first time I've been asked a question about myself in this building since the overly nice boss showed me around on my first day. I try to not fall over in shock.

"It was *great*," I tell him.

"Good."

"I mean, I never really stay in a town very long, so it's unusual for me to have friends to do things with, but they kept me busy all weekend."

"Good."

"They're all super nice. And they all have these adorable kids and it just seems like everyone loves everyone and they are all just raising those kids exactly as they should be."

"Good."

I can tell he's stopped listening to me. He's back to clicking around on my computer.

I look out the window, thinking.

I wasn't raised a Christian. Sometimes I wonder what it would have been like to have known Jesus from the beginning. Would I have turned out differently? Would I have picked a job that kept me in a stationary place rather than clinging to the first one that promised a constant getaway?

"You look depressed for having such a great weekend."

I blink and look over at him. He's looking at me but as soon as I make eye contact, he shrugs and goes back to the computer.

Still. It's the first time that someone in this office has seemed even remotely concerned about me.

"Were you raised here?" I ask him.

"No."

"Where did you grow up?"

"Trinidad."

I rack my brain. "Colorado?"

"Yes."

"So same state. Does your family still live there?"

"Yes."

"Do you get to see them often?"

He makes a sound that might be a laugh, I'm not totally sure. But he doesn't say anything afterward so I don't know how to take it.

He suddenly pushes the chair away from the desk and stands. "You're all connected. I'm not sure why it disconnected over the weekend, but it's working now. You may need to leave your laptop here."

"I try to work from home though."

He shrugs.

"Well. Thanks uh..." It suddenly hits me that I don't even know this guy's name.

He looks at me through his hair. "Andrew."

"Andrew. Thanks."

"Yep." He leaves.

And we've just set the record, folks, for how many words have been spoken aloud to another human being who works in this office.

Wednesday afternoon, I'm in the middle of figuring out how many overtime hours a Mr. Ron Hannerson had charged last year when there's a knock on my open door.

"Hi friend!"

I look up to see Laurie and Hannah standing there, holding a plastic grocery sack.

"Hey!" I grin and I wave them inside. "Where are the kids?"

"Ryan got off work early," Laurie says, pulling a chair over and sitting on the other side of my desk.

Hannah waves at me. "No thank you."

"No chair?"

"This baby is coming out."

I jump up, panic coursing through my veins. "Now?! Here? Why are you here?"

Laurie rolls her eyes, digging in the grocery sack. "No, he's not coming out now. Hannah just wants him out so she's in her 'I refuse to sit or lay down or drive like a normal person' stage."

"First of all, we don't know it's a boy. Second, you know

what they say about car seats and their effect on the birthing position of the baby," Hannah retorts and then starts lightly jogging in place, holding her stomach as she does.

I stare at her and I know my eyes are as big as coasters. I mostly know this because my contacts immediately start drying out. I start blinking repeatedly and shaking my head over and over again.

"No, no, no," I say finally. I run around the desk, still blinking, and make Hannah sit in the chair beside Laurie. "No, no. There are no babies being born in my office today. No, no, no. No."

"Atta girl, Annie. Maybe you can talk some sense into her. Goodness knows I can't. Dessert?" Laurie emerges from the plastic sack with three Styrofoam containers and my mouth starts watering.

It's weird when your eyes are too dry for your contacts to properly work while you are simultaneously dealing with a drooling problem.

I sit back down at the desk and Laurie hands me a plastic fork.

"Merson's?" I ask.

"Where else?" Laurie says, passing out the containers.

I pop open the top of my Styrofoam container and there's a hefty slice of carrot cake inside, drowning in enough cream cheese frosting to thinly ice my entire desk.

I am going to need to begin running again if I continue to hang out with these people.

I take one bite and mentally set a 5:30 alarm for tomorrow morning, trying to remember where I stashed my running shoes.

The cake is totally worth the early morning wake up.

I take a deep breath. "Wow. Shawn really knows his desserts."

"You need to stick around long enough to try his summer lemon raspberry cake," Laurie says. "I don't like to deviate from chocolate, but this cake is seriously one of my top five favorite desserts."

Hannah is back up, swaying back and forth, looking at her phone. "This says to try eggplant parmesan," she says.

"For what?"

"To try and induce labor."

"I've eaten eggplant parmesan a million times and I've never gone into labor afterward," Laurie declares.

"Neither have I," I offer.

Both of them look at me and then burst out laughing.

I grin.

Hannah, still smiling, finally sits again of her own volition and just rubs her hands over and over her extended stomach. "I'm just so ready for this little one to come," she says. "I can't wait to see if it's a boy or a girl, I can't wait to finally hold him or her, I can't wait to easily fit in my car again and—"

"Here comes the real reason," Laurie interjects, licking her fork.

"I can't wait to sleep on my stomach."

Laurie nods. "Yep." She looks at her friend. "You're not even technically due yet, Hannah. It will happen. Just be patient."

"Easy for you to say. You were not patient when you were this close with Corbin. Or Cannon, actually."

"Well, it's not me so I have no trouble giving you advice." Laurie grins cheekily at Hannah and then turns to me. "So. Annie," she says, her tone business-like.

"So. Laurie."

"Let's talk about you."

I squirm. I don't particularly like talking about myself.

And I really don't like talking about certain aspects of myself, especially relating to my past.

Hakuna matata. Pumbaa was right in his view of the world.

"What about me?" I ask cautiously.

"This job thing." Laurie waves her hand around the office. "How tied to it are you?"

"Well, I mean, it pays for me to live…"

"What if we found alternate means of paying for you to live? Would you consider staying here?"

I narrow my eyes at her, sensing that there is more to her question than she's asking. "What are you asking me?"

"Just tell her the whole story, Laur. I'm sure she'd appreciate you not beating around the bush."

"I'm feeling her out, Hannah."

"You guys realize that I can hear you, right?"

"Annie," Laurie says again, pointing at me with her fork. "We need your help."

I take another bite. "Help with what?"

"I can't tell you."

Hannah rolls her eyes.

"Well, uh…then, I don't know that I can help you," I say, slowly, because I have no idea how to respond to that.

"She's not going to just agree to something without hearing what it is!" Hannah says loudly.

"She might! She can trust us. We are very trustworthy."

"She doesn't know that!"

"I really can hear everything you guys are saying."

Laurie sighs. "Okay. Here's the deal but you have to promise not to breathe a word to anyone because it's not really public knowledge yet. Ryan is quitting his job at the end of the month and starting up his own contracting business."

"Finally," Hannah interjects.

"He's already got feelers out for staff and we have a good amount saved up to cover the first few months when business will likely be pretty slow, but we don't have someone to do our books yet."

"Which is where you come in," Hannah says.

"Wait, are you offering me a job?" I ask.

"Unofficially, yes. We need a bookkeeper slash secretary and I think you would be perfect for it. I have no idea what you currently make and I'm sure we cannot offer you nearly that much, but I think our salary would be pretty reasonable and it would also let you stay in town forever." She grins at me hopefully.

"And it would mean that you could start seeing—"

"—if you liked living somewhere permanently," Laurie interrupts quickly, danger flashing in her eyes as she looks at Hannah.

"Am I missing something?" I ask slowly.

"Yes."

"No."

They both speak at the same time and I set my fork down.

"Okay. What's really going on here?"

Laurie sends a glare Hannah's way. "Only the secretary job, Annie. I even brought the official job description. I mean, you'd have to interview for it and whatever, but you would totally get it. If you think you might be interested in the job and staying in town, you should definitely come for dinner tomorrow night so Ryan can talk to you about all the details."

She passes me three sheets of paper stapled together. At the top, it says: *Palmer and Sons - Administrative Assistant Job Description.*

"You're starting the boys kind of young, don't you think?" I ask, taking the papers.

She grins. "Ryan is nothing if not forward thinking when it comes to his boys. He's already looking into football scholarships for Corbin. The kid is a monster. I'm pretty sure Ryan's first thought when he saw him right after he'd been born was just the word 'linebacker'."

I smile.

"Apparently planning other peoples' futures runs in the family," Hannah says, rolling her eyes.

Laurie just grins at me and takes a huge bite of her dessert.

Chapter Eight

By Tuesday afternoon, I'm convinced that even if Ryan and Laurie offered me a job as a plumber whose job would entirely consist of unclogging toilets, I would take it, if only so I could talk to the people who owned the toilets while I was working.

Nothing like a job where you don't talk to anyone to make you realize maybe you weren't as big of an introvert as you thought you were.

Or maybe it's just the fact that I actually have friends now. I look down at my phone as I leave the office after not speaking to any of my coworkers all day. There was a point about three o'clock that I was tempted to throw my laptop on the floor if only to be able to call in the shaggy-haired tech guy to say his seven words to me.

The phone screen lights up as I push the button.

Hannah Knox – 2 messages

Laurie Palmer – 3 messages

Hallie Merson – 1 message

Laurie was double checking I was coming tonight to discuss the potential job, Hannah was seeing if I was available this weekend for the Sunday lunch, Hallie wanted to know if we could do dinner Thursday since Shawn would be closing at the restaurant again.

Thirty seconds after getting off work and my social calendar is completely full.

I text everyone back and tell them all yes, I'll be there.

I get to Laurie's house at exactly six o'clock and my knock is met at the door by the older son. Cannon, I think.

"Hi," I say.

"Hi," he says, staring at me through the three inch crack in the door.

"Can I come in?"

He just looks at me. "Are you a stranger?"

"No, I'm Anne – Annie. Remember? I came here on Sunday for the barbecue?"

"I don't like barbecue. What did I eat?"

"I think you guys got hot dogs," I say. "And macaroni. Remember?"

"What color shirt was I wearing?"

Good grief, it's like twenty questions to get into these people's house for dinner. I rack my brain, trying to remember. There were so many kids though that I honestly don't remember seeing Cannon there at all.

"Uh," I say.

"Cannon? What are you doing, buddy?" The door opens wider and Ryan's face appears. "Annie! Hey. Sorry, I didn't even hear you knock."

"Oh, that's okay."

"Cannon, bud, remember Annie?"

"Hi," he says again.

I grin.

"Come on in, Annie. Laurie's feeding Corbin and then we'll sit down for dinner."

I follow them into the house. Laurie is on the couch, surrounded by pillows and toys and spit up rags and she's got a blanket over her shoulder, Corbin's little legs sticking out the other side. "Hi Annie," she says. "Sorry, I've just got a couple more minutes."

"No problem. I'm in no rush."

"Sorry – I didn't see Cannon answer the door until Ryan went over there."

I smile. "He's cute."

"You can sit if you want," Laurie says, nodding to the loveseat.

I push a hand-knit blanket over and sit down. "Who is the knitter?" I ask, fingering the soft yarn.

"Joan. She started after Ryan and I got married and made a blanket for each of the grandkids and then went a little nuts on the family. I think I have six blankets here that she's made. She finally started making baby blankets for the hospital. I think she's made almost forty."

"Holy cow."

"Yeah, she's amazing." Laurie pulls Corbin out from under the blanket and hands him to me, along with a rag. "Would you mind burping him for me while I finish up dinner?"

She doesn't really give me the option, because she just up and leaves and I'm sitting there, frozen, hands locked around this kid because I just know he's going to break into a million pieces or burst into tears.

He looks up at me and gums his fingers, grinning a cheeky, toothless smile.

"Hi," I say, carefully rearranging my grip so I can pat his back.

I can't decide if I'm more scared of him crying, shattering into pieces or spitting up all over me.

"So, how was your day?" Laurie yells over at me from the kitchen.

"Uh. Fine. Thanks."

Maybe if I angle him facing out, he'll at least spit up on the floor. But then if he slips off my lap, he'll smash into the wood floor.

This is a no win situation.

I have no idea how moms do this all day long.

The doorbell rings and Cannon runs for the door. "I'll see who it is, Mama!"

Ryan comes in, frowning. "Were we expecting someone else?"

Since it's me and the baby in the room and I'm the only

one between the two of us who understands his question, I shrug. "I'm not sure."

Cannon opens the door and starts giggling a minute later. "You're funny, Mr. Zach," he says.

"See? You even know my name. I'm not a stranger," I hear Zach tell him.

"My mom said that I can't even let people I know in. Especially if she's in the shower."

"And thank you, Cannon," Laurie says, hurrying over. "Come on in, Zach."

"Hey guys," Zach says, walking into the house. He sees me on the couch and smiles. "Hey Annie, how's it going?"

"Good."

My honest answer: "I feel like I'm clutching this baby like he's about to spontaneously combust."

But that answer seems like a little more information than what he's looking for.

Laurie grins at Zach. "You've met Annie, right?" Surely she remembers introducing us and the lunch we spent together.

He shakes his head. "Seriously? We're basically old friends now. Right, Annie?"

Laurie beams.

"Sure." I'm distracted looking at Ryan. He's closing the front door and looking at Zach, then at me, then at his wife and he finally just shakes his head.

I'm sensing a set up.

"Come in, come in! Sit, sit!" Laurie cheerfully demands.

I look at Laurie and how happy she is and how she leads Zach into the living room and quickly plops on the big couch, dragging Ryan and Cannon down with her and leaving Zach no choice but to sit by me.

Zach seems totally easy and normal as he settles on the cushion next to me on the loveseat. He casually reaches over and takes Corbin from me like he holds babies on a daily basis. Corbin giggles a wide-open-mouth laugh at him and Zach makes a goofy face back at him, which then gets Cannon laughing.

"Oh Zach, you are just so good with babies. And toddlers. And just children in general, I guess," Laurie says.

Ryan sends Laurie a sidelong look and just sighs. "So. It's nice to have you *both* here," he says, but he's not looking at us. He's looking at his wife.

Laurie ignores him. "So. How was your day, Zach?"

"Eh. Normal. We had a staff meeting for most of the morning and then I spent the afternoon at the office working on Sunday's service."

I have no idea what a worship pastor does during the hours of the week that aren't nine to noon on Sundays. The only thing I know is that people make a living doing it, so it must involve some kind of work.

"Annie actually came here tonight to find out more about the job opening up at Ryan's business," Laurie says.

"Are you thinking of staying here?" Zach asks. There's nothing but friendliness in his tone, but Laurie pounces like he just proposed.

"Well, I sure hope she does. Don't you, Zach? I'm so glad that you think she should stay too! Maybe between the two of us, we can convince her."

I'm pretty sure Zach never mentioned wanting me to stay but I'm not going to point that out at the moment. Ryan sits on the couch and just continues to shake his head like a bobble head doll on the hood of an off-roading Jeep.

He's going to get a headache if he keeps this up.

Or maybe if *she* keeps this up.

There's a *ding* from the kitchen and Laurie hops off the couch. "Dinner is ready! I made lasagna. I hope you guys are hungry!"

"Lasagna sounds great," Zach says, standing with the baby. I follow him and Laurie into the kitchen. Ryan goes down the hallway with Cannon to help him wash his hands.

"Don't get your hopes too high. It's just a frozen lasagna. But you know who loves to cook? Annie. I bet her lasagna is amazing," Laurie says.

She's a sneaky one.

"So you're a chef, huh?" Zach asks me, shifting the baby to his other arm and smiling at me.

I shake my head. "Not really. Every so often, I get the urge to bake something." I can feel my cheeks coloring and it has nothing to do with Zach and everything to do with being the center of attention.

Despite my newfound liking of being around a bunch of people, I still am not a big fan of everyone's eyes on me.

"Don't be so modest," Laurie says, brushing her hands off before sliding them into oven mitts.

The only thing I've ever made that Laurie has eaten are

those little caprese bites I brought to the barbecue. And those were basically just me threading tomatoes, cheese and basil onto toothpicks and then drizzling a balsamic reduction over it.

Anyone with opposable thumbs could have made it.

"It's really nothing. I mean, I'm not the next Paula Deen or anything."

Zach smiles at me like he knows I'm embarrassed.

Lovely.

Laurie pulls a bubbling casserole dish out of the oven and slides it onto a couple of wooden blocks to keep it off the counter. She then gets a big glass bowl full of salad and sets that and a loaf of bread on the counter.

"All right. Let's eat."

"Wow, this looks so good," Zach says. "Thanks again for inviting me over for dinner."

"I'm glad you both could come."

Ryan returns with Cannon and nods to Laurie. "I should probably say the blessing tonight since I'm not sure how many of us here have clean hands and a pure heart," he says.

She grins at him.

Apparently Ryan shares my opinion on this dinner.

"Lord, we thank You for this food and we thank You for these friends. We pray that You bless the food to our bodies. Amen."

It's short and sweet and Laurie squeezes her husband's hand before taking the baby from Zach. "Dig in, guys."

We fill our plates and then settle at the table. Cannon sits on a booster seat and Laurie plops the baby into a highchair that is slightly tilted back and hands him a pacifier and a toy.

"So let's talk about Annie's new job," Laurie says, putting her napkin in her lap.

"I don't know that it's my new job," I protest. "I haven't interviewed, I haven't heard anything about the hours or the salary or even whether or not I'm a good fit..."

"Trust me. You're perfect for it," Laurie says.

"You don't know me as a professional. I could be a terrible person to work with," I say.

"I have a good sense about people and I highly doubt that."

Ryan smiles at me. "I guess I can at least give you some details about the job. Obviously it would be here in town. Right now, we'll be working out of the mother-in-law quarters in my backyard. I've got it all set up as an office. Eventually, the goal would be to have a little farther commute than just twenty steps."

Laurie shrugs. "I'm good with twenty steps. Then you can change all the nasty, explosive diapers."

Zach grins at her.

Ryan ignores her. "Anyway, it would be a normal nine to five job, or eight to five I guess if you wanted an hour lunch break. I'm okay with that too. And I'm willing to discuss the salary. Whatever we decide on, there would definitely be room for growth in that. I don't know what you make right now but I wouldn't think it would be too far off from that."

"But best of all, you wouldn't have to keep moving all the time!" Laurie exclaims.

"True," I say. I'm pushing the lasagna around on my plate. It's delicious but for some reason, my stomach keeps clenching up at the idea of staying here permanently.

Permanent.

It's the scariest word I've ever heard.

It was scary when I was twenty and I colored my hair for the first time and it's even scarier now that I'm so used to constant change.

I'm not sure why. My whole life, I've complained about just wanting a place to settle down and now the opportunity is sitting right there on the table in front of me next to the salad and I'm completely terrified.

Chapter Nine

"Shoot."

I mumble the word under my breath as I'm clicking around on my computer at work Thursday afternoon, one hand holding my head. It's everything I can do to not pull my hair out.

"Come again?"

I whirl around in my chair and Mr. Phillips, the boss of the company, is standing in my office doorway.

"Oh Mr. Phillips! Hi," I fumble standing, trying to awkwardly smooth down the fist marks from my hair.

"I didn't take you for a cussing woman," Mr. Phillips says.

"I'm sorry?"

"Just now. You cursed the computer."

"Oh no, sir. I just said 'shoot'. Like a basketball? For whatever reason, your network hates my laptop."

"Well now, that's odd," Mr. Phillips says and puts his bifocals on his face. He sits in my chair and squints at my computer.

I have a feeling that he doesn't have a clue what he's looking for.

I have a much stronger feeling that I'm right when he almost erases my music library from my hard drive.

"Uh, I'll just call the tech guy back in here," I say, quickly grabbing the computer mouse from him.

"That would probably be for the best. So. How is your time here? Is there anything you need or want that could make your job easier? An assistant? Some coffee?" He tries to stand and the chair squeaks horribly. "A better office chair?"

"Honestly, sir, it would probably be a good idea if you and I scheduled a time to meet here in the next week or so. We need to talk through some of the ways I've found for you to scale back some of your expenditures."

"Oh, fine, fine." Mr. Phillips is waving his hand like it's no big deal that they are in debt up to the top of his thinning gray-haired head. "Whenever you like, dear."

I already know that if I don't schedule it this minute and then forward a reminder of our upcoming meeting to Mrs. Stoufferson, it's not going to happen.

I pull out my agenda and look at next week. "Friday at two?" I ask him.

"Oh no, that won't work. My granddaughter is performing in *The Little Princess* at her ballet school."

"Her performance is at two on a school day?"

"Oh goodness no. It's at five-thirty. The ballet school is never to take the place of her academics. But I have to get off early so I have a chance to buy her some roses and get a good seat in the auditorium."

It's becoming more clear to me why this company is in such jeopardy. I study him with a long look and he very obviously avoids eye contact with me.

"Sir," I start.

"Fine," he says, rubbing his forehead. "I'll put you down for Friday."

That was easy enough. "Thank you."

He leaves quickly, probably so I don't start in on some of the topics of our meeting. Which I was not going to do. I've already got a long list in my notebook of points I need to cover with him.

I sit back down at my desk, pull it out from the desk

drawer and find a pencil.

Too much time off work across the board.

It's like these people don't even have sick days they have to save up. I ran into one guy in the hallway yesterday who told me that he was heading out to catch the end of the SportsCenter highlights on TV.

I'm fairly certain he had no idea who I was or he likely would not have said that.

Unless he was just hoping to get a severance package.

I click around on my computer for another ten minutes before just giving up. It's almost five o'clock. Already there has been a steady stream of people clocking out early despite their late clocking in times. The odds of Andrew the Tech Guy still being here are very low.

Besides, I have dinner tonight with Hallie again.

I start packing up my stuff, thinking.

Laurie has texted me eight time since the dinner at her house on Tuesday night. Mostly about Zach and how it was so wonderful that we were hitting it off and wasn't he just the nicest guy and didn't I want to stay in town?

I didn't know what to think.

On the one hand, yes, Zach is a nice guy. He is great with the kids that are everywhere in this group of people and he seems pretty relaxed and easy going.

Two qualities that can either be a blessing or a curse.

But on the other hand, I still didn't know if I was going to take the job with Ryan. And beyond that, wasn't it the guy's responsibility to initiate a relationship?

Not that I would accept if he asked me out.

The whole moving thing.

Or not moving.

I rub my aching head.

I knock on Hallie and Shawn's door at exactly six o'clock. I even had time to run back to my apartment and change into comfier clothes. Hallie had texted me and told me she was likely going to be in sweatpants and we might eat dinner on the floor so to not wear a skirt again.

I obeyed. I am wearing yoga pants, a fairly worn tank top and a hooded lightweight jacket since the whole time I was here last time, I felt like we should be running into eight Siberian huskies who were abandoned by Paul Walker at any moment.

She opens the door and an icy arctic blast hits me in the face.

I should have added a scarf and gloves.

At least I brought a warm dessert.

"Hi!" she says, beaming all brightly. She's holding her daughter and her little baby bump has popped out more. If I didn't know she was expecting, I still wouldn't think she was pregnant but since I know, I feel like I can comment.

"Hi Hallie. You look cute."

"Oh gosh." She rolls her eyes and closes the door behind me. She's wearing leggings and a long sleeve shirt again. She sets her daughter on the floor and tugs at the shirt which is tightening on her belly. "I totally feel gigantic."

I'm pretty sure I look like she does right now after I eat a large meal.

Better to just not say anything.

"So how are you?" she asks me, going into the kitchen.

"I'm fine." I follow her and she's busy cutting two huge sandwiches in half and setting them on paper plates.

I set my bag on the counter and unload the contents onto her counter. I brought mini fruit cobblers and a small quart of vanilla ice cream.

"Oh wow," Hallie says, looking at the ramekins. "What in the world did you bring?"

"It's just a fruit cobbler," I tell her.

"No there is no such thing as *just* a fruit cobbler. That looks amazing!"

"It's just cut up berries tossed in some sugar and a pie crust." I used to go to a church in Pennsylvania and the woman who first showed me the art of the mini cobbler was about ninety-three years old. She could barely move her fingers because her arthritis was so bad. And I'm pretty sure she was almost blind.

They were the easiest things ever to make.

"They're really just mini cobblers," I tell Hallie again. "They're super easy to make."

Hallie hands me a plate and a glass of iced tea. "Have you noticed you do that often?" she asks me, leading us back into the living room.

"Do what?"

"Belittle yourself or something you did."

I just look at her as I settle on the floor, leaning back against the couch. I set my plate on my lap and put my iced tea next to me on the floor.

Well.

I don't know what to think.

Hallie turns on a TV show for Rachel with two-dimensional Disney characters bouncing around and nods to me. "Let's pray really quick. Lord, bless this food and bless my friend. Amen."

I guess we aren't talking about her comment anymore.

Good. That's just awkward.

I take a big bite of the sandwich, mostly because it's huge and I almost have to unhinge my jaw to get my mouth all the way around it. It's super soft Italian seasoned bread filled with rotisserie chicken, spring lettuce, sun-dried tomatoes and some amazing sauce.

"Oh my gosh," I say after I swallow. "What is this?"

"It's my chicken sandwich," Hallie says, grinning at me. "This is what keeps Shawn coming home at night. Well, except for tonight."

I laugh.

"See how I did that?" Hallie asks.

"Did what?"

"It's okay to be proud of what you've done or made," she tells me.

I guess we are still talking about this.

"So I know you were raised in a military family, but where is your family now?" Hallie asks me, totally changing the topic.

I think I'd like to go back to talking about the way I apparently belittle myself.

"Oklahoma," I say since I'm not one hundred percent certain where my dad is. "My mom and her husband live in a suburb outside Tulsa." They actually live in the exact same house my mother grew up in. My grandparents sold it and moved into a nursing home and after they died, my mom happened to drive past her old neighborhood and randomly saw it for sale and talked Ned into buying it.

As weird as it is, it makes sense to me. It was the only place that a woman who craved home so badly the entire time she was married to my father could remember feeling that way.

So, of course she bought the house.

"That's cool! I have family in Tulsa too. Three cousins and

their families. Shawn and I want to make a trip out there because none of them have met Rachel."

It's a good opening to change the subject before we get into some history that doesn't need repeating – either in action or word.

"Were you raised in the Midwest then?"

Hallie shakes her head. "No, actually, I was a California girl. San Diego. We moved here when my dad bought a business. He's in the paper industry. My parents live a few miles outside of town. They love the Colorado thing this town has going on."

I nod. "Neat."

"Yeah."

We sort of lapse into silence and both of us watch the Disney cartoon for a few minutes with Rachel.

"Have you ever talked to Hannah?" Hallie asks me.

I look at her. "About something specific?"

"Yeah. Her upbringing."

"No."

"Hmm." She nods and looks back the TV. "You should."

I leave after we lick the cobbler bowls clean and Rachel is in bed.

"I'm so glad you came over, Annie," Hallie says, walking me to the door. She picks up a blanket and a few toys on our way over to it.

"Thanks for having me. Your sandwiches are amazing."

"As are your cobblers."

I fight the urge to argue her point and I just nod. "Thank you."

"You're welcome. Have a good night, friend."

I slide into my car and drive the few minutes back to my apartment. Climb the stairs, unlock the door, lock it behind me and sit on the couch.

I feel like I have two choices on the sofa next to me. On the right, I have the job with Ryan's company, the friends I've made, the possibility of living somewhere for longer than just learning all the closest coffee shops and then packing back up.

On the left, I have what I'm comfortable with. My current job, my current apartment for the next few months and then the prospect of moving on to a new city. Meeting new people. Finding new coffee shops. Not having to get more than an inch or two thick in conversations.

And maybe it's just these particular people, but I've never

had friends I've made in different cities who have asked me so much about my past and where I'm from. This is at least the second conversation I've had with someone.

There is something to be said for acquaintances.

Particularly when you don't want people too close.

Chapter Ten

I wake up Saturday morning slowly.

This is the life. No alarms, no agenda, no place to be right then. I stare at the ceiling and take a couple of deep breaths.

Yes, Lord. This is wonderful. Thanks.

My new plans for the day are as follows:

1. Read my Bible while drinking a pot of coffee. Yes. A whole twelve-cup pot.

2. Go for a run to combat all these desserts I've been eating lately. I'm not twenty-one years old anymore.

That's it. That's all I've got planned this whole, lovely day. I feel totally at peace, totally content, totally willing to continue to just push aside the mental question of whether or not to look more into Ryan's job offer.

Yes, he will likely need an answer soon but probably not today.

So today will be great.

I look at the clock and it's almost nine. I reach for my cell phone and click over to the weather app.

Forty-two degrees.

This town seriously goes from summer to winter.

What happened to fall? It's my favorite season and we didn't even really get one. The mountains in the distance had snow on them yesterday.

My phone buzzes in my hand and I look down to see a text from a number that I don't have programed into my phone.

Hi Annie. It's Zach. What are you up to today? Could I interest you in a cup of coffee?

Uh-oh.

My stomach clenches tight and all peace I was just feeling ten seconds ago dissipates like the warm weather we were just having.

Coffee.

With Zach.

I take a deep breath and sit up in bed, rubbing my hair which has kinked in a hundred different directions. You know those dogs that look like they have dreadlocks and their hair just sort of pokes out everywhere?

That's what I look like in the mornings.

Ponytail elastics are my friends if I don't immediately take a shower upon getting out of bed.

I look at the text again. On the surface, it seems pretty normal. Friendly. Like this isn't the first time he's ever asked me out to coffee.

Is he technically asking me out to coffee?

I read it yet again, one word at a time.

Hi Annie. It's Zach. What are you up to today? Could I interest you in a cup of coffee?

I remember working with a secretary one time who thought I was mad at her every time I sent her a text message and didn't include a smiley face emoticon.

Seriously. One time I wrote Rebecca this text: *Have you ever eaten a cranberry bagel?*

She met me at work the next day with thirteen cranberry bagels and told me through tears that she never meant to eat that cranberry bagel at her desk the other day without buying one for me too.

I'd never even noticed her eating a bagel at her desk.

Worse was when it would take me a few hours to respond

to one of Rebecca's texts and she would immediately start texting like every two seconds.

Are you mad at me?

Did I say something wrong?

Umm…I guess you are mad.

Are we even still friends?

She was the definition of a high-maintenance texter.

I feel like I'm channeling Rebecca right now as I stare at Zach's text. There aren't any smiley faces in it. There aren't any exclamation points. Maybe he's feeling chained into going to coffee with me because of Laurie? Maybe he actually really doesn't like me? Maybe he actually doesn't like coffee?

No.

He's a man and he's in ministry at a church. I haven't spent tons of time around the men's ministry at any church but you only have to be a Christian for about ten minutes before you realize that the drug that fuels our nation's churches is hot, dark caffeine.

So, he's obviously interested in coffee.

He might be actually interested in me then.

If anything, my stomach gets tighter.

I haven't had too many dates and the ones I've been on haven't been ones to write down in my journal, if you know what I mean. Most of them involved either a blind date thanks to someone at church or work and the ones where I've actually met the guy first, I went expecting them to be terrible.

And they all were.

I mean, is it really so hard to just open the car door for me?

I remember going to a singles' Sunday school class at a church in Atlanta about six or seven years ago and the pastor taught the majority of the lesson on why it was extra super important to have a list of qualities of what you were looking for in the opposite sex. At the time, it seemed like good advice. He even compared it to a "shopping list" so you didn't end up coming away from the store of Future Spouses with something that was not on your list.

I'd gone home that night and written seventy-six qualities that I wanted in a man.

I'm pretty sure I was down to about three.

Christian, Funny and Male.

I sigh at my phone and climb out of bed. Better to face this with a cup of coffee. On the one hand, saying yes to a coffee date with Zach is not a big deal. We would likely go, get a drink, talk about meaningless things and then I would go back home.

On the other hand, I feel like I would basically be saying, yes, I'm available for a potential relationship because I'm going to be staying here permanently.

And there's that word again.

I brush my teeth, gasp at my hair and yank it up in a high, sloppy bun on the top of my head. I pull on my yoga leggings and a long tank top and a fleece jacket.

Might as well embrace the weather.

I stare at the coffeemaker for a few minutes and then go to the bedroom, grab my running shoes and lace them up.

Maybe some fresh air will help clear my head.

The last time I'd been to Laurie's house, I'd seen the prettiest little trail out by her house, so I jump in my car and drive the few minutes over to where I saw it. It looks like the trail goes along a small stream.

Perfect.

I park the car, pocket the keys and my cell phone, do a couple of stretches and take off.

I'm a good twenty minutes into my run before I can really

stop focusing on not heaving in my breaths and start thinking about other things.

Like Zach.

Or not Zach.

Or maybe Zach.

I huff out a breath and look at the stream I'm passing by on my left. It's so peaceful out here. If I were Laurie and lived right next to this, I would be out here every spare minute I could take. There are thick trees to my right and the leaves are starting to turn gold and red.

In a few weeks, it will be absolutely gorgeous out here.

God, I think I'm overreacting here.

Part of me thinks the Lord responds to me with a heavenly, *Ya think?*

Especially because right at that moment, I nearly collide with Laurie.

"Hey!" Laurie looks up at me, surprised and pulls her headphones out of her ears. She grins and even though I'm about eighty percent certain she did not brush her hair this morning, she looks adorable. She's wearing long, tight running pants, a bright blue jacket zipped all the way up to her neck and her hair is in a long, beachy-style ponytail. She's not wearing any makeup.

"What are you doing here?" she asks me as I come to a stop next to her.

"Running," I huff, lacing my hands over my head. Obviously I need to do more of it. Laurie was probably running too and yet she's not even winded.

"Oh you're one of *those* people," Laurie says, rolling her eyes. "I'm out here walking purely for the quiet. Ryan told me to hit the road this morning and get some alone time so here I am."

"Headphones?"

She shows them to me, grinning. "Noise cancelling. I didn't even want to hear any of the stream trickling by. I listen to enough of that white noise crap through the monitor whenever the kids are sleeping."

I laugh.

"You look the part of a runner," I tell her.

She grins, obviously proud. "Well. Thank you. The point is to convince the people you pass that you're just taking a break from your run so you totally belong out here on a running trail." She nods to me. "I didn't know you ran here."

"Today is the first time I've ever done it."

"Are you a runner?"

"Someday I will be," I say.

"Running from something then today?"

This girl is way too perceptive for her own good. That much seeing-through-people power doesn't work well in someone who is likely to abuse it.

Like Laurie totally does with the matchmaking.

"Eh," I shrug because no way am I telling her that Zach asked me to coffee and I went on a run instead of writing him back.

She looks at me with her all-seeing gray eyes again and nods. "Want to walk with me and catch your breath for a few minutes?"

I really don't because I'm about one hundred and twelve percent certain that she's going to weasel the truth out of me, but it seems rude to say no, so I nod. "What about your quiet time?"

"Eh," she shrugs, pocketing her headphones. "Adult conversation will always take the place of quiet time. You can only make up so many answers to Mickey Mouse Clubhouse questions before your mind starts turning into something resembling more of cooked oatmeal. And I cook a lot of oatmeal, so I know what I'm talking about."

I smile.

We start walking the way I was running and Laurie keeps up a good pace. It's definitely not a stroll. It's good though, because the point was to get a little bit of exercise today.

Particularly if I go meet Zach for a five hundred calorie drink.

I miss my early twenties metabolism.

"So. What's the run for?" Laurie asks me, catching a long reed from the side of the stream and picking it as we walk past.

"I'm trying to not be so high maintenance."

She snorts. "Honey, if you're high maintenance then I'm a whole maintenance staff over here. And you obviously don't know Hannah well because she sort of takes the cake when she's pregnant."

Actually, I could kind of see that.

"Okay, well, I'm worried that I'm prone to overreacting."

"There is nothing wrong with overreacting," Laurie declares, pointing at me with the reed. "Sometimes you have to overreact in order to be heard. I have this saying. 'Volume always trumps logic'. And it's true. Any situation I've ever been in, the one who is the loudest always wins."

I could see how this was the case.

"Laurie, how did you and Ryan meet?" I switch subjects quickly before she starts asking me what I'm overreacting about.

She grins. "We met over a bag of Oreos."

Somehow this doesn't shock me.

"He came to our Bible study and we ended up sitting by each other."

"And the rest was history?"

"Mm," she shrugs. "Kind of. I was too busy trying to set up my friends to notice that he liked me at first so it took some manipulating by them to make it happen, but I'm glad that it did. Ryan is..." She shrugs, looking for the word. "Ryan is mine," she says finally and I hear everything she's trying to say in that one word.

There's my stomach tightening up again. For wanting it so badly it's ridiculous that I'm so scared when someone actually shows interest.

I must have a heart with a split personality.

"Come on," Laurie says, waving her hand toward a tiny trail that leads off the big one. "We'll go steal some decaf from

Hannah."

"She lives over here?"

"Right down the street."

"That must be nice."

"It is until she gets into one of her baking moods and uses up all my eggs and sugar," Laurie says.

We walk along the path and a little white house with a blue roof suddenly appears out of the trees. It's like Laurie's house and sits on a huge grassy field. Laurie squints at the house.

"Oh good, she's home."

"Shouldn't we call first?" I get anxious just dropping in on people. Particularly married people.

Laurie shrugs. "She never calls me first."

We walk right up the back steps and Laurie doesn't even bother with a knock but just walks right in the back door which leads into the kitchen.

I cringe. "Are you sure it's okay to —"

"Hey," Brandon says, walking into the kitchen holding a pink plastic cereal bowl. He speaks like he walks in on people just entering his house without any notice every day. His feet are bare, he's wearing ratty jeans and a college sweatshirt and his hair, which I've only seen gelled and combed, is flicking around all crazily on his head.

"Hey," Laurie says.

"Want some corn flakes?"

"Gag," Laurie says, making a face. "Ryan made pancakes."

"And he didn't call us?"

"It was at six this morning."

"We were up," Brandon nods. His daughter comes into the room then and waves at Laurie.

"Hi Auntie Laurie."

"Hey Nat."

She looks at me.

"I'm Annie," I say, smiling at the child.

"Hi."

"Hi."

"Where's your wife?" Laurie asks Brandon.

"Living room."

Laurie walks out of the kitchen. I smile politely at Brandon and then follow her out while Brandon starts pouring a bowl of corn flakes.

Hannah is sitting cross-legged on the floor in front of the TV where a largely pregnant woman is doing the downward dog yoga move.

"Breathe into that baby, ladies!" she says perkily from the position.

"I think you're supposed to copy what they are doing on the DVD," Laurie says.

Hannah looks up at Laurie like she's totally used to her just randomly showing up at her house. "That woman can't be really, truly pregnant. There's no way she could bend like that if she really were."

Laurie squints at the TV. "She looks like she is."

"Well, I think it's a bodysuit like they use in the movies."

"Yeah, but her stomach is showing."

"Makeup." Hannah smiles at me. "Hey Annie."

"Hi Hannah."

"Well, we didn't come over to watch you not work out," Laurie says.

"Why did you come over? Did I know you were coming over?"

"We ran into each other on a walk and we decided to see if

you had any decaf we could make." Laurie plops on the couch behind Hannah.

I like how she's only used the word *we* when it was definitely her sole idea.

Hannah shrugs. "You know where I keep my coffee. You can find out if I have any decaf way easier than I can since it will take me at least five minutes to get off the floor."

Laurie nods. "How many cups for you?" She directs the question to Hannah.

"Just one."

"Annie?"

"Probably just one for me too," I say.

Laurie shakes her head. "Weaklings." She leaves the room and I can hear faint murmurings of her conversation with Brandon in the kitchen a few moment later.

"So. Annie," Hannah says, arching her back. "How's your weekend going?"

"Good. Fine." Better not mention Zach to Hannah either. I imagine the secrets she has from Laurie are few and far between.

She nods. "Good."

I'm remembering Hallie's comment about finding out

about Hannah's family sometime and now seems as good of time as ever.

"Hannah," I start slowly.

"Yeah?"

Now I don't know how to ask the question without just seeming nosy. "Um, so, I actually...well, I was wondering..."

Hannah grins at me. "Annie," she stops me, holding up a hand. "I'm stuck on the floor, the baby is kicking me right in the bladder, I didn't sleep more than about twenty minutes straight last night and I've been having false labor all morning. Trust me. There is no question too weird to ask. Want to know what brand of deodorant I use? Whether or not I have hemorrhoids? The grossest thing I've touched in the last twenty-four hours?"

"No, no, no," I say, shaking my head and holding my hands up because I really did not want to know at least two of those answers.

"What's up then?"

"Hallie had just mentioned that I should ask you sometime about your family."

Hannah blinks and a gentle look comes into her eyes. She pushes onto her hands and knees and then grabs the edge of the couch and pulls herself up, moaning. "Ugh. This baby better be twelve pounds for how much weight I've put on." She pauses. "Actually, I don't want a twelve pound newborn." She nods to me. "Let's go out front. It will take Laurie awhile to make the coffee anyway if she and Brandon continue to argue over which *Spider-Man* version was the best."

I follow her out front.

Chapter Eleven

Hannah slowly sits in one of the wooden rocking chairs on her front porch and I take a seat in the other one.

"So," she says. "Why did Hallie mention my family?"

I shrug. "She just said I should talk to you about it."

Hannah looks at me for a long time before finally looking away and staring out at the long, dirt drive surrounded by grass leading up to their house.

"So, I wasn't raised here," Hannah says finally. "I actually moved here to get away from my family situation."

"I'm sorry," I say, wondering why Hallie had me ask Hannah to dredge up painful memories.

"My parents got divorced when I was nine," Hannah says. "They dragged me through a custody battle until I was eleven and that's when the courts decided I should go live with my dad." She rubs her temples. "It was a horrible decision but we had to do what they said, so I moved in with my dad and spent the next four years living with him and his string of girlfriends. Then Mom took Dad back to court and I ended up moving back in with her and changing schools and everything that went along with that when I was sixteen. Mom was no better."

She sighs. "I moved out the summer I turned eighteen and picked the absolute farthest possible college I could go to in the country. After college, I needed a job and had always heard good things about Colorado, so I decided to just drive through the state and apply for jobs along the way. I ended up at Brandon's studio, I met Jesus, basically got adopted by the friends out here and I never looked back."

I did notice the propensity to just be grafted in by these people, Laurie in particular.

"I'm sorry Hannah."

"What's your story, Annie? I've noticed that you tend to clam up whenever the past is mentioned."

It's my turn to stare at the driveway.

Hannah's voice gentles. "You know," she says. "Sometimes the best thing to do is just let it out. The best thing I ever did was finally open up to someone about everything. It won't fix the situation, but sometimes it can fix the way you respond to it."

"My parents divorced when I was seventeen," I say, finally. My voice is quiet, subdued. I don't look at Hannah. I'm still staring at the driveway though to be honest, I'm not really seeing it.

"I'm sorry, Annie."

"It was seventeen years later than they should have divorced," I say.

Hannah hums an acknowledgement of my statement but doesn't say anything. She just rocks in the rocking chair and we both just look at the front yard.

"Dad was in the military. We moved a lot. I didn't really have any friends. Neither did my mom. It got to her big time. My parents fought a lot." I look down at my hands. "They yelled a lot. For years, they just yelled at each other. Mostly about moving constantly. Every so often, Dad would get deployed and we would go to stay with my grandparents in Oklahoma. But those years were few and far between."

"Oh Annie."

"Then, when I was about to turn eighteen, Dad came home one night and told us that we were all moving to Virginia after we had just unpacked the last box from our last move. He'd previously told us we were going to stay there for at least four or five years. Mom got mad and they started fighting."

I shut my eyes. The sounds of that night still echoed in my brain. Glass shattering, my mother screaming.

The neighbors called the cops and by the time everything was sorted out, it was way past three in the morning. The very next day, Mom packed up all of her clothes and all of my belongings while I was at school and when I got home, she handed me a train ticket and my suitcase and told me we were leaving.

"So, Mom took me and left him."

"Where did you go?"

"We moved to Oklahoma." We'd lived with my grandparents for the remainder of the school year and I went to Mom's old high school. I graduated on May 16th and on May 17th, I was driving to California for college. I applied to the farthest schools I could think of in both directions.

I've only seen my dad three times since then. I've only seen my mother a handful more times than that.

"Anyway." I shrug. "I met Jesus in college, I got hired by the company that brought me here and that's pretty much it."

"So your mom left your dad because of his constant moving?"

"Among other things."

"Do you ever..." Hannah's voice trails off and she looks at me. "Do you ever wonder if that's why you are so reluctant to stay in one spot?"

I frown and my stomach twinges. "What do you mean?"

"I mean, do you actually enjoy moving all the time?"

I look at her serious blue eyes and then back out at the driveway, squinting into the sun.

For years, I have been comfortable saying that I am a loner. After the way I was raised I don't know how to be anything else.

But now...

I look at Hannah finally. "I don't know."

She nods. "Just keep thinking on it. I think you're in this town for a reason, Annie. But whether it's just for a short time or for forever is something that you have to figure out." She groans and pushes herself up and out of the rocking chair. "Let's go get some coffee."

I follow her as she waddles into the house.

Laurie and Brandon are standing in the living room, both holding cups of coffee, both staring at the TV, eyebrows furrowed.

"Looks like I lost the TV to football again," Hannah says to me.

"What?" Brandon asks her but doesn't take his eyes off the TV.

"What game is on?"

"How in the world...?" Laurie's voice trails off as she tilts her head, watching the TV.

Hannah and I exchange a glance and then walk around behind them. The largely pregnant woman that Hannah was watching workout is in the middle of some weird criss-cross position that does not look possible with a stomach that big.

"See?" Hannah says. "I swear she's not really pregnant."

I am sitting in the driver's seat, parked outside my apartment, staring at my phone.

Finally, I work up the nerve to text Zach back.

Coffee sounds great.

No, that looks flat.

Coffee sounds great!

That looks too excited like I've never been on a date before.

How come someone hasn't invented a punctuation mark that is between a period and an exclamation point?

Coffee sounds great – when is a good time for you?

There. I just avoided ending the first sentence.

Ask a question with a question. Jesus totally did that all the time.

Now to wait. I just look at the phone for a good three minutes before I decide it is ridiculous to still be sitting in my car, so I walk up the stairs to my apartment. I'm unlocking the door when my phone buzzes in my hand.

It's Zach.

How about two o'clock?

It's almost noon right now. That gives me two hours to eat lunch, get showered, find something cute to wear and put some makeup on.

And settle my nerves.

I dig through my fridge and find a wrinkled apple and a

questionable stalk of celery. I really wish I had more time to cook. Especially when the weather gets colder. One of my favorite things to create are soups.

I eat quickly and then run for the shower. Thirty minutes later, I'm clean and dry, I've blow dried my hair and I've slathered about four pounds of lotion on my skin. I came to Colorado from Tampa. In Florida, I never used lotion. Here, I feel like if I sneeze too hard my skin is just going to shatter into about eight million shards.

So I pile on the lotion and I'm extra careful when I sneeze.

I wish I could get some curl to stay in my hair but I remind myself that there are lots of people out there who wish they could get their curly hair to stay straight and start putting on some makeup. The grass is always greener, right? I remember a girl I knew in the sixth or seventh grade who had the most beautiful, curly red hair and she complained about it all time and just constantly told us how much she wanted straight hair.

I finish up my makeup and now it's time to figure out what in the world to wear. It's a little chilly out and it's cloudy. Cloudy days are my favorite.

I end up pulling on brown leggings and tan tall boots, a

short, straight cream-colored skirt and I layer a hooded dark rose cardigan over a brown cami. I look like the fall color palette, but I'm warm and cozy and dressed up enough that if it's a date, I'm dressed appropriately and if it's just a coffee hang out, I'm still dressed casually.

So much pressure for one little outfit.

I grab my keys and go back downstairs to my car about twenty minutes before two. There is nothing wrong with being a few minutes early.

I drive the three minutes to Merson's and sit in the car for a couple of minutes before deciding to just wait inside.

Shawn isn't there but his assistant manager, a nice guy almost out of college named Darrell is. Shawn introduced me to him a couple of days ago. He seems nice if not nearly as friendly as Shawn. He's an engineering major, so I doubt he's sticking around Merson's for the long haul.

Today, though, I'm really thankful that it isn't Shawn behind the counter. The last thing I need is the crew getting all worked up about me having coffee with Zach. Because it's just a friendly coffee and there's nothing to report.

Right?

Right.

I almost suggested meeting somewhere else but I didn't want Zach to think I was embarrassed to be seen with him.

There's a chance that I might be way overthinking this.

I wave at Darrell, order myself a pumpkin spice tea so we don't have the whole "do I pay or you pay or do I offer to pay" awkwardness and go sit at one of the corner tables.

Random fact about me: I always, always have a magazine in my purse. It's one of the reasons why I don't carry small purses because I can't fit my magazines in them. I love the home design magazines or the fashion ones but my real love affair is the cooking magazines. I could read those all day.

I pull out my latest edition of a cooking magazine advertising new fall foods and between that and the pumpkin spice tea I'm finally starting to relax when I hear a soft laugh right above me.

"I guess we both had the same idea," Zach says. He's standing right in front of my table in straight cut jeans, a plaid green shirt and he's holding a book.

I squint at the title. *42 Reasons To Have a Djembe In Worship Music.*

"What's a djembe?" I ask, pointing at the book and using all my knowledge of phonics to pronounce it.

Zach starts laughing. "It's pronounced 'jim-bay'. It's like a little drum."

"Oh. There are forty-two reasons to use it in worship music?"

"So far, there has been a lot of repetition, so I'm betting there are really only fifteen reworded over and over." He nods to my tea. "You were supposed to let me buy that, just so you know."

"Sorry."

"Next time. Can I at least interest you in dessert?"

My stomach is stuck on the words *next time*, so I think it might be too much for it to handle those two words and a piece of pie. I shake my head even though I know the second I leave here I will immediately be starving to death since my lunch was the apple and celery stick. "No thanks."

"I'll be right back."

I try to get back into the article I was reading about the world's best apple crumb pie but I can't focus on the words in front of me.

I have got to get a grip.

I bet Laurie and Hannah and Hallie were never this nervous when they used to go out on dates before they got married.

Maybe this is why I'm still single. I'm just so ridiculously awkward around anyone who could potentially show interest in me.

Deep breaths.

Zach comes back over a minute later holding a cup of black coffee and a plate with a gigantic slice of red velvet cake on it.

It looks amazing.

"That looks delicious."

"Shawn makes the best red velvet cake you've ever had," Zach says and then sets two forks on the table. "Just in case you change your mind," he says, nudging the second fork toward me.

"Thanks." I close my magazine and put it back in my purse.

"So. Annie McKay."

I nod. "That's the name."

He forks off a bite of cake. "Tell me about yourself. I know you work in finance. Are you hoping to continue to work in that area? Are you going to take Ryan and Laurie up on their offer?"

Ah, the million dollar question. "I'm not sure yet," I tell him.

He nods. "It would be a big adjustment from the job you currently do, wouldn't it?"

"Almost everything would be different."

"What wouldn't be different?"

"I imagine I'd still sit at a desk."

He grins. "Knowing Laurie, I wouldn't count on that. She's anti-desk. You might get a couch though, which I would prefer anyway."

"You're anti-desk as well?"

"Honestly, Annie, the only use I have for a desk is to stack stuff on it. Bruce, the janitor at church, is forever griping about how he can't even dust my desk it's so bad."

I smile. "So you're not a neat person."

He fakes a shocked, sad look. "I'm neat. I get told at least once a week how neat I am." Then he grins. "Oh you mean *tidy*. Nope. Not so much."

A long time ago, when my list of what I wanted in a future husband was still in it's lengthy form, *Cleanly* and *Picks up after himself* were both on there.

Maybe that's a bad sign.

Or maybe it's just a sign that I need to get rid of the list once and for all – even if it's only a mental list at this point.

Zach smiles at me, taking another bite of cake. "I can just tell this by looking at you. You're a clean freak, aren't you?"

"I don't know if I would say *freak*, necessarily."

Zach gives me a look like he doesn't believe me.

One time I worked with a girl named Tanya who went on vacation to the beach and brought everyone back a seashell and she had written a reason why she enjoyed working with us on a piece of paper and tucked it into the shell. It was super kind of her but the shell leaked sand like a nine year-old kid's Converse shoe. I was so glad when I finally got transferred out of there so I could chuck the seashell.

No pun intended. You know, Converse...chucks...

I shouldn't be allowed in public unsupervised. At least I thought through this story and subsequent joke before I said it out loud to Zach.

Although now it's all awkward because I've been thinking for so long.

"Okay, so I enjoy things being clean," I say, thinking of my bare apartment and empty office. He grins.

"I totally knew it."

"How?"

"You've been sitting there wiping up every crumb that dares to fall on your side of the plate for the last five minutes," he says.

My hands are immediately banished to my lap.

"You know, I graduated from seminary and I had to take a few psychology classes in order to graduate."

"Even to be a music pastor?"

"Even to be a music pastor. That way I can simultaneously strum and diagnose."

I laugh.

"Anyway, they say that extremely organized and clean people are really just a different version of OCD but we don't notice it because society accepts that version."

"I could see that." I stop and think as he eats another bite of cake. "Wait. Did you just call me OCD?"

"Pretty much, yes." He grins at me. "Isn't this the best first date you've ever been on?"

I grin. And lace my fingers together tightly under the table, feeling like a junior-high girl. *He totally just said the word date!*

"So how did you end up here?" I ask him.

"In Merson's? I asked you to meet me here and then I got in my car and drove it here."

"You are an incredibly frustrating person to talk to."

"Well, thank you."

I rephrase the question as I roll my eyes. "How did you end up in this town? As a music pastor?"

"You want the long version or the short version?"

I shrug. "I have nowhere to be."

"All right then. A long time ago on a cold winter night, a woman, after twenty-six miserable hours of labor, delivered a healthy, adorable seven-pound, twelve-ounce boy and his father, through tears of joy named him Zachary."

I hold up my hands. "I changed my mind. I want the short version."

"No one is ever interested in my long version."

"Sorry. By nowhere to be, I meant that at some point, I'd like to go to sleep tonight."

Zach's eyes are twinkling as he grins. "The short version is that I always loved music. My dad likes to tell me that even when I was just a few months old, I would bounce to the beat if a song was on. When I was four, I asked for a guitar for Christmas and that was it. I started playing the guitar at church in the youth group when I was in the sixth grade and by the ninth grade, I was leading music there. I always knew I wanted to be a pastor, so right after high school, I went to seminary and next thing I knew, I was graduating with my M. Div and absolutely no job prospects."

"Always a warm, welcoming way to enter the real world."

He laughs. "Exactly."

"So what happened next?"

"I did what any kid straight out of college with a pointless except in one career field major does. I worked at Starbucks and started a band."

I grin. "Ah."

"I found a bunch of buddies who were in the same boat as me after seminary and we played at different retreats and bars and at one point, we even released a CD."

"Seriously?"

"Dude, we were big time."

"What was your name?"

"It was Zach back then too."

I rub my forehead, trying not to reward the awful joke with a smile. "I meant, what was your band name?"

"The Unemployable But Very Well Educated M. Divs."

"Makes sense."

"We thought so. We ended up shortening it to the M. Divs though. The full version didn't fit on the CD cover."

"You performed in bars?"

"Yep. I mean, we mostly played at Christian retreats and stuff, but we had a buddy whose family owned a pub and grill type of place and they had us come play for them a few times." He grins. "We made two hundred bucks a night and unlimited chips and queso. Best deal we ever got."

"So when did you get the job you have now?"

"A few years ago. I'd already gotten a previous music pastor job a couple of years before that but it was part-time, the band had broken up and by that point I was getting pretty tired of working at Starbucks and I had to work there in order to keep my apartment and not become the Employed But Living on the Street M. Div."

"That's kind of a long band name too."

"Exactly."

I want to ask him how he's still single because so far he appears to be normal, funny, not previously divorced, good-looking and he has a job. There aren't too many men my age who fit all of those categories. Most of the men I've been introduced to recently have been divorced with kids somewhere.

I've seen too many Disney movies to take on the role of stepmother. Have you seen what they become?

"So. Do you feel ambushed by the Laurie crowd yet?" Zach asks, sipping his coffee.

"Ambushed? No." I think about how all-encompassing they have become in my life. "Maybe a little bit overwhelmed at times."

"They don't leave a lot of room to breathe sometimes," Zach grins.

I watch as he takes another bite of his red velvet cake. He's not eating it all slobbily, he's dressed really nice and his eyes are starting to wrinkle on the corners showing a lifetime of laughing.

He's really a nice looking man.

Seriously. How is he still single? Especially with a friend

like Laurie?

"She's never tried to set you up before?" I ask.

"Who?"

"Laurie."

"Oh." He grins. "Oh, she's tried. She tries about every three or so months. About two years ago, she swore to me for *weeks* that this new girl was the absolute perfect girl for me, she got crazy 'Zach-vibes' every time she was around the girl and we just had a million things in common."

"What happened?"

"Well, we did have tons in common. She likes board games, thinks every good home should own a copy of *Tom Sawyer*, loves seafood and also thinks it's weird when people wear pants that have belt loops but don't wear a belt." He shrugs. "But then, you know, we also have Grandpa Henry and Grandma Lois in common too."

I start laughing. "What?"

"Yep. I walked in the restaurant for the blind date that Laurie had set us up on and it was with my cousin, Heidi."

I'm still giggling. "You didn't know she was in town?"

"Oh yeah! We'd hung out several times. She crashed at my

house for like a week before her apartment was ready, actually. Now *that* was a fun scenario, trying to convince all my neighbors that their upstanding, moral and pastoral neighbor hadn't gone the way of fornication but that the beautiful blond girl coming in and out of my house was really my cousin." He shrugs. "Apparently Laurie just hadn't seen us together."

"Okay, that's funny."

He grins at me, hunched over his coffee, his eyes twinkling.

"So. Seafood."

"Love it." He nods. "You?"

"Hate it." I make a face. "Can't stand it, actually."

"No! Even popcorn shrimp? Everybody likes popcorn shrimp."

"I'd rather eat my napkin."

He starts shaking his head. "This does not look good, McKay. What are your thoughts on *Tom Sawyer?*"

"I've never read it."

"You've never read —" He stops and clutches at his chest with the hand not holding his coffee mug, mouth open. "Oh Annie, that's the single best writing ever penned other than the

Bible!"

"I saw the movie. I think."

"Movie?"

"I think Jonathan Taylor Thomas was in it."

He just stares at me.

"Oh come now. You grew up in the early nineties. Jonathan Taylor Thomas? JTT?"

He blinks at me.

"The kid on *Home Improvement*?"

"Weren't there three kids?"

"The middle brother. With the hair that everyone wanted."

Finally I see a light turn on in his eyes. "Oh," he says, drawing the word out. "I do remember the hair."

"Mm-hmm."

"*He* played Tom Sawyer?"

"Yep. Quality movie."

"Are you—"

"I'm joking, yes."

He sighs and shakes his head again. "Just not good, Annie. So if you don't like seafood and you haven't read *Tom Sawyer*, what do you like to eat and read?"

"Desserts and *Anne of Green Gables*," I say right away.

"Thus the reason you turned me down for the dessert here," Zach grins.

"Well." To be honest, my stomach has completely settled down and I'm now wishing I'd taken him up on his offer. There is a plate of the most delicious looking salted caramel blondies sitting directly in my line of sight inside the wonderful glass-door-covered wall.

"So your favorite book is also your favorite movie," he says and I'm touched that he remembered our conversation from the insane lunch we had with the Laurie gang after church.

"It's pretty great," I nod.

"What's your favorite dessert?"

"It depends on the season."

"You're one of *those* people." He grins at me. "It's fall. What's your favorite right now?"

"Anything pumpkin. Or caramel. Or both together."

"I'll remember that. So. What else?"

I shrug. "What else about what?"

"What's been your favorite job?"

"As an auditor?"

"Have you been something else?"

I nod. "I had all kinds of jobs in high school and college. Not anything quite as interesting as an unemployed band member with my fellow unemployed pastor-wannabes, but..."

He grins. "Like what kind of jobs?"

"I was a cashier at a craft store, I've been a server at a restaurant. I did paperwork at a car dealership for a year or so."

"That sounds like an insanely fun job."

"That's me. Insanely fun." I look over at the blondie again and hope Zach hears the truth behind the sarcasm.

Zach is fun and crazy and a little on the goofy side. Compared to him, I'm the most boring person on the planet. I have a feeling that if I went to his house, the walls would be painted all kinds of psychedelic colors and I prefer all home furnishings to be in the cream-ish to brown-ish color family.

Boring, boring, boring.

"So what has been your favorite job then?"

I stare at the blondie while I think about it. "Honestly, probably the server. It wasn't a chain restaurant and sometimes on slow days, the cook and I would spend hours experimenting with different ingredients."

"The owner didn't mind you guys doing that?"

"Are you kidding? She loved it. That's how we came up with some of our bestselling entrees."

He smiles. "So in another life, you would own a restaurant?"

I don't think he realizes that he just touched on my closest held dream of my long list of what-ifs and wish-I'd-done-differentlys.

I play it cool. "Mm. Maybe someday." I look away again, trying to shove down the panicky feeling that sometimes climbs up in my esophagus when I think of the future. "Probably not."

"Why not?"

"Zach, I'm not a kid fresh out of college anymore."

"Neither am I." He shrugs. "I still have things I want to do though. It's not like you turn thirty and your life is over."

No, but changing gets a lot harder.

He drains the rest of his coffee. "I'm going to get a refill. Sure I can't get you anything?"

Now it just seems weird to tell him I really do want

something, so I just shake my head. "I'm good, thanks."

"Be right back."

While he's gone, I check my phone and then my email. Some companies I work with are quick to get me everything I need and try to get me on the road as quickly as possible.

This company is not like that.

Shockingly, Mr. Phillips rescheduled our meeting that was supposed to be on Friday to Monday. But he promised to at least send me some of the documents I needed from him.

There is nothing new in my email box except for a coupon for a pizza place in Indianapolis.

I probably should go through and clean my email address off of some lists I've managed to get myself on over the years.

Zach sits back down in front of me and he's holding his cup of coffee and a plate with a salted caramel blondie on it. He grins at me and sets it in front of me.

"You didn't have to do this," I protest even as I pick up the fork.

"Are you kidding? You've been eyeing it this entire time. The least I could do is get it for you."

I smile as I take a big bite. It's every bit as delicious as it looks. "Thank you Zach."

"You're welcome Annie. And don't give up, you know? Life can still surprise you. You never know. You might get that restaurant someday."

I look at him as he sips his coffee.

Yes. Life can still surprise me.

Chapter **Twelve**

Sunday morning and I'm standing in my apartment bedroom staring into the tiny closet. I've blow-dried my hair and put on makeup but I can't find one single thing to wear.

And I just did laundry yesterday.

This is all Zach's fault.

As we left Merson's yesterday, he grinned, flipped his keys over his finger and said, "Looking forward to seeing you at church tomorrow, Annie."

Which now that I think about it, sounds just friendly and like he meant nothing other than what he said.

Maybe it was the *way* he said it. All familiar and sweet, like we were more than just casual acquaintances.

But now I can't wear just *anything* to church.

Good grief. I am way overthinking this.

This is so not like me. I am the planner, I am the one who always knows what's going on, I am the one who is unemotional and fairly detached. I don't often get nervous – it's a trait that comes in handy when I'm suddenly the one in charge of laying off people.

Something about this town is getting to me.

I look at my closet again and straighten my posture.

This is ridiculous. I am twenty-eight years old, for heavens' sake!

I stand up, grab the first shirt I find which ends up being a cream-colored baseball-style sweater with navy blue sleeves and my distressed jeans. I find my pair of knockoff Sperry's in the bottom of my closet and call the outfit done.

Maybe it's on the casual side for church but I am not going to become this girl who sits around and obsesses about these kind of things.

I pour myself a thermos of coffee, grab my Bible and head out the door to church. I am going to need to stop by the grocery store on my way home. I never made it there yesterday.

I pull into the church parking lot a few minutes later and find a spot pretty quickly. This church has an amazing coffee bar area and last week, they had those little chocolate-covered Hostess mini donuts that are so terrible for you but so good at the same time.

"Hi Annie!" I turn as I'm about to go inside and catch Hallie's wave as she and Shawn walk up. Shawn is carrying Rachel, Hallie has the diaper bag over her shoulder.

"Hey guys," I say, waiting for them to catch up to me.

"You're here early," Hallie says.

"I didn't have anything in my house for breakfast," I say, wincing. "I was going to try and snag a donut before the service started."

Shawn grimaces. "Oh Annie."

"I know. Not super healthy."

"I don't care that much about the health aspect. But those donuts are disgusting."

Now I just look at Shawn. "Have you ever had a Hostess donut?"

"Have you ever had one of my homemade donuts?" he counters back.

"Shawn does make great donuts," Hallie nods.

"I've never seen donuts at your store."

"They're terrible for you so I don't make them often," he says. "You don't even want to know how much oil it takes to cook them."

"You're right."

"What?"

"I don't want to know." I sigh. "So I should just starve this morning?"

Hallie shakes her head. "Oh good grief. Don't listen to him, Annie. Shawn just gets a little temperamental when it comes to quality breakfast foods. You should have heard some of our conversations about my cereal choices when we first started dating."

"You were eating store brand corn flakes!" Shawn bursts. "They tasted like when you forget to unwrap the straw before you put it in your mouth!"

Both of us just look at him.

"Does this happen to you often?" I ask Shawn.

"Yeah. What she said."

"The point I'm making, ladies," Shawn says, rolling his eyes, "Is that you only have one chance to start the day off right when it comes to the foods you eat. Now. Do you really want the start to your day to be packed full of all kids of artificial ingredients?"

"Hey guys," Laurie says, suddenly materializing in front of us. "What are we talking about?"

"Artificial ingredients," Hallie tells her.

"Oh, I know all about those," Laurie nods.

"Know about them." Shawn is mumbling now. "Laurie, with the foods that you eat, you basically *are* an artificial ingredient."

"Hey, I resemble that remark."

He laughs at her. Then Shawn looks at me. "Go get a donut. Goodness knows I don't want to be responsible for you fainting of hunger at church."

"I doubt I'd faint," I say. "But my stomach might growl really loudly and that would be kind of embarrassing."

They all laugh and I go to the coffee bar to get a donut, smiling the whole way there.

I'm never the one to leave the group laughing.

I feel totally confident as I walk, totally comfortable in my own skin, totally happy with who I am and I'm even good with the lousy outfit I'd finally thrown on this morning.

I have honestly never felt this way before.

Maybe because I've never had good friends really before.

"You know, I heard that if you leave one of those in the sun for three days that it doesn't even change the appearance of the donut."

I look up as I'm stuffing my face with one of the three little donuts I picked up and Zach is standing there grinning at me, pouring steaming coffee into a Styrofoam cup.

All confidence shatters like a dried up leaf under the heel of a perfect fall boot.

"Oh, uh, hi there," I say, sputtering on the crumbs and trying to napkin-off my chin as I also balance the other two donuts in my hands.

He grins at me, obviously enjoying the show. "Skip breakfast?"

"I didn't have anything in my apartment to eat," I tell him. "I've got to go grocery shopping today."

"Hey! What do you know, I need to go too. Maybe I can tag along and we can go together." He grins at me and then checks his watch, holding up a hand to my reply. "Sorry, Annie, I really have to go. Time to start work." He winks at me and leaves and I stand there, sighing over my ridiculousness and then choking on the crumbs still stuck in my mouth.

Lovely.

Some little kid comes over and hands me another napkin. "Here you go, lady," he says. He's got his hair spiked up in a faux hawk and he is maybe five years old.

It's sad when a five year-old beats you in the style department.

I walk back over to the group, a shell of the woman who left them.

"So. How are the artificial donuts?" Shawn asks me. He's exchanged Rachel for a pager in the time that I was gone.

"Oh. They are fine."

"You okay?" Hallie asks me, looking concerned.

"You look upset," Shawn says.

"How's Zach?" Laurie asks me, coyly.

I sigh.

Church is fantastic, just as it was the week before. Today, though, the regular pastor is apparently out of town and Nick, one of the people who was at lunch last week, is standing up there preaching.

I like him. He leans casually against the pulpit, using his hands to talk and sounding more like we are sitting across from each other at Panera, sharing a cup of coffee, rather than preaching in front of a large congregation.

And it is a large congregation. I sneak a peek around during the sermon. Almost every chair is taken. There are quite a few more people here today than there were last week.

"What are we hoping to leave here?" Nick asks, looking around the room, making eye contact with several people. "Who are you influencing, whether for good or for bad? When people think of you after you are gone, what are their memories going to be of?"

I clutch my Bible, too convicted to even write down sermon notes. I stare right at Nick and my mind is racing.

"My grandfather passed away about three months ago," Nick says, folding his hands together. "He lived a very long, very fruitful life and he loved the Lord very much. But you know what? He didn't keep that love only for Jesus. He loved and loved and loved. He loved my grandma. He loved my mom and her brothers. He loved me and my cousins. He loved his coworkers. He loved his neighbors. And all of them showed up to the funeral. We had an open mic at the funeral and you wouldn't believe the stories I heard. I mean, heck, we had a guy show up who had met Gramps in the grocery store and Gramps led this guy to Jesus right there by the canned beans!"

The audience all chuckles softly.

I just grip my Bible harder.

"Over and over again, I heard how Gramps loved Jesus and how he loved people. A woman came who met my grandfather because he bought her three little kids Chick-fil-a one day when she didn't have enough money for their lunches." Nick shakes his head. "Gramps lived and breathed these verses by Jesus. '"A new command I give you: Love one another. As I have loved you, so you must love one another. By this everyone will know that you are my disciples, if you love one another."'"

He looks out at the congregation again. "So, I'll ask again. Who will be at your funeral? And what will they be saying? Let's pray."

Nick prays and a few seconds into the prayer, I hear Zach softly strumming his guitar.

My eyes are closed tight, but my grip hasn't loosened on

my Bible.

If I died this afternoon, what would my funeral look like?

Goodness knows they wouldn't need a lot of food for it.
I've blamed my constant moving on this, but I've managed to slip
in and out completely unnoticed by most people in ten different
states. I would be willing to bet that nine times out of ten, most
people I've worked with – even those where I've been there a year,
can't even remember my name now.

My throat closes tight.

My own dad doesn't even know where I am right now.

"Amen," Nick says and Zach takes the microphone as
Nick steps down off the stage.

"Let's all sing in response to our Lord Jesus' call on our
heart," Zach says and starts playing a much more contemporary
version of "Abide With Me" than I remember.

The service ends and people begin visiting with the people
around them. Laughing, talking, lots and lots of hugging,
handshakes and smiles.

Hallie elbows me as she stretches. "Well. That was good
and convicting."

"Yeah." It's all I can manage around the huge lump in my

throat.

Shawn stands to go talk to the other guys and Laurie scoots down. "Good grief, I had totally forgotten how much I missed hearing Nick preach," she says.

"He's good," I say.

"He's gifted," Hallie nods. "He's always been gifted. Half this church is here because of the amazing singles' group he used to teach."

Laurie nods, looking around. "Apparently word got out about him teaching today because there are a lot more people here than usual." She shakes her head. "This church is going to explode out the doors when Nick takes over."

"He's taking over?" To hear preaching like that every week...

Laurie nods. "Pastor Louis is retiring at the end of the year. He's been grooming Nick, whatever that means. Nick's been the associate pastor for a couple of years now and he'll start phasing in more and more."

"Wow."

"Yeah. It's going to be just like old times to be able to listen to him again every Sunday." Laurie grins. "Just a slightly bigger classroom."

"Hey guys." Hannah waddles up, one hand behind her back.

"There you are. I thought you'd gone into labor and hadn't told me," Laurie says.

"I gathered that from your thirty-two texts." Hannah rolls her eyes as she sits down in the seat behind mine. "No baby. Just couldn't get out of bed."

"Tired?"

"No, I literally couldn't get out of bed. Brandon had to finally shove me from behind while I gripped the edge of the mattress."

I start giggling and Hannah gives me a look. "Just you wait, Henry Higgins. Your turn is coming. And then it will be my turn to laugh while I sit there all skinny and fit."

I laugh more. "Oh Hannah. I'm sorry."

"He's never coming out."

"You know, you always refer to this child as a boy. What if she's a girl?" Hallie says.

"Then we'll stop calling her 'he'."

"*Hola*, mates." Zach is suddenly in front of us and

straddling the seat directly before me, grinning at me and then drumming his hands on the back of the chair to the beat of the background Chris Tomlin song playing softly over the speakers.

"Hi," Hallie says.

"Hey," Hannah nods.

"Aren't you supposed to be greeting people?" Laurie says.

"I am greeting people. Did you not hear my greeting? I even threw in a little cultural influence in there," Zach says, grinning at her. "And besides, it's actually Nick who gets to greet people today." He nods to the back of the sanctuary.

We all turn as one accord to look in the back. Nick has a pained smile on his face as he shakes hand after hand as people file out of the room. "Have a good day. Take care. God bless." I can read his lips as people leave. A few old women come and hold his hand in both of theirs, talking very passionately to him, likely about the phenomenal sermon.

I can't say I blame them.

Laurie giggles as we all turn back around. "Nick has to love that."

I glance back again. "Does he not like greeting people?"

"He doesn't like shaking hands."

I watch him for a little while longer and I can see the wince in his expression every time someone grabs his hand.

"Germaphobe?" I ask.

"I'm pretty sure he carries a flask of Purell everywhere he goes," Laurie says.

"I don't think they are called flasks, Laur," Hallie says.

She shrugs. "But that's basically what it is. Shakes someone's hand, gets a little hit off the flask..."

"You are terrible."

"There's totally alcohol in Purell too."

"Seriously, Laur."

I look back at Nick and watch the sweat beading on his forehead as he shakes another lady's hand who isn't letting go.

Poor guy.

"He was never like that until their littlest son got RSV as a newborn," Hannah tells me, rubbing her stomach. "Then he became the king of clean."

Laurie is watching the line out the sanctuary and as soon as there's a break, she books it down the aisle.

Zach watches her and laughs. "She's just mean."

I glance back and she's shaking Nick's hand like an

annoying cartoon character, over and over and extremely exaggerated. He finally tosses her off of his arm and immediately piles enough Purell for an army of six year-olds who all have a bad case of the flu in his hands and rubs and rubs and rubs.

"So," Zach says.

Ryan and Shawn walk up then, both with their kids. Brandon is a few aisles away, talking to another man, his daughter standing beside him, twirling in her pretty skirt.

Laurie comes up behind me and sets her hand on my shoulder. "Lunch?" she suggests.

"Merson's again?" I ask.

"No, we let Shawn have few weeks off in between lunches so he doesn't get too sick of us," Hannah says.

I smile.

"Have you ever been to Vizzini's?" Laurie asks me.

I shake my head. "Like the guy in *The Princess Bride*?" I ask.

Laurie's hand squeezes on my shoulder. "I knew I liked you. Isn't she great?" She pretends like she's addressing everyone, but I know she's only looking at Zach.

"What kind of restaurant is it?" I ask, trying to save the

poor man from having to make a reply.

"Italian, mostly," Laurie says. "It's great. You will love it."

I nod. "Sounds good."

"Work for everyone?" Laurie asks.

Hannah nods and shoves herself off the chair. "Works. I read on Pinterest that eggplant parmesan can start labor and I think Vizzini's has eggplant parmesan on their menu."

"Well, that sounds good and gross," Laurie says.

"Just because you don't like to mix your vegetables with spaghetti sauce doesn't mean the rest of us feel the same way," Hannah replies, walking over to Brandon.

"Really, when you think about it, Laurie, spaghetti sauce basically is a vegetable," Zach tells her, also standing.

"And now you sound like a Chef Boyardee commercial," Laurie tells him.

He laughs.

"And really, spaghetti sauce should actually be considered a fruit sauce because tomatoes are technically a fruit," Laurie tells him as I stand up.

We start walking to the doors.

"That reminds me of a quote I saw once about the

difference between knowledge and wisdom," Zach says.

"'Knowledge is knowing that tomatoes are a fruit and wisdom is not putting them into a fruit salad.'"

Chapter Thirteen

By the time lunch is over and I'm finally heading to the grocery store, it's almost three o'clock. I've laughed and smiled so much that my cheeks are going to be killing me the rest of the night and I'm stuffed to the tip top of my head with lasagna, breadsticks, salad and at least three more glasses of sweet iced tea than any sane person should ever drink.

What can I say? It was good and the refills were free. Though I'm pretty sure they had to brew at least another pot just for me.

I pull a shopping cart out of the cart corral thing, dig my list out of my back jean pocket and push my sunglasses onto the top of my head.

I actually like grocery shopping. Especially when I have nowhere else to be and I'm doing well as far as the grocery budget goes. And since it's just me and I keep getting raises since I'm the only person who works for my company who is insane enough to have this job, I have a little money to burn on food.

Maybe I should not work late one night and actually cook something.

Maybe I could even have people over to my apartment.

My heart kind of skips around a little bit at the thought of actually entertaining people. Whether from sheer terror or excitement, I'm not sure.

"No, no, Annie, the Lucky Charms are on Aisle 12."

I look behind me and Zach is grinning at me from behind his own shopping cart.

I'd forgotten that he needed to go shopping as well. I guess he lives in the neighborhood, because I'm at the store that's only three blocks from my apartment.

"Lucky Charms?"

"Part of every balanced breakfast," he says, nodding to the cereal aisle.

"I guess that depends on your definition of 'balanced'."

"Well, I mean, sure, you have to add fourteen celery sticks, a grapefruit, three glasses of skim milk and forty-two multivitamins to make it truly balanced, but really. Let's not squabble over definitions."

I grin.

Lunch was…interesting. The more I am around Zach, Laurie and the weird group of friends she's assembled, the more I like them.

But my goodness. Some of their conversations are just odd.

"What's on your list?" he asks, nodding to the piece of paper I'm clutching.

"Oh. Um, milk, bread, eggs, peanut butter, tomatoes, fruit, salad mix—"

He holds up his hands. "Never mind, I don't really need or want to know. How about I'll go get my cereal and the stuff I need for the week and I'll just meet up with you in a minute?"

I nod. "Sounds good."

I start in the produce and I'm only barely bagging my green onions when Zach shows up with six items in his cart.

"I thought you had to get the stuff you needed for the week," I tell him.

"I have it."

I look at his cart again. A loaf of bread, two cartons of eggs, a gallon of milk and two boxes of Lucky Charms.

"Please tell me you don't eat Lucky Charms for every meal."

"I don't eat Lucky Charms for every meal."

"It's not good to lie, Zach."

He grins. "I don't have them for *every* meal. Just breakfast and dinner. With some scrambled eggs."

"Oh Zach."

"What? Lucky Charms are good and they have…" He pulls the box out of the cart and looks at the side panel. "Only ten grams of sugar per serving. Hey! Fifty percent folic acid though!" He does a little fist pump into the air. "Not even sure what you need folic acid for, but Annie, I've got it. And at two bowls a day, I'm getting one hundred percent of my daily needs!"

I just shake my head.

He peers into my cart. "What is in all the plastic bags?"

"Produce, Zach."

"Fruits and vegetables?"

"Oh good! You've heard of them."

"Heard of them? Honey, I've even *eaten* them on occasion." He grins at me.

I look at Zach. He's wearing straight-cut, dark-rinsed

jeans, leather work boots and a white T-shirt under a buttoned down shirt. He's rolled the sleeves up to his elbows.

Zach isn't a big man but he's not small either. He's got broad shoulders but not a big waist. And he's pretty tall. Not as tall as Brandon, but I've met very few men who were as tall as Brandon.

Zach doesn't look like he only exists on sugar cereal.

Maybe he's one of those weird freaks of nature who can just eat garbage and stay in good shape.

I am not such a freak.

I put a head of romaine lettuce in the cart.

"What are you making this week?" Zach asks me.

"Chili," I say, deciding that I'm going to make it as I say it.

"That sounds good."

"I'm going to experiment with it."

"It. Meaning a family recipe?"

I can tell he's trying to find out more about my family.

Definitely not going to get into that particular topic in the middle of the grocery store next to a pile of oranges.

I shake my head. "Just one I've played with for awhile."

He nods, obviously hearing my reluctance to talk about it.

"You can come try it if you want," I offer quietly.

"Done," he says immediately. "You name the day."

"Friday?"

He smiles at me, eyes twinkling. "Friday it is. Just tell me what I can bring."

"Not Lucky Charms."

He laughs.

The week passes by slowly and very quietly.

Very, very quietly. I think I can count on one hand how many people I've talked to since Sunday.

By Thursday, I am about ready to hijack my network myself if only to have the shaggy-haired Andrew come in so I can talk to him. Everyone is avoiding me and I know that they are because I mentioned the dread "L" word when I had my meeting with Mr. Phillips.

Layoffs.

Hey, it's not my favorite word either. And it's not my fault they are in this mess.

I plunk down at my computer after throwing away the paper towel from my lunch of a peanut butter and jelly sandwich and look at my cell phone.

Last Sunday night, I had texted Laurie, Hannah and Hallie and invited them and their respective husbands to join me and Zach for chili. All of them said they could come. And I'd bought enough ingredients for it that I could probably feed this entire office building for a day or two. I had no idea where they were all going to sit in my tiny apartment, but I figured we could use my couch and porch chairs if we had to.

But then on Wednesday, Hannah and Brandon had canceled, saying that they couldn't find a babysitter. Then Hallie canceled yesterday, saying she had forgotten Shawn was already planning on closing Friday night and she was going to stay home and go to bed early because she hadn't been feeling good lately.

And Laurie had texted a few minutes ago, asking me to tell her the time again. I can pretty much see the text she's likely writing at this moment.

"Oh, sorry, I double booked us for that night. Sorry."

My phone buzzes and it's a text from Laurie. I open it.

So I definitely had it in my phone calendar for earlier and my

babysitter canceled and Ryan wants to do some work on the company idea
since he's going to be pitching the idea to our bank Saturday morning.
Sorry. Have fun though!

I look at the text, look at my computer and narrow my eyes at the numbers in front of me.

Sure.

I immediately pick up the phone and press the dial button next to Laurie's name.

"Hello?" She sounds out of breath. I can hear pots banging around in the background and a baby yelling.

"Laurie?"

"I'm sorry, hang on, I can't hear you. Hey! Cannon! Settle down, dude, you're being way too loud!"

I'm not sure that yelling at someone is the best way to communicate that they need to be quieter. But I also am not a mother, so what do I know?

The sound of the pots and pans settles down and the only noise is the baby now. "Okay, sorry about that," Laurie says.

"It's okay."

"Annie?"

"Right."

"Did you get my text? We can't make it tomorrow. Sorry about that."

"Yeah, that's a bummer."

"Well, I mean, it's just one of those things with Ryan working late and all."

"What?"

"Oh sorry." I can tell she's turning the phone away from her face again. "Cannon! Goodness, son, could you play your piano at another time? You're making Corbin cry even louder!" She sighs into the phone. "Sorry."

"No, I mean, I could hear you fine. Why can't you come?"

"Ryan. He has to work late."

"I thought your babysitter canceled."

"Right. And the babysitter canceled."

"Laurie." I draw her name out.

"Just one of those things, you know?" she says again. "Okay, well, tough luck about tomorrow but I'm sure we'll get to do it again soon and yeah, just let us know when you decide about Ryan's job offer. Talk to you soon. Bye!"

The phone clicks in my ear.

I pull my phone away from my head and just look at it,

shaking my head.

She is not as sneaky as she thinks she is. Obviously she found out Zach was coming and made everyone else cancel their plans.

What am I supposed to do with the ingredients that I bought that are all going to spoil now?

And plus there's the whole Zach is coming to my apartment and it's now going to be just me and him.

That is way too intimate of a setting for a second date. It's not even just a little bit too much. That's like a giant, flying leap into way too intimate, especially for me. A group of friends is one thing. One guy is totally different.

I rub my hands into my hair and growl under my breath.

What am I supposed to tell Zach now?

Sorry, man, but turns out you're the only one who is coming so I'm going to have to cancel because you make me nervous.

Awkward.

I get an idea then and I send out a group text to Laurie, Hallie and Hannah. If Laurie can play dirty, I can too.

Hey all. So bummed to hear you guys can't come to my little chili dinner tomorrow! Since everyone already had plans, I think I'm

going to just reschedule dinner to next week. Same time, same place.
Does that work for you all?

I send it, smile to myself and tuck my phone in my purse where it can buzz away with Laurie's objections while I keep working.

And object she did.

I check my phone as I'm climbing into my car that night and there are seventeen texts in the group message I'd sent out.

Weeding through those is going to be just so much fun.

Ninety percent of them include something to the tune of "Oh, wow, we all canceled? So sorry about that, I had no idea... well, maybe you could just still make chili for whoever is still supposed to come?"

I write back.

It's totally fine. I think most of the ingredients will last until next week and we can just do it then.

A minute later, my phone rings.

"Off work?"

"Hi Laurie. Yeah, I just got off work." I smile as I unlock my car door.

This is totally killing her. I can just tell.

"So, uh, who all did you invite to this dinner?"

"Just the group. But really, I have no problem moving it to next week. Actually, that might be better anyway. I've had a long week and it would probably be good to just crash tomorrow night."

"Oh?"

"Yeah." I sigh. "This job stinks."

"I know of a good one that has your name written all over it."

I half-laugh. I'm still thinking through the job offer. Every time I make a decision one way or the other, I get so worried that I'm making the wrong decision that I can barely sleep.

"No, I mean, seriously. I wrote your name on the dust that has gathered all over the desk in that little mother-in-law quarters that Ryan is going to use for his business." She sighs. "At some point, I might find time to actually go dust it, but for now, the seat is saved for you."

I laugh. "Thanks. And thanks for putting up with me

taking a little bit to think about it."

"Sure. Although, we will kind of need an answer by the end of the month."

I nod. "Understood."

"So. Party is next week then?"

"Next week."

"Okay. I hope you get some rest."

"Thanks."

We hang up and I look at my phone and frown.

Maybe she really did have all those excuses. I was fully anticipating her putting up a big fuss about how we should keep it tomorrow night.

Weird.

Chapter **Fourteen**

After much debating, worrying, cookie dough eating and gnashing of teeth, I finally crafted the absolute perfect text to send to Zach last night to let him know that chili was off for tonight.

Zach, it sounds like everyone else had plans or had babysitter troubles, so I moved the chili party to next week. Hope you can still come. –Annie

It was the hoping he could still come part that kept me up in cold sweats all night. What if he read too much into it? What if it sounded like I wanted him to come?

Which was silly, because of course I wanted him to come. Did I want him to think I didn't want him to come?

Then I just got so confused that I finally fell into a very troubled sleep where I dreamed about falling into a giant lake filled with chili and getting fished out by Zach, only to have him take one look at my face and toss me back in, where I had to hang onto a gigantic pinto bean in order to survive.

I woke up gripping my pillow for dear life.

I have got to figure out how to relax.

I take a quick shower and then stumble out to the kitchen to make the coffee. I get the coffeemaker percolating and then go over to my kitchen table and sit down, stretching and yawning.

I pull my Bible across the table and open it, reaching for my notebook and pen as well. Ever since Nick's sermon, I've been making a list of ways that I can improve on my legacy that I leave when I'm gone.

I think one of the biggest things I've realized is that this is something I can work on now. I always thought that "legacy" had to do with children and grandchildren and great-grandchildren, which obviously I do not have. I don't even have the capability of that right now.

But children don't automatically equal legacy and they definitely don't automatically equal a good legacy. And the more I read, the more I feel like children, while they contribute, don't have as much to do with legacy as do some of the other things that Nick talked about.

Kindness, generosity, sharing the gospel.

I open to 1 Corinthians and read in the first couple of

chapters for a few minutes, ending with a hot cup of coffee and running for the door so I'm not late to work.

I do my customary wave to Mrs. Stoufferson who does her customary ignoring of me and walk back to my office.

My phone buzzes right as I sit down.

It's from Zach.

Finally. I was starting to channel my inner Rebecca again and get all obsessive about how he had received my text.

Well, not how he had received it. I know he got it on his phone.

Just how he had received it *emotionally*.

I cradle my head in my hands. I am losing it.

Hey, no problem! I heard that everyone else had plans. Hey, so I was thinking since we are the only ones without anything to do tonight, would you like to still get dinner with me?

Well. This was an unforeseen turn of events.

I look at my phone, look at my computer, look at my empty office and then back down at my phone before finally clicking the lock button and sticking it back in my purse.

If he can take forever to write me back, then I can take a little bit too. Besides. I'm at work. And I'm about to lay down the law about wasting time at work so it doesn't seem right for me to be texting when I'm getting mad at everyone else for doing it.

These people seem to believe that being in the building equates to working and sadly, this is not the case. Ever, for any job, but especially here when they are so crazy underwater it's not even funny.

I remember when I was fifteen I decided to get a job to earn a little extra so I could buy some clothes that I wanted. I walked two miles after school every day to this little café and spent the rest of the afternoon washing dishes until it was time to head home for homework and bed. One day it got really slow there and a couple of the servers were just messing around in the back instead of tending to their tables or the front register and since I didn't have any dishes to wash, I just went out there and took care of things.

The owner saw, immediately promoted me to waitress and I got a fifty percent raise.

I definitely learned the value of not sitting around on the job that day.

I spend the rest of the morning working. I've now got a list of employees who are taking far too much time off work. Time to start enforcing the "time off work at work" policy, which includes the oh-so-fun job of monitoring bathroom and water breaks.

I feel like a third grade teacher when I have to do these things.

Finally, at lunch, I pull my phone back out and click to reply to Zach.

That sounds fun!

I push send before I can think too hard about it or analyze what I'm writing too much.

I'd brought a peanut butter and honey sandwich and a small zip-top bag of baked potato chips for lunch.

Speaking of the third grade and all.

I'm just putting the first chip in my mouth and unwrapping my sandwich from the paper towel when there's a knock on my door. "Anyone hungry in here?" Laurie sticks her head in and I immediately smell something heavenly wafting through the door.

"Hi Laurie," I smile.

She comes in and sets a bag from Merson's on the desk in front of me. "I figured you were probably eating something that wasn't nearly as good as this," she says, grinning at me.

228

"Thanks. Where are the boys?"

"Ryan took the afternoon off."

I'm aghast that she's here with me. "Shouldn't you be with your family then?" I ask her, freezing where I was in opening the Merson's bag. Sweet thing to do or not, there are priorities!

Laurie shrugs. "They get Mom Time all day everyday. It's important for the boys to have Daddy Time too. Plus I wanted something majorly unhealthy for lunch and I'm trying to set a good example for Cannon."

I grin. "Merson's isn't a good example?"

"Not when I'm ordering stuff like this," she says and pulls out two boxes. I open one and find what must be Shawn's version of the Monte Cristo sandwich.

Oh. Goodness.

I lean close and take a big whiff of the sandwich.

"Oh my gosh," I say when I finally stop inhaling in.

"Have you had one of these yet?"

"No." I'm back to smelling.

"So it's basically amazing. He makes like French toast with the bread, stacks a ton of Brie and ham on there, heats the whole thing back up, dusts it with powdered sugar and serves it with this." She pulls two tiny round containers out of the bag.

"Raspberry peach sauce. You have not lived until you've had Shawn's homemade raspberry peach sauce. The man is a culinary master."

I grin. "Let's eat."

"I'll pray." Laurie grabs a chair and slides it over, sits and then bows her head. "Lord, thanks for this food and for this friendship and we pray that any calories therein are not ones that stick permanently to our thighs. Amen."

"Amen," I echo, grinning.

"And I brought salted caramel bars for dessert."

"I feel like a turkey getting fattened up for Thanksgiving," I say, picking up the sandwich.

"Trust me, two bites of that sandwich and you won't care anymore."

She's right. The bread is sweet and crispy, the Brie is perfectly melted over the thinly sliced and piled high ham and the raspberry peach sauce...

"Oh dear graciousness," I say after the first bite of the sauce.

"Yep."

"This stuff…"

"Yep." Laurie shakes her head slightly and swallows. "I told Ryan that for my birthday, I just want like one of those huge whiskey barrel planter things full of this sauce. I might even just take a swim in it."

I laugh.

She takes a few more bites. "So."

"So?"

"Sorry about tonight," she says. "I really do want to taste your chili."

I wave a hand. "It's fine. I don't totally understand babysitter issues, obviously, but I'm sure that good sitters are hard to come by."

"You have no idea. Normally I would just take the kids to my sister Lexi's house when our usual girl can't do it, but Lexi and Nate have a mandatory foster care meeting with the state tonight and my dad doesn't handle crying very well. And I feel like adding two more kids to Laney's circus is just not very kind."

I wave my hand. "Really, Laurie. It's fine."

"But, I mean, I know that it's a pain to invite people with kids over anyway. We went to these people's house from church one time when Cannon was a baby and he spit up bright green peas and exploded out of his diaper all over their brand new light beige carpet."

I make a face. "Ew."

"It was disgusting. And it was everywhere. And they moved from here soon after and I just have always felt terrible about that. I mean, I've never seen a diaper explosion like that before or since."

Here's the thing about parents: They have no concept of being grossed out by diapers or spit up and love to tell stories about it. Especially when people are eating.

This raspberry peach sauce is too good to be ruined by diaper stories.

"We can change the subject now," I say, gesturing to my food.

"Oh yeah. Sorry. Anyway, I think you should still make chili tonight but just make it for people who don't have kids."

"Like who? Your dad and his wife?"

Laurie grins. "Are you kidding? Dad would never eat something so unhealthy and so suspect as someone else's chili. What if you sneezed in it? What if you spit in it? Does he know with one hundred percent certainty that you used hand sanitizer every time before you stirred?"

"I often spit in my chili as I'm making it, so that's a good call on his part."

She grins. Takes a bite. Looks around the office nonchalantly. "I bet some of your coworkers don't have any plans tonight. Or you know, maybe Zach."

Ah-ha.

She's a sneaky one, coming in here, bringing me what is basically a fried piece of brie and sugar to dip into the most amazing sauce on the planet, getting all my defenses down and then suggesting Zach come over.

I just look at her, eyes narrowed.

"I mean, I know he loves chili. And the poor guy hardly gets to eat home cooked food and I know this because one time he got the stomach flu and Ryan took some soup over to him for me and he said that Zach's kitchen only had Fritos and Lucky Charms in it." Laurie sighs sadly. "I worry about him sometimes. I mean, he's such a wonderful man. So good with my boys, so great with the worship band. But he just doesn't have too many friends."

Zach doesn't really strike me as a guy who is aching for

friends.

"Really."

"He doesn't go out very much, I know that. Well, I mean, with people. I think he actually eats out almost every day." She shakes her head all slowly and dramatically. "Do you know how much sodium is in restaurant foods? He's eating himself into an early heart attack, not to mention the financial strains of eating out all the time, and I just feel so helpless. I mean, we've all had him over for dinner a lot just to try and keep his strength up, but sometimes it's just like what you were saying earlier and we just need some time just as a family."

She is good.

Too good.

Now I feel completely guilty and like the worst person on the planet for thinking it would be awkward to feed Zach a home cooked dinner tonight. Especially since he's on the verge of a health breakdown as well as financial ruin.

"Anyway," Laurie shrugs with a sigh. "I just think you guys need to stick together. We're all married and caught up in budgets and water bills and vacuums that stop sucking right when the dog is in the middle of shedding enough coats to cover Cruella de Vil and her four sisters but y'all are free and easy and totally unhindered by life."

I feel like Laurie may not remember her single days too clearly. I don't feel free, easy or unhindered. Whatever she meant by that.

She shrugs. "Just think about it."

"Okay." I'm not sure what else to say. Especially since I'm drowning in guilt.

Guilt and raspberry peach sauce.

There are worse things to drown in, I would imagine.

I wait until Laurie is all the way out the door before I pull my phone out to text Zach again.

I just stare at the blinking cursor for ten whole minutes before I finally start typing.

Hey, so, I still have all the stuff to make chili and some of it will probably go bad before next week. If you want to, we could just make chili at my apartment.

I push send after reading it four times. And then I just grip my phone.

Who am I? I never invite men over to my apartment. I never invite men anywhere ever. Period.

My phone buzzes and it's a reply from Zach.

Sounds great! What can I bring?

I've seen his grocery cart and while I don't mind Lucky Charms occasionally for breakfast if I'm staying at one of those cheap hotels where the "continental breakfast" only consists of dry cereal, terrible coffee and suspicious looking eggs, I'm not really such a big fan of it that I want it for dinner.

But that's just me.

Still, I know that when I go places for dinner, I don't like to show up empty handed, so I write him back.

Great. How about a salad or something?

It's easy enough to go to the grocery store and pick up a bag of pre-mixed salad. Surely even Zach can do that.

Perfect. See you soon, Annie.

I lock my phone, put it back in my purse and cradle my head in my hands on my desk.

I don't even know who I am anymore.

Chapter **Fifteen**

I get home in time to do a little bit of straightening before I have to go right to browning the meat for the chili. I am making it with ground turkey because it's a little bit healthier, so I add a bunch of spices to cover up that fact.

Plus if Zach is really in such a crucial health state, the turkey is a better choice anyway.

Zach knocks on the door at exactly six o'clock and I'm still in my work clothes. I was hoping to get the chance to change before he got here. I'm wearing my leggings, a long dress-style tunic that I belted at the waist and a sweater with my tall boots. I've pushed the sleeves of my sweater up to my elbows since I've been cleaning and cooking like crazy.

I wipe my hands on the kitchen towel and go to open the door, my heart thumping in my chest.

I'm trying to tell myself to look at him like any other friend I would have over to the apartment for chili.

So tonight, in my mind, Zach is Hallie.

"Hey," he says, grinning, when I open the door.

Hallie. He's exactly like Hallie.

"Hi," I say, opening the door a little wider so he can come inside. He's carrying a grocery sack that looks like it contains more than just a bag of salad. "What did you bring?"

"I thought you wanted me to make a salad."

"They sell bagged salads."

He shakes his head and goes to the kitchen while I close the door behind him. "Oh no, Annie. We are doing this salad up Zach-style!"

"You aren't going to put Lucky Charms on it, are you?"

He rolls his eyes. "Ha. You are just hilarious. Have a little faith, will you? And point me towards your sharpest knife and a good cutting board."

I give him my favorite knife that I splurged on a few years ago. It's exactly like the knives they use in all the Food Network challenges and I always feel like a master chef when I'm dicing something.

Zach pulls a bright green Granny Smith apple out of the bag and starts hacking away at it.

"Are you going slice those or—?"

"Uh-uh," he says, pointing the knife over at me. I immediately raise my hands and step to the other side of the kitchen. "Let the master work. You go do whatever needs to be done for the chili."

"Yes, master."

"That's better."

I go over to the stove and lift the lid on the chili. It smells good. Homey. Not that my childhood home ever smelled like chili, but that's beside the point. It's the perfect smell to make everything feel fall-like and happy. I stir the chili once or twice and then check on the cornbread I'd put in the oven about ten minutes ago.

It looks great.

"So what all is going in this salad?" I ask, looking over at him. It's weird having someone else cooking in my kitchen with me.

"You'll find out," he says.

"Should I be worried?"

"Probably."

I laugh.

He looks back at me and grins. "How was your day?"

"Fine. Long. Laurie brought me lunch from Merson's though, so that was nice."

He turns and gives me a funny look. "She brought me breakfast from Merson's."

"Really?"

"Yep. She and the boys just randomly showed up at the church with cinnamon rolls and coffee."

I narrow my eyes. "Really."

"Yeah. Said she was sorry they couldn't make it tonight."

I stir the chili again and shake my head. "Zach," I say, finally.

"Yeah?"

"I think we are being played here, my friend."

He grins. "Well, I don't know what gave you that idea. She's only been shoving us together since you first walked in the door at church."

That was true.

"I'm just thankful you aren't my cousin," Zach says and goes back to thwacking at something on the cutting board with the knife.

Seriously. It's like he's never held a kitchen knife before.

"You know, you can make that a lot easier on yourself," I say.

"Hey! Remember the rules. Zach makes his salad. Annie makes the chili." He gestures with the knife. "Let me be all Master Chef Zach and woo you with my Salad of Incredible Edibleness."

"Fine."

Here's something I don't tell too many people: I can't stand people speaking in the third person.

The scene in *The Wedding Planner*? When Matthew McConaughey's character is talking about himself in the third person during the dance class?

Makes me crazy. I know women who swooned during that scene and I was about ready to reach into the screen and hit him with a grammar book.

So it takes everything in me to not comment on Zach referring to himself by his name.

I. Just say *I*. Or me. Or my. Or something else.

"Okay!" Zach finally says and sets down my expensive knife that he apparently has no idea how to properly use. "The salad is done."

"So is the chili." I reach into the oven with an oven mitt and come out with the cornbread. "And the cornbread."

"This is a feast!"

"Don't eat too much," I say, setting the cornbread on a hot pad on the table. "I was wanting to try some ginger molasses cookies that I found a recipe for online so I have some of those as well."

He grins and carries the salad bowl over to the table. "Even better."

I serve up two bowls of the chili and set them on the table as well as a bowl of sour cream, some grated cheddar cheese to put in the chili and two plates for the salad and cornbread.

"I'll pray," Zach says when we've sat down. "Lord, bless this food, bless Annie and please let the salad turn out well since it's the only dish here that I'm concerned about. Amen."

I laugh and lift my head. "It looks fine."

He'd piled chopped apples, pecans and what looks like bleu cheese on top of some romaine lettuce and tossed it with some sort of vinaigrette.

"We'll see."

"You have to have faith that it's going to be fantastic," I

tell him. "That's the key to selling yourself as a chef."

"I always knew that was Bobby Flay's gig."

I grin.

We talk small talk over the chili and Zach's salad turns out to be really good.

"So what exactly does a music pastor do?" I ask as I'm putting our empty bowls in the sink.

"What do you mean?"

"I mean, I've always been curious. You work full time, right?"

He nods.

"But really, your job is only those couple of hours during services on Sunday, right?"

He grins. "So, look at it like this. You do presentations in your job, right?"

I shrug. "I mean, sort of. I'm about to do a big company-wide thing on not wasting time."

"So, think of it like Sunday mornings are my weekly presentation. If I don't spend all the hours before Sunday preparing, then worship on Sunday goes just terribly."

"But I mean, what do you *do*?"

He grins and stands to help me clear the table. "Want my weekly schedule?"

"Well, I mean, I've just always wondered."

"We worship pastors do tend to have an air of mystery and intrigue," Zach says, looking through all of my cabinets.

"Can I help you?"

"Where do you keep your plastic wrap?"

I point to the drawer.

"Thanks. Okay. So Monday morning, we have an all church staff meeting for most of the morning. We talk about issues that came up during church services, prayer requests, things that need to be taken care of, stuff like that. On Monday afternoon, I work mostly on scheduling and picking songs for the next week's services."

"Okay."

"Tuesday, I have a meeting with just the other senior pastors. So just Pastor Louis, Nick and the youth pastor, Craig. Then I spend Tuesday afternoon teaching music at a local Christian school. I go there Thursday afternoons too."

I look at him, surprised as I put the lid back on the chili to wait for it to cool enough to put in the fridge. "You teach music?"

"Well, I mean, it's not rocket science."

"What grade?"

"Kindergarten through third. I spend about an hour with each class." He shrugs. "It's pretty great. The kids are cool and all the teachers there are these ladies who all have grown kids and they basically think I'm starving to death since I'm single and live alone and so they always bring all kinds of breads and soups and casseroles for me to take home."

I shake my head. "Wow. Taking advantage of poor old schoolteacher ladies."

"Well, I'm not one to feed into people's myths, but that's one I don't mind," he says, grinning. "So Wednesdays I spend working on the songs and service line up and I coordinate with Louis or Nick or whoever is teaching on Sunday to make sure that the songs go with the sermon and then I have rehearsals Wednesday night, Thursday night and Sunday morning right before the service starts."

I nod.

He shrugs. "Then I get Friday, at least in the afternoon, off and I'm at the church by six to set up on Sunday morning."

"That's early."

"It's my favorite time to be there, though."

"Really?" I am dubious. I realize that men can typically get showered and ready and get themselves out the door faster than women, but still. In order for me to be somewhere by six in the morning, I would have to wake up at four-thirty just to have time to shower and make sure I was awake enough to drive.

Which sounds good and horrible.

"Oh yeah," Zach says and leans up against my counter while I start our dishes soaking. I'll do them after he leaves tonight. "I'm the only one in the building. It's quiet, it's dark and there just this great sense of what is about to happen in there. You know, being a music pastor is a huge honor because it means that I get to help guide people in the worship of Jesus. I mean, that's *huge*. So I love Sunday mornings. I walk in and just get excited about what I know is about to happen."

There's a sweet feeling blooming in my chest. Zach is a nice guy but beyond that, I can tell that he genuinely, one hundred percent loves Jesus.

I wish more guys knew how attractive that was for a girl.

I turn off the water and go to get the big container of cookies that I'd put on the counter and I hear the water turn back on.

"So. Now it's your turn," Zach says, rolling up the sleeves of his blue and white pin-striped, button down shirt.

Oh boy. Not only does this guy love Jesus but he's going to roll his sleeves halfway up his arm.

I am convinced that there is not much more attractive in life than a man wearing a button down shirt with the sleeves rolled part way up.

And now he's doing my dishes.

And whistling.

A hymn, nonetheless.

Time to change the thought processes. Hallie. Remember Hallie? I have got to focus on treating him like I would treat Hallie.

He's looking at me like he's waiting for something and I realize that I completely forgot to respond to his last question. "Oh!" I say and try to hide my sudden fidgeting by grabbing a washrag and heading over to wipe off the table. "My schedule?"

"Right. Is your job a normal nine-to-fiver?"

"Pretty much." I shrug. "I sometimes go in early or stay late depending on the day, but yeah." I wipe the table down and Zach is just finishing the dishes.

Cleaning up after dinner goes a lot faster with some help.

"That's cool. Do you like it?"

"Like what?" I am having the worst time focusing. I blame the sleeves.

"Your job."

"Oh! Oh yeah. Well, not really. Sometimes, I guess."

He grins at me. "That sounds good and convincing."

"Sometimes it depends on the moment."

"So what kind of moment are you in now?"

Honestly? I'm trying hard to remind myself that I really don't know that much about this guy so it's completely crazy that I find him as attractive as I do right now. And plus, it's just been me for so long. And I'm about to be moving again likely in a few months. And I'm half considering taking Ryan up on his job offer just to get to stay here because of Zach and that scares me to death.

Though it would probably validate Laurie's entire existence.

"I'm not sure," I say, answering Zach's question while trying to tell my brain to quiet down.

He finishes with the dishes and now we are just kind of standing awkwardly in my kitchen. It seems weird to serve dessert so soon after finishing dinner but I have no idea what to suggest that we do. I don't have any games and most of my movies are just chick-flicks or BBC miniseries that I doubt that Zach would be interested in watching. So I wring the dishrag in my hands and try desperately to think of something to talk about.

This was such a bad idea. Such a terrible, awful, no good idea. I am going to immediately write Laurie a long letter why this should never happen again and how she is never allowed to organize me and Zach being together again.

I am so much more rested alone.

"Um. Want to sit?" I ask because I have no idea what else to ask. "I think I might have some tea. Or coffee. I have coffee."

Zach smiles at me like he knows I'm completely nervous.

"I have a better idea," he says and takes the dishrag from me. "Let's go for a walk."

"A walk?" I repeat.

"Right. That thing where you put one foot in front of the other? Like that annoying song on that kids' Christmas movie about St. Nick's early life?"

"No, I mean, I know what a walk is but I live in an apartment."

"Right. I noticed when I parked that there were a lot of cars outside." He grins. "You don't have to only live in a house to go for a walk. You actually live about two blocks from one of the best biking trails in town."

"I don't have a bike."

"That's something that we might have to remedy." He nods to my outfit. "Are you comfortable walking in that?"

I look down at my dress, leggings and boots and nod slowly. "I mean, we aren't going to run or anything, right?"

"Only if a bear comes."

"There are *bears*?!"

"You are a little on the gullible side, Miss McKay. Grab a jacket. It's a little chilly out tonight."

I turn and walk into my bedroom and get a jacket. I pull it on top of my sweater and go back out to the living room. Zach is standing by the door, smiling at me. "I'll just need to stop by my car and get my jacket too," he says as I open the front door.

A cold blast of air hits us as we walk outside and the warm, snuggly feeling you always get after a meal of chili and cornbread is immediately gone.

Oh, this is such a bad idea. Zach jogs down my stairs and

disappears inside the driver's door of an old, steel gray Jeep Cherokee. He reappears and pulls on a brown leather coat.

He's too attractive to still be single.

"This way," he says, waving me over. I put my hands in my coat pockets and he does the same, which is nice of him because it's just plain weird enough to go on a walk with someone of the opposite sex without also having to figure out what to do with your hands.

"So are you seriously considering Ryan's job offer?" Zach asks, nodding toward a sidewalk along the main road I take to get to my apartment.

I walk and consider. "Yes. No."

"You sound about as convinced as you are about whether or not you even like your job."

"It's hard to decide," I tell him. "Part of me is just used to this life. I move somewhere, I fix a company, make a lot of people mad at me and then I move on. Part of me actually looks forward to finding out where I'm going next and what neat things I'll get to see in the new place."

"Do you spend time touring around the places you live?"

I nod. "Sometimes. It depends on the city. Obviously

there's not a lot to do here…"

He grins.

"But it's always kind of fun in the big cities to find these little niches in the city that no one else knows about."

"Like what kind of places?"

"Like where I came from in Tampa? There was this little café that had a coconut chai latte that was just amazing. It tasted like summer on the Caribbean and I would get one and go park at this place overlooking the Bay and I would just watch the sunset and it was just me and God and it was perfect."

"Sounds like a great place."

I nod. "It was."

"You must have been sad to come here."

I shrug. "I was curious, that's for certain. I'd never heard of this town and I can guarantee that it's the smallest town I've ever lived in. And that says a lot because I've lived a lot of places."

Zach nods.

Throughout the conversation, he's been semi-steering me in the right direction, reaching out to gently lead me by the elbow as we turn down different paths. We finally end up on this asphalt-paved trail that cuts off the road and leads up through the hills and into the more wooded area.

Maybe he wasn't really kidding about the bears.

We are keeping up a pretty fast pace. There are solar lights marking both sides of the path every few feet and we haven't been on the road more than a minute or two before two bikes whiz past us.

"On your left!" the lead biker yells.

I gasp and Zach again reaches out to grasp my elbow.

"Sometimes they come by pretty fast," he says. "Though it's getting kind of late for them to still be out."

"So you're a biker?"

He grins. "Only in the pedal form. I would love to get a motorcycle but my mother would disown me and as a guy in ministry, what can I say? I need the inheritance."

I laugh.

"Plus I think Pastor Louis might draw the line at that one."

"Where do you go bike?"

"On these trails. There are actually trails all around this town. The last mayor was big into the outdoor sports and recreation and he spent a ton of taxpayer money adding all sorts of trails and bike paths and parks to the city. Which everyone enjoys now but at the time, they couldn't stand how much money it was costing him, so they voted him out of office."

"Poor guy."

"Politics. He picked a hard profession."

It's completely dark now and except for the glow of the moon through the trees and the tiny solar lights on the path, I can barely see anything.

I unconsciously walk a little closer to Zach.

"How far are we going?"

"Are you getting cold?" he asks me. "We can go back anytime. I just wanted to show you something. It's about another ten minute walk though. Are you doing okay?"

"I'm fine. You aren't taking me out to some clearing in the middle of the woods to kill me, are you?"

"I sure hope not. I actually like these jeans and I've heard killing people is a messy job. And I'm not the best with getting stains out of laundry."

"I've heard lemon can help."

"With getting stains out of laundry or killing people in a less messy fashion?"

I grin. "Laundry. I haven't heard too many 'death by

lemon' stories."

"I don't know. My sister has two kids and you would have thought her youngest was dying by the way she reacted any time she tasted lemon as a toddler."

"It's an acquired taste."

He shrugs. "I couldn't really blame her. I don't like the taste of lemon either."

"Really? Not even lemonade?"

"Not even lemonade." He reaches for my elbow again as another bike flies past us. It's sweet and I can tell he's doing it almost without thinking.

It makes me feel protected.

Though I am getting nervous about being out in the woods after dark. Not necessarily about Zach and his potential for murder but aren't there bears in Colorado? Or at least mountain lions? Or much worse, snakes?

I am not a reptile person. Or a bear person. Or a large mountain cat person.

Actually, I'm just not really an animal person at all.

I scoot even closer to Zach and he doesn't let go of my elbow and instead nods to a little path in the dirt between the trees. "Here it is."

"Seriously, Zach. I don't know that I know you well enough to trust you in the dark in the woods."

"But isn't the intrigue killing you? Don't you want to know why I'm taking you down this little dirt path in the woods?"

"You aren't a vampire, are you?"

He gapes at me in mock shock. "I don't know what you are talking about Bella — I mean, Annie."

I laugh.

We walk along the dirt path and without the lights, it's hard to see all the twists and turns. I nearly fall on a tree root and when I put my hands out to steady myself, Zach just reaches for my hand.

"It's not too much farther," he says in a low voice.

His hand is warm and rough and my stomach is immediately somewhere in the vicinity of the heels of my tall boots.

I'm having trouble swallowing.

I focus on taking steps and keeping up and try to ignore the way his hand gently cradles mine but still somehow provides enough support that I'm not tripping over everything anymore.

I'm looking down at my feet and the path just suddenly stops.

"Here we are."

I look up and I didn't even notice that we were coming to the edge of a taller hill. The valley and tiny town are below us and the city lights glimmer in the dark.

"Oh." I catch my breath and look around. It's completely dark so I can't see much other than the town lights flickering below us, but if I stare hard enough, I think I can make out the little river running through town.

"There's the church," Zach says, pointing. He's still holding my hand and I don't really know what to make of that.

It's not like I'm going on a lot of life experience with this. The last time I held a guy's hand, I was fourteen and at the one and only school dance I ever went to. My teacher told all of us painfully shy kids that if we all went together, she would give us extra bonus in our grades. And since that was the same year I took earth science, I needed the bonus points.

In hindsight, it may not have been completely legal for the teacher to do that.

No wonder I never became something that involved the

knowledge of earth sciences.

"What are you thinking about?" Zach asks me.

"What occupation uses earth science?"

He starts laughing. "Well, so much for the magical moment," he says, letting go of my hand. He's grinning, though, so it doesn't seem like he minds me shattering it there.

Meanwhile, I am rubbing my temples, embarrassed and very thankful for the darkness.

I should not be allowed in public settings.

Zach is still smiling. "I would imagine most science related fields need some knowledge of earth sciences. You know, like botanists and stuff."

I nod. "Probably."

"It doesn't seem like you would make very much with a career in botany."

"Most likely not."

"Unless you were employed by someone like Disney World or something."

"I'm sorry?"

"You know, those Mickey Mouse pumpkins they grow? And watermelons? I think they have a whole greenhouse that sources a lot of the food they serve in the parks."

I shake my head. "I had no idea. I've never been to Disney World."

"You lived in Tampa! That's only a couple of hours away!"

I shrug. I wasn't about to go to what I've always heard is the happiest place on earth by myself.

That just seemed weird.

Plus, I am not a big roller coaster person. And doesn't Disney World have roller coasters?

Zach shakes his head. "One of these days, you need to go."

"I'm sure I will. Someday. Maybe."

He smiles. "So. Cold yet?"

I am freezing but I'm trying not to let the shivers overtake my entire body. I'm regretting my decision not to change clothes. Leggings are not necessarily known for their excellent warmth.

I nod instead of reply because I don't want my teeth to start chattering.

"Let's head back."

We start walking back to the path and again, he reaches for my hand as we start walking over some of the rougher terrain.

We get back to the path and he doesn't let go.

"So what does your weekend look like?" Zach asks. He keeps up a pretty quick pace, probably so we can get back to my warm apartment as fast as possible.

I shrug. "I don't have a lot. Laurie invited me over tomorrow for something at her house."

"Me too. Around four?"

I nod.

"Well, that's good and shocking that she invited us both." Zach grins and squeezes my hand lightly.

"Then just church."

He finally lets go of my hand when we reach my apartment stairs. I climb up, unlock the door and hurry into the warm room. I go immediately to the stove and turn on my teapot.

Tonight definitely calls for the tea I've been hoarding for over a year.

"Caramel chai tea?" I ask Zach, reaching for the old cookie tin that I keep all my tea in. I never drink tea unless it's cold and dark outside. During daytime hours, I am a coffee girl.

Unless it's iced tea. There was a lady who had moved from Texas at the church I went to in Tampa who always made gallons of sweet iced tea on Sunday mornings and it was hands down the best iced tea I have ever had. I used to get a cup as I was walking out the door to go home. I asked her one time if I could get a recipe for how she made her tea and she just rolled her eyes, shook her head and drawled, "Honey, if you aren't born with the knowledge, there is no way I can teach you."

I'd never heard the word *born* said in six syllables before I met her.

"Chai tea?" Zach asks.

"Yeah. Chai."

"Like would you like to chai this tea?"

"Or would you like some chai tea."

"Let me just chai to think about that for a minute," he says, grinning and leaning his arms on the high counter over my sink. "What does chai tea tastes like?"

"You've never had it?" I am aghast that someone could get so old and never have had chai tea.

Though I met a girl my age who had never had a peach, so I guess that one takes the cake. She'd even grown up in an upper-middle-class California.

"Nope," Zach says cheerfully. "Can't say I've ever chai-ed it."

I just sigh while he grins even wider.

"It's kind of cinnamon-y and spicy," I tell him. "This one is a loose leaf tea and it's not decaf but it's never kept me up."

"Sure. I'll chai it."

"Zach."

"I mean, I'm not opposed to chai-ing it but I can't promise that I'm going to think it's tea-lightful."

"Zach."

"What would you brew if you were me? Chai it or leaf it to someone else?"

I cover my face with my hands and attempt not to give his horrible jokes the benefit of a smile. "Are you done?"

"I'm chai-ing but I'm having trouble coming up with more tea-rrific jokes."

"Zach!"

He laughs.

Chapter Sixteen

I wake up slowly on Saturday and I think I'm still smiling from when I went to bed.

What a wonderful night.

I get up and go get my coffee started brewing and settle in front of my computer on the couch. I've got a big presentation I'm giving to the company on Monday.

How to Stop Wasting Time and Increase Productivity.

The topic is just enthralling.

I am clocking right along at this company. I'm estimating maybe two months left of work here.

I check my email and there's my normal two-months-in email from my employer.

Hey Annie,

Just checking to see how things were progressing at the power company and how much estimated time you had left. A new assignment just came in that we are saving for you. Hope you are ready for some warm weather.

Best,

Steve

Steve is actually the one who originally hired me to my job. He's nice in a non-personal, all business kind of a way. Which is fine with me because his personal life is interesting. Steve is in his sixties and I'm pretty sure his current wife is still too young to drink alcohol.

Best to keep that relationship on the business track alone.

I email him back and think about moving to a warmer climate as I pour my cup of coffee and look out the window. It will be November here soon and most of the trees outside my window are in their full fall glory. Soon, the leaves will be crunching under my boots and I'll get to dig out my box of scarves that I never needed in Tampa.

I think about the cold walk I took last night and the warm hand that held mine.

Then I just get sad.

Laurie and Ryan's job offer fills my mind again.

Maybe...maybe I could stay.

No.

Even thinking the word *stay* makes my whole spine straighten and my fingers start to itch.

I don't know how to stay in one place.

There's a sign on Laurie's doorbell when I walk up to the porch at four that afternoon.

Come in, we are either out back or talking too loud to hear the doorbell.

I know very few people who can say this with such truth as Laurie and her children.

I open the door and the small house is empty but the back sliding door is part way open and I can hear people laughing and talking out there. I step outside and even though I'm pretty punctual, there are already quite a few people here. Brandon and Hannah. Shawn and Hallie. Lexi and her husband, Nate. Laurie is filling glasses with ice on the table by the backdoor and Ryan is leaning over the grill. The kids are all running through the yard. A cold breeze is blowing right through me, coat and all.

How are these people not freezing?

"Annie!" A chorus of my name rings out and I get this warm, wonderful feeling deep in my stomach.

How is it that I can enjoy being with friends so much and yet be so terrified at the thought of staying here with them?

"Annie, can you help me get more stuff from inside?" Laurie asks me.

"Sure."

I follow her inside and she hands me a bag of red Solo cups and a stack of paper plates with little nutcrackers marching around the edge.

She grins. "I couldn't resist. Aren't they cute?"

"It's not even Halloween until next week."

She waves a hand. "I could do without Halloween. It's Christmas that I really care about."

"I guess I'm with you there."

Laurie is all over her kitchen, pulling out plastic silverware, napkins, condiments. "So how was your night last night?" she asks nonchalantly over her shoulder as she digs in her fridge.

She's totally fishing for a dish on Zach and I decide to have a little fun since she's been ridiculous about setting us up.

I shake my head and sigh. "It was pretty much awful."

Her jaw drops as she emerges from the fridge with a jar of sliced dill pickles and another small jar of relish. "No!"

"Yeah, pretty terrible." I lean against her kitchen counter and sigh again. "I mean, he's a nice guy and all but he's a little weird."

"Well, Annie, I mean every guy is a little on the strange side." She sighs and nudges the fridge closed. "You didn't have *any* chemistry? At all?"

I think about the way his hand felt holding mine and swallow back the immediate formation of a colony of admiral butterflies that find a home in my stomach.

"Nope," I lie. "No chemistry at all."

She makes a growling sound in the back of her throat. "Oh, I could have just *sworn* that something was there!" She sets her pickles on the counter and huffs. "I mean, I seriously could have sworn. Like the day that I met you, I totally knew you would be perfect for Zach." She rubs her head and sighs at the pickles. "And I'm not often wrong, Annie."

"Oh I believe you," I say because I really do believe her.

"I mean, I put together Shawn and Hallie—"

"Wait, you arranged their — ?"

"Happiness?" she interrupts, looking up at me. "Yep."

"I was going to say marriage, but okay."

"Eh, happiness, marriage. It's all one and the same to a single person."

"And to a married person?"

She grins. "Oh we don't tell single people that kind of stuff. The goal is to get people to the altar, not have them running from it."

"Who is running from the altar?" Ryan comes into the kitchen and takes the barbecue sauce off the counter.

"Annie."

"I am not," I say, shaking my head at Ryan. "I'm just asking if married people find marriage as fulfilling and happy as single people think marriage will be."

Ryan shrugs and looks at his wife. "I mean, a lot probably depends on the time of the month that we're in." He grins and ducks Laurie's slap on his arm.

"Hey!"

Now he's dancing around the kitchen, narrowly missing being hit by his wife as he goes back toward the door. "Or, you know, like whether or not they are pregnant or nursing or had a bad haircut or watched a scary movie the night before or 'accidentally' shredded my favorite pair of jeans in the laundry—"

"They were disgusting!" Laurie yells at him. "They were so badly torn that Mrs. O'Neil across the street could see your underwear through them when you were in our backyard!"

Ryan grins and goes back outside but sticks his head back in once more, grinning unrepentantly. "Or when she thinks that moth balls are the same as dryer balls and—"

"Enough!" Laurie yells.

He closes the door on his laugh.

She sighs at me. "Laundry may not be my strong point."

I laugh. "Oh Laurie."

We walk outside carrying all of the stuff Laurie had been pulling out and pile it on the long table right outside the door. Meanwhile, all of the couples at the table are talking about marital happiness now.

"I don't know. Are we still happily married?" Brandon asks Hannah, who is rubbing her stomach with a concentrated look.

"Not when you keep asking me every ten seconds if I'm in

labor."

"Are you in labor?"

She rewards his question with a glare that makes my water completely freeze over. He grins.

"Are you having contractions?" Laurie asks, watching her friend.

"I don't know."

"What do you mean you don't know?"

"I mean, I don't know," Hannah bites out. "I ache all over all the time. And I have to pee like every twelve minutes and it takes me another twelve minutes to stand back up from the potty. They seriously did not have pregnant women in mind when whoever it was invented the toilet."

"It was probably a man," Hallie offers.

Hannah grimaces and rubs her stomach harder.

"Seriously, Hannah, now you're scaring me too. You are not allowed to have this baby on my back porch, no matter how much I love you."

Brandon watches his wife and shakes his head. "And here we go again."

"She's in labor?" I ask, feeling this mix of fear, excitement and lots more fear. I've never been around someone who is about to have a baby. I've watched some of the Discovery Channel programs and bawled through them at the miracle of birth, but I've never been this close to it before.

"She won't admit it until the baby is crowning," Brandon says.

"Good grief, Hannah." Hallie rolls her eyes. "I have one good contraction and I'm driving myself to the hospital."

"I hate hospitals," Hannah bites out.

"It's because you don't have a great doctor," Laurie tells her. "You should go with Dr. Hamilton. She's great."

"I hate doctors."

"Or Dr. Menelli. He's fantastic," Hallie says.

"I hate men."

Brandon nods to his wife and looks at his watch. "Okay, honey, we've reached the point where you hate everyone. Can we go to the hospital now?"

"No."

He sighs.

Laurie shakes her head. "Hannah."

"It's probably just indigestion."

Shawn grins. "You haven't eaten yet."

"It's pre-indigestion." Her face creases in a frown and she huffs her breath out, holding her stomach. "It's pre-gestion."

"And now you are making up words." Brandon looks at his watch again. "And we're at three minutes apart. Seriously, Hannah, if you don't let me drive you to the hospital right now, I will make Dr. Kemry come here."

"I already said you can't have the baby on my back porch," Laurie says.

Ryan smiles gently at Hannah. "It's probably time, friend."

She sighs and her face eases from it's tightness. "Fine."

"Fine?" Brandon is up from the chair, keys in hand and is helping Hannah up before she even really finishes saying the word. "Great. Great. Bye guys. We will call when we know something."

He steadies his wife and then runs to the yard and carries his daughter back with him.

"All right, Nat, we love you very much," he says as he gets closer. He gives her a huge hug and kisses her cheeks and all of a sudden, Hannah is sobbing.

"Oh, let me hold her," she says, reaching for Natalie with one hand while holding her stomach with the other. "Oh my baby girl. Our last few moment as a family of three."

Zach pokes his head out the door, grins at me and comes and stands over next to me as the rest of the friends all try their best to give Brandon, Hannah and Natalie a little bit of time of their own.

"What's going on?" he whispers, obviously catching onto the seriousness of the moment.

"Hannah's in labor," I whisper back.

"Good grief, *finally.*"

I grin and then shush him. "This is a big moment."

"Well yeah. She might be able to walk correctly now."

"No, I mean, they are saying goodbye to Natalie."

"What's wrong with Natalie?"

"She can't go to the hospital with them," I say.

Zach shrugs. "I say she's getting the better deal then."

"Shh!"

Hannah finally turns, swiping away tears after smothering Natalie with kisses and hands me her cell phone.

"You don't think you'll need this?" I ask her.

"Can you take a last picture of us as a family of three?" Even as she says it, she starts crying again.

Laurie and Brandon are the photographers here so I'm not sure why I am holding the cell phone instead of Laurie but then I glance to my right and see Laurie holding Corbin close while she's crying and nod.

Even Hallie is swiping away tears.

Now I feel like a bad friend for not being more emotional about this.

"Sure," I nod. I wait until Hannah has gathered herself again and she smiles through teary eyes, cuddling Natalie close to her cheek, Brandon on the other side. "There," I say, handing her back her phone.

"Okay. Let's go," Hannah nods, kissing Natalie one last time. "Laur?"

"She's fine, Hannah. We're good." Laurie comes over and puts her hand on Natalie's head. "Now go have my niece or nephew before you birth them right here on the porch."

"Or in the car," Brandon urges her toward the door. "I'm not nearly as prepared as the Lamaze people thought I was."

Hannah smiles, takes a deep breath and then waves to

everyone before crunching over in a contraction again as Brandon hustles her back into the house and out the front door.

We all just kind of stand around and look at each other for a few minutes before Zach finally clears his throat. "Why don't we just say a prayer for Brandon and Hannah right now?"

It's an incredibly sweet thought and one that everyone is automatically nodding and muttering their agreement before joining hands.

I hold Zach's hand and Laurie's free hand as she cradles Corbin with the other arm. Ryan puts his arm around Laurie and the baby and then reaches for Hallie's hand. We make a circle around the table and I peek open my eyes just once as Zach starts to pray.

A warm sweetness is blooming deep in my stomach.

Here I am, circled in prayer, praying with friends for another friend.

There's just this most wonderful feeling surrounding us and I totally know that Jesus is right here with us.

"Lord," Zach says like he's talking to Shawn who is right next to him. "We just want to ask you to watch over our dear friends right now as they are about to have their newest baby.

Surround them in your care, protect them, keep both Hannah and the little one safe and Lord, we just pray that you bless this little baby with a heart that loves You and follows You. Amen."

"Amen," we all murmur.

I'm sad when the prayer ends.

Zach squeezes my hand once and slowly, reluctantly lets go. Then he smiles at me, just for a hint of a second, before going over to talk to Ryan who is back to manning the grill.

I turn, feeling a smile on my face and bump right into Laurie who is staring at me, eyes narrowed, face serious.

"Um. Laurie?"

"Kitchen," she demands and stalks inside.

Hallie looks at me. "Wow. I'm glad I'm not you."

I wince and follow her inside, closing the door slowly behind me before turning to face her, grimacing.

"Okay, so I don't know what I did but—"

"I SAW THAT," she yells and the baby jumps in her arms but doesn't cry. Laurie's face is the picture of overwhelming joy as she does a happy dance in the kitchen with Corbin.

"Wait, you're not...what?"

"I totally saw that! He definitely held your hand for like an extra five whole seconds! And he smiled! And you smiled! You are such a liar!"

Her tone is accusatory but her face is all smiles. And she's still dancing around the kitchen with Corbin.

I'm assuming she's not actually mad that I told her there wasn't any chemistry then.

Or if she is mad, she has the weirdest way of showing that.

I'm not sure what to say so I just stand there until her dance is over. She takes a deep breath and then grins at me before shaking her head.

"You little stink. You should have told me that it went well!"

"What?"

"Dinner! This totally all happened at dinner the other night, didn't it?"

Ryan sticks his head in the door as I open my mouth. "Hey, honey, we've got like two minutes on the burgers. Can I get the seasoning salt?" He looks at her face. "What happened? Hannah didn't have the baby in the car, did she?"

"No, no, no. This has nothing to do with Hannah." She frowns. "Though I might text Brandon and just make sure they

278

made it to triage." She pulls her phone out of her back pocket and types something really quick. "No, this is about Annie. She's about to tell me that the dinner that she and Zach had together the other night is the reason that they are all sparkied and chemistried today."

"I'm not sure those are real words," I tell her.

"Please don't say anything," Ryan says to me, close to begging. "She had a brief few years where this didn't happen and now we're back to arranging everything and meddling in everything."

"And doing a pretty great job at it too!" Laurie fist pumps the air.

Ryan sighs. "The seasoning salt. Please."

Laurie chucks it to him and he sighs at me once more before going back to the grill.

"Please," he whispers.

The door closes and Laurie rolls her eyes. "He's always been a little on the dramatic side."

Knowing what I know about this couple, I really don't believe that Ryan is the dramatic one of the pair.

"So?" she asks excitedly, sitting on one of the stools by her kitchen counter and setting the baby on her lap.

"So?" I parrot, not sure what she's wanting from me.

"Dish, dish! How was dinner? What did you make? What did you talk about? Was it love at first bite?" She grins at me. "See what I did there?"

"I see," I nod. I shake my head. "There's not much to tell, Laurie."

"There is always something to tell. Besides, you are my most favorite new friend and Zach is just like the greatest worship leader on the whole planet. You know, the moment I first met Zach I just knew that I was going to find him the perfect girl for him to marry someday."

"Whoa," I say, holding up my hands. "Marry? Laurie, we've barely even been on one date! I don't even know if we have been on one date!"

"Coffee and then dinner? I'd say that's two whole dates."

I just look at her. "I don't know what to say."

"You don't have to say anything, Annie. Don't you worry. I've got this all worked out."

"You really do, don't you?" I sort of feeling like one of those marionette things that they used in the *Sound of Music*, only instead of Julie Andrews pulling the strings, I've got Laurie up there moving my arms and legs around.

I think I would have preferred Julie Andrews.

Laurie's phone buzzes, she looks at it, smiles and types out a quick message before looking at me grinning. "Today is a great day, my friend. You and Zach actually have chemistry, my beautiful son Cannon can now recognize his name written down and Hannah made it to the hospital on time."

"That's good. I mean about Hannah. And Cannon, I guess, too."

"Dinner!" Ryan calls into the house.

Laurie picks up the baby and waltzes for the door, humming the song from *Cinderella* as she leaves.

So this is love...

I squinch my eyes tight, rub my temples and follow her outside.

At eleven forty-five that night, my phone chirps with a text and wakes me up. I grope for it in the darkness, my eyes bleary from sleep. Finally I find it, click the button and it brings up a very bright picture that makes me yelp. Once my eyes stop watering, I have to squint at in order to see.

It's a baby wrapped up in a striped blanket with a little hat, laying on a white sheet.

Introducing Declan Curtis Knox. 7lbs. 12oz. Mom and baby are doing great.

I squint once more at the picture, then at the clock, click out a quick congratulations and go back to sleep.

So much for delivering in the car.

Chapter Seventeen

By the time I wake up the next morning, there are thirty-two text messages on my phone.

No wonder I slept so badly last night. I probably subconsciously heard the buzzing of it vibrating on my nightstand the entire night.

Somehow, I got stuck in a group message between Laurie, Hallie and two other numbers that I didn't have in my phone. All about who is going to bring dinner to Hannah when and is anyone available to go to the hospital to visit them today and by the way, Hannah was really craving Brie now that she could eat soft cheeses again so someone should bring that.

Which only makes me curious what soft cheese does to a baby in-utero.

Does soft cheese equal soft bones or something?

I pour myself a thermos of coffee and head out the door for church. I'm so tired that I went for the I-don't-care-anymore outfit of ballet flats, jeans and a cardigan over a tank top. If nothing else, I'll at least be comfortable as I try not to fall asleep during the service.

I get to church with a couple of minutes to spare, so I go inside and head straight for the chocolate-covered mini donuts.

Shawn still hasn't made donuts for me, so I don't even feel bad as I shove three of them one after another into my mouth.

"Hungry much?"

I turn and Zach is standing there grinning at me. I swallow the last bite as he reaches for a Styrofoam cup.

"I got stuck on a group text last night," I tell him by way of explaining the donuts.

"I hate those. That's the worst part of owning a smart phone."

"You're telling me."

"What group?"

"Laurie, Hallie and two other people I don't have listed in my phone. All about Hannah and her new baby."

"Did she make it to the hospital?"

I am surprised. "No one texted you?"

He shakes his head. "Nope."

"Oh. Yeah. She made it. She had him around 11:30 last night, I guess. It was a boy. They named him Declan."

"Hmm. Declan." He shrugs. "Okay then."

"You don't like the name?"

"I'm just more of a fan of regular names."

"Like what?"

He shrugs again. "I don't know. Annie." He grins.

I smile and I can feel my cheeks warming. "You know, I had never been called Annie before I met Laurie."

"You're kidding."

I shake my head. "No, I'm really not."

"She changed your name?"

"Well, I mean, she didn't change it, she just added an *ie* to it."

He starts laughing. "She is something else. So do you even like being called Annie? What did you grow up being called? Anne?"

I nod. "Just Anne. Yeah, I mean, it's fine." Truth be told, I actually have grown pretty fond of it. With how much has changed in my life over the past few weeks, Annie just seems like a good change as well.

New person, new name. I'm just changing all over.

He pours a cup of coffee and takes my elbow, moving us out of the crowd trying to get to the coffee and donuts. "So, what's your middle name?"

"I don't have one," I tell him.

He raises his eyebrows as he sips his coffee. "You what?" he says after he swallows.

"I don't have one," I say again.

"How come?"

I shrug. "I guess my parents decided I didn't need two names."

"So when you're filling out paperwork and it asks for your middle initial, you just leave it blank?"

I nod. "Yep."

"I didn't even know you could do that."

"What's your middle name?"

"Thomas."

"Zachary Thomas Murphy."

He nods. "That's the name. Thomas is my dad's name. So interesting story, my parents had a really hard time getting pregnant with my sister, so they almost named her Corrine

Thomas Murphy after my dad because they were pretty convinced that she was going to be their only baby and the name Thomas has been in my family for over a hundred years. But my mom decided that she just couldn't name her baby girl Thomas and a year later, they found out I was coming as a complete surprise."

I smile. "That's so cool."

He nods. "So, you should let me take you out to brunch after this service. That is, if you haven't filled up on those little donuts."

I grin. "I didn't get breakfast and I was sort of starving."

"Oh, you don't have to explain anything to me. I eat those every Sunday. I just have a hard time with figuring out where to stop with them, since it takes like eight to equal one regular donut. So while I'm trying to figure out the ratio, my stomach is just like, 'I'll have six more, thank you.'"

I smile. "I would like that."

"Six more mini donuts?"

"Brunch, weirdo."

He grins. "And done. I'll see you after service, Annie."

Somehow he finds my hand and gives it a quick, warm squeeze as he leaves.

I don't even hear her sidle up to me.

"So, brunch?" I hear in my ear and I jump about ten feet. I grab my chest and turn to see Laurie standing there, grinning like a kid who just got her favorite colored gumball out of the machine.

"Laurie!" I gasp. "Good night!"

"Actually, it's good morning," she points out. Then she rubs her cheek and pokes at her messy bun on the top of her head. "Though, honestly, it feels like it should be the night again. Corbin didn't sleep worth a flip and you guys kept replying to my text messages."

"I can guarantee it was not me replying," I say.

"Well, anyway, it was a long night. So. Brunch?" she says again, still with that same smile.

I take a long drink of my coffee and shrug rather than reply.

She just grins wider. "Uh-huh. You can't fool me, Annie McKay. I have been in this game for far too long."

"What game?" Ryan asks, coming up behind her and pocketing a pager.

"The Game of Life, Love and Happiness," Laurie says, dramatically sticking her pointer finger in the air. "You may call me the Spin Master."

"Why the Spin Master?" I ask.

"Because. I spin people where they need to go. Or maybe *to whom* they need to go."

Ryan sighs. "Here we go again."

"He asked her out to brunch!" she says, all giggly to Ryan.

"Are you going?" he asks me.

"Of course she is going! You don't turn down free food! That's the cardinal rule of single womanhood. And he totally likes her and she totally likes him, so of course, *of course*, she is going."

"How do you know?"

"That she's going?"

"That he likes her?"

Somehow, I have become just an accessory to this whole conversation about my future. I stand there and sip my coffee, wondering if I should comment or not.

Nah.

Laurie huffs her breath out, rolling her eyes. "Ryan. He used the word *brunch*. A man doesn't use the word *brunch* unless he is super serious about a woman."

"I use the word brunch all the time."

"Because you are married. To a *woman*."

Laurie likes to over-emphasize words sometimes.

"So what do men who aren't serious about women call the meal in between breakfast and lunch?" Ryan asks.

Laurie opens her mouth and then closes it, waving a hand. "You are just being difficult."

He laughs. "And yet, somehow, you continue to love me."

"Sure. Sure. Keep telling yourself that, buddy."

"You adore me." He shakes his head and sips his Styrofoam cup of coffee. "You know it, I know it. And you know how I know it?"

"How?" I ask, since Laurie is too busy rolling her eyes to respond.

"Because she asked me this morning if I wanted a *bagel*," Ryan says. "Women don't use the word *bagel* unless they are very serious about a man."

I start laughing and Laurie just shakes her head at her husband, obviously trying not to give him the benefit of a smile. I can hear Zach playing the opening strains of "Come Thou Fount" through the opening and closing door as people go in and out of the sanctuary.

Laurie just sighs at Ryan. "You are incorrigible."

"And you are cute. Come on, Spin Master. Let's go find our seats."

I grin.

I follow them inside and they sit next to Shawn and Hallie, who have a whole bunch of seats saved in the same row we sat in last week. Hallie grins at me and picks her Bible off of the seat beside her.

"Here you go, Annie. I saved you a seat."

I smile and settle next to her. Shawn grins at me and we all stand as per Zach's instructions to sing. Shawn puts his arm around his wife's waist and Hallie leans up against him, one hand in the air as she sings, eyes closed, and one hand on the tiny bump on her abdomen. I sneak a peek to the other side of them and Ryan and Laurie are holding hands as they sing.

I look back up at the stage as we switch verses and Zach nods and moves to the beat as he strums his guitar. His eyes are closed and he's just completely in the zone of worshiping Jesus and I suddenly realize how very attractive this guy is.

Oh boy.

This has never happened to me before. I mean, yes, I've

found different men attractive and whatever, but it's never been based on something so intangible like this and it's definitely never been something that could potentially be reciprocated.

I can't decide if it makes me want to stay in this tiny town or to call up my boss, Steve, and get him to move me out of here pronto so that I have no chance of potentially getting hurt here.

The marriage that impacted me the most – my parents' – wasn't really an experience that any of us enjoyed.

I sneak another look at the two couples I am standing next to. Somehow, these people make being married seem normal and fun. Not painful and heart-wrenching.

I close my eyes and sing the words, praying them as I sing. "Let thy goodness, like a fetter, bind my wandering heart to thee. Prone to wander, Lord, I feel it, prone to leave the God I love; here's my heart, O take and seal it, seal it for Thy courts above."

The song ends and I look up at the stage as Zach plays the closing chords. He nods to the congregation and starts strumming the next song but as he does, he looks down from the stage and sends a small smile my way.

I'd be lying if I said my chest didn't feel like someone had mod-podged my ribs together. I suddenly have a very hard time getting a full breath into my lungs and focusing on the words up on the screens.

"Bless the Lord, oh my soul," sings Zach and the congregation joins right in. Since I was having trouble focusing anyway, I just close my eyes and listen. The place is packed this morning, probably because my bulletin states that Nick Amery is teaching again.

Several hundred voices all singing to Jesus is enough to wake even the tiredest, most confused soul.

I sometimes wonder how many of my problems could be solved just by being a little quieter and listening more.

I join in the singing for the second verse and soon the music is over and Nick is taking the stage.

"Today, we are going to pick up where we left off at the beginning of John 14. Remember that we just heard Jesus' new command that He has given His disciples about loving one another. Today, we're right back where we were in finding out some of the last minute things Jesus had for His disciples."

Nick clears his throat and starts reading from his Bible. The verses are posted on the screens. ""And if I go and prepare a place for you, I will come back and take you to be with me that you also may be where I am. You know the way to the place where I am going." Thomas said to Him, "Lord, we don't know where you are going, so how can we know the way?"'"

He stops and nods to the congregation. "So, with that, I have a three point sermon. I wanted to have a forty-seven point sermon on this small section, but Ruby told me that you would all have stood up and walked out."

Everyone chuckles.

Nick teaches for forty minutes. "Do you know where you are going?" he asks a little while later. "Not just in eternity, though that is an important question as well. But do you know where you are going today? This afternoon after church?"

Brunch. The word sticks in my mind.

"And if you know where you are going, do you know what purpose it has? Don't live your life without purpose. This life is too short, this time passes too quickly. Figure out where you are going, know where you are going to be and then *live*. Meet people, talk to people, create friends, lead people to Jesus, spend time cultivating relationships, get married, fall more in love, have babies, stay up all night with them, send them to school, keep the flame alive with your spouse, and just keep *living*." He looks out over the crowd. "Are you living? Or are you just existing?"

He closes us in prayer and unlike last week where everyone was up and chattering pretty quickly, I think everyone is a little sobered by his lesson. So we all slowly stop nodding and quietly pack away our Bibles and pens before we start quietly visiting.

"Wow," Hallie says, one hand rubbing her stomach, as she shakes her head.

"Yeah," I breathe.

"Talk about convicting."

"Yeah." I don't totally trust my train of thoughts yet enough to say something more than that.

All I can think about is my job. And Ryan's job offer. And the future.

And Zach.

And this town.

And Zach some more.

"So. What are you up to today, Annie?" Hallie smiles at me. "Would you like to come with us to the hospital to see little Declan?"

Laurie leans over. "She's got plans, Hallie."

"I would love to," I say at the same time.

Laurie narrows her eyes at me. "What about your plans?"

"The plans are only for this morning. What time are you going to the hospital?"

"I was thinking around two or three," Hallie says, looking back and forth to me and Laurie. "I was going to try and go during Rachel's nap time. Does that work for you, Laur?"

She nods. "That works for me."

"Annie?"

"I think that will work."

"Okay!" She smiles brightly. "How about we meet at the restaurant and we can all drive over together."

"Merson's?" I clarify.

She nods.

"Sounds good."

Zach comes up then and smiles at everyone before grinning especially big at me. "Hey."

"Hi." I'm sure my cheeks are basically the same color as my cranberry colored sweater. "Music was fantastic."

"Thanks. It's all those hours not working coming out."

I grin.

Laurie starts talking to Hallie about something and though it's an obvious ploy to get her attention so Zach and I can talk, it's not unappreciated.

"So. Still up for brunch?" he asks me.

I nod.

"Where do you want to go?"

I shrug. "Where is good?"

"Merson's, but they are closed today. There's a pretty good little café on the other side of town that I've been to a couple of times before I started going to Shawn's place. Or we could always do Vizzini's, though that's not really brunch."

"The café sounds good," I say because as much as I like Italian food, I can only eat it every so often before it just doesn't sound good to me. I knew a girl one time who could happily eat at Olive Garden every day of the week, but more than once or twice in a month and I never want to eat there again.

Zach nods. "Why don't we just take my car and we'll swing back by here for yours after lunch?"

"Sounds good."

He smiles at me. "Let me just pack up the instruments and I'll be back."

We are heading to the restaurant a few minutes later. Laurie was all smiles when we left.

"She really enjoys matchmaking, doesn't she?" I say as Zach holds open the passenger side door of his car for me.

"Oh man. It's her most favorite thing to do. I still remember the very first time I ever met her, she walked straight up to me and asked if I was single. I would have been a little weirded out if she hadn't been gigantically pregnant with Cannon at the time."

I laugh.

He goes around and climbs in the driver's seat and starts driving us toward the café and we talk about everything and nothing at the same time.

It's easy to talk to Zach.

We get to the café and we are right in the middle of the lunch crowd, so we have to wait a couple of minutes for a table.

"Most of these people are here because Merson's is closed," Zach tells me as we lean up against the wall close to the door. All the waiting benches are taken and the place smells like eggs, potatoes and bacon, unlike Shawn's which usually smells like something sweet baking.

It's not a bad smell, but just different.

I decide that a sweet smelling bakery/café lends itself much better to drinking coffee and hanging out there. In places that smell like meat, I feel like I need to eat and get out.

"What are you thinking about?" Zach asks me, looking over with a smile. "You've got a weird look on your face."

"Do you think that places that cook bacon want you to stay and talk or do you think that they are more in the business of turning over tables?"

Zach starts laughing. "What?"

"Well, I mean, Shawn's place kind of encourages people to just stay and hang out and talk and order more food."

"Yeah."

"But this place seems like a place where you should just come, eat and get back on the road."

Zach looks around and finally nods. "I can see that."

Over the noise level of the people here, I can hear very faint music playing and I lean off the wall a few inches to listen better. "They're playing Christmas music!"

"Seriously?" Zach shakes his head. "It's barely November."

"They have a tree over there!"

"How sad."

"Sad? Christmas is happy! You aren't happy when you see Christmas trees?"

Zach opens his mouth and I hold up a hand.

"Answer carefully, Zachary. Our future friendship depends on your answer."

He grins. "Okay. Yes, I am made very happy when I see a Christmas tree."

"Thank you."

"*After* Thanksgiving though. It's too early for Christmas decorations and they keep coming out earlier and earlier. Soon, we will be decorating for Christmas in September."

I shake my head. "Not as long as pumpkin spice lattes exist. People get a little too crazy about fall to just jump ahead to Christmas."

"So is Christmas your favorite holiday then?"

I shrug. "Isn't it everyone's?"

"It's not mine."

"What's yours?"

"St. Patrick's Day."

I just look at him. "Are you serious?"

"Sure. The little green guy with the red hair? He's pretty awesome."

"The leprechaun?"

"Right."

I just look at him for a few more minutes before he finally grins and I shake my head. "You are an odd duck, Zach."

"Thanks. I'd hate to be predictable."

"Zach, party of two!" the host yells and we push ourselves off the wall and follow him to a table in the far back corner of the restaurant.

We get our seats and I take the menu the host is handing to me. "Thanks."

"If you need anything, Clay will be your server. Have a good lunch."

He disappears and Zach smiles at me across the table.

"So. How did you like church today?"

I sigh. "It was convicting."

He nods. "I thought so too. So, cool story, Nick actually used to be a singles' pastor at the church. I think he's retained his ability to not make every sermon about having a family. Know what I mean?"

I nod. I've been to many church services over the years that were all about how to keep harmony in the home. Not a hard thing to do when it was just me in my home and I rarely disagree with myself.

"What did you find convicting?" Zach asks me.

Part of me likes that Zach doesn't just stick with the surface conversations and part of me wishes that he would.

I look at the menu without really seeing the words in front of me as I contemplate what to say to Zach. It's hard to put something that is based on so much feeling into actual thoughts and words.

I open my mouth to start.

"Good morning, how are you guys?" A younger guy with a name tag that says *Clay* is in front of us, holding a pen and paper. "What can I start you guys off with?"

"Coffee please," I say when Zach nods to me.

"Same here."

"And a water," I add on.

Zach smiles. "Same."

Clay nods. "I'll be back."

"You were about to say something?" Zach says when Clay leaves.

I take a deep breath and try to gather my thoughts again. "So. I've been thinking a lot about the job Ryan offered me."

Zach nods. "I know."

"And it sounds like a good job." Ryan had emailed me the actual requirements and the benefits and salary information this past week. I'd printed it out and stared at it during dinner several nights.

"But?" Zach prompts.

I sigh. "I'm just…" I shake my head and look up at him, not sure how much I can actually say to him.

Yes, he's a friend. Yes, he's a nice guy. But he's also made it fairly clear that he's potentially interested in more than just friendship and I don't want him getting the wrong idea here.

What is the wrong idea? Do I even have a right idea for him?

Zach smiles a gentle smile at me and leans a little closer to the table. "Listen, Annie, I just want you to know that I'm going to put into practice my seminary degree here and in particular, the part where I learned how to counsel people. The floor is yours and

I promise I will have zero condemnation or opinions for you."

"No, I mean, I want your opinion."

"Really." He doesn't say it like a question.

"No, really."

He shakes his head. "No opinion. So start over and just know that you can speak as freely as you want." He waves a hand around. "We don't know anyone here. You just say as much as you want to without fear of anyone hearing or finding out."

I smile at his unsaid promise not to mention anything to Ryan or Laurie.

Clay brings the coffees and sets a big bowl of half and half containers in the middle of the table. Zach orders an omelet with a side of biscuits. I order the yogurt parfait and a side of cinnamon toast.

Clay nods and leaves. Zach looks at me and nods, pulling his coffee closer, forearm on the table, hunching over his cup slightly. "Go for it."

"I don't know if I want to take the job," I say. Saying it out loud makes me feel completely ungrateful.

Zach nods. "Okay."

"Not that I don't like this town or the people here or

everything that goes along with it," I say quickly.

"Right."

"But..." My voice trails off as I look around the restaurant.

"But?"

"I'm just so used to things like they are."

And there it is. Right there in the open space between us on the table.

Zach nods. "I understand. Change is scary."

"It's very scary." I rub my hand through my hair. "I'm not big on change."

"Says the woman who moves to a new location every six months."

I smile. "It does sound ridiculous coming from me, doesn't it?"

He shrugs and sips his coffee, smiling at me. His hair is flicked up in a sticky-up style, his eyes are warm and understanding. His chin has a light dusting of whiskers on it.

He really is a very good looking guy.

"It's not ridiculous. It would be a huge change to go from no roots to roots."

"Yeah."

He watches me for a minute and then purses his lips before speaking. "So, Annie, you've never really mentioned too much about your family."

I shake my head.

"I mean, I kind of gathered that you aren't close with them."

"You could say that." Especially considering I don't even know where my dad is right now.

"Do you think that might be some of the reason that you are hesitant to settle somewhere?" He asks the question slowly.

I sigh. "Maybe." I look around the restaurant again. "Maybe I'm just not the staying kind," I say.

He studies me for a long time. So long, that I start getting a little uncomfortable under his stare.

"Mm," he says, finally. "No. No, I don't think that's it."

"You don't think what is it?"

"Someone told you that and you've pulled it into who you are, but I don't think that you really aren't the staying kind. You fit too well into the group of friends here that you've been forced into and I think it just scares you to think of not having that excuse if something were to happen."

Who knew that brunch came with a side of therapy?

I just look at him and Clay appears with our food. "Omelet and biscuits for you, sir. Toast and parfait for you, miss. Can I get you anything else?"

"No, thanks," Zach says, smiling nicely at the waiter.

"Enjoy your meal." He leaves.

Zach reaches a hand across the table. "Can I pray for the food?"

I stare at his hand for a good twenty seconds before I carefully set my hand on his. He holds my hand gently and closes his eyes. "Lord, please just bless Annie today. I pray that You give her clarity and wisdom as she tries to figure out what she's going to do with this job offer, but more than that Lord, I pray that You just give her a deeper understanding of her purpose. Amen." He squeezes my hand and then shuts his eyes really fast again. "Oh and bless the food. Amen."

I grin.

Chapter **Eighteen**

The week races by. I spend my entire Monday in a company-wide conference to discuss work place habits. I even made up a little presentation with graphics to drive the point home.

On one slide, there was a big x crossing over a cartoon of a man sitting on a toilet reading the paper.

This is what my job has come down to.

I sent Ryan an email that very same night and told him that I would like to discuss the job on Friday evening and I would have a definite answer for him by Saturday.

But Friday came way faster than I had anticipated.

Probably because I was so busy. Tuesday, Zach took me out to dinner. Wednesday, I hurried home from work, whipped up a quick soup with a side of macaroni and cheese for their toddler and took it over to Hannah and Brandon. Thursday, Zach called at seven o'clock and asked if I knew that *Cupcake Wars* was coming on in an hour since I'd mentioned that I liked to watch it and then he randomly showed up at my apartment with a box of gourmet cupcakes right as I turned on the TV.

If he's trying to win points, he was doing a great job of it.

But now, all of a sudden, it's Friday and I'm leaving work to go meet Laurie and Ryan at their house and I still have no earthly idea what I'm going to do.

Now to just pray that God gives me the wisdom between tonight and tomorrow.

I ring their doorbell and hear a faint "Come in!" from inside the house so I open the door.

Corbin is laying in the middle of the living room surrounded by toys and staring at me and I hear a "just a second, Annie!" coming from the back of the house.

Finally, Laurie and Cannon walk out and Cannon is wiping wet hands on his jeans.

"Sorry," Laurie says to me. "We still aren't fully independent in the bathroom yet."

Cannon just grins at me.

I smile. "It's fine." I kneel down on the floor next to the baby and chuck his little cheek. "Hi there, buddy!"

"Can you grab him for me? It's almost time for him to eat but I've got to get dinner finished up."

I nod and pick up the baby. He grins a toothless smile at me and I stand and follow Laurie into the kitchen with him.

"Ryan is on his way home," she says. "They were running a little behind today. I guess one of the guys didn't show up this morning."

"That would be frustrating."

She nods. "Sadly, it happens a lot in construction. So. Do you know if you are going to take the job or not?"

Laurie is nothing if not direct.

"Not a clue," I tell her, deciding to just be direct with her as well.

She nods. "Well. I'm praying for you and for you to figure out your purpose here."

There's that word again that Zach used when he prayed for me at brunch last weekend.

Purpose.

I smile at Laurie. "Thanks Laur."

"So, I'm making this casserole tonight and I have no idea what I'm doing," she says, squinting at her laptop which is perched up on the high counter.

"Where did you find the recipe?"

"Where else? Pinterest. I don't even remember how I used to cook before Pinterest. I probably didn't. Goodness knows I wasn't raised to cook. Unless it involves brewing lemongrass tea — which by the way, *blegh*. Dad is not the best in the kitchen."

"Not the world's best chef?"

"Let's just say that Emeril doesn't need to be worried about anything," Laurie says. She sighs at the computer. "Anyway, I only started attempting to cook because it was costing too much money to eat out and unlike myself, Ryan actually likes to have more for dinner than a bowl of cereal."

I grin.

"Cardamom?" she mutters at the computer. "What is cardamom? I don't have cardamom. I don't even know what it is."

"It's a spice," I offer.

"Like pepper?"

"No," I say, slowly, trying to think about how to describe it. "It's sort of like a mix between ginger and cinnamon. It's used in spice teas a lot."

"So why am I putting it in a chicken casserole?"

"I don't know. Why are you putting it in chicken casserole?"

"Because that's what the recipe says to do." Laurie motions me over and points to the laptop screen.

I lean over the counter and study the computer screen. "Laurie, this is a recipe for chai cupcakes."

"No, it's not. It's for chicken enchilada casserole."

I look at the stuff she has in her bowl. Shredded chicken, diced green chilies, chopped tomatoes and then she has flour and apparently sugar, baking powder and salt, judging by the containers on the counter by the bowl.

"Oh boy," I say. I scroll up on the page and there's a very delicious looking picture of a cupcake, the frosting twisted up high, half a cinnamon stick tucked into it as decoration.

This was definitely not a chicken enchilada recipe.

"Did you push the back button or something?" I ask her.

"No. I haven't ever even looked up chai cupcakes. I was making the enchiladas and Corbin started crying, so I went to check on him and..." her voice trails off and her eyes get big.

"Cannon," she mutters.

"You think he was playing with the computer?"

"Most likely. He's gotten really into electronics." She sighs at the bowl. "So do I have to toss this?"

I look at the amount of flour and sugar in the bowl and the baking powder and salt and purse my lips. "Maybe we can just sift some of that out. But we might be turning this into chicken enchilada pot pie."

"Great. I've never made a pot pie before. I don't even know what you need for a pot pie."

"Do you have milk and butter?"

She nods.

"Then we probably have everything we need." I push up my sleeves and wash my hands in her kitchen sink. "Okay. First thing we are going to do is make a roux."

"Like Kanga's son?"

"I'm sorry?"

"Roo? Kanga's little guy on *Winnie the Pooh*? The little kangaroo? And side note, but am I the only one who has ever noticed that Roo doesn't have a father? He's like the *Winnie the Pooh* version of the Immaculate Conception."

I laugh. "No, a *roux*. It's French, I think. It just means we are going to melt down butter and then whisk in flour so we can make a thick sauce to put over the chicken and veggies before we put them in a pie crust."

"I don't have a pie crust."

"I think you have the ingredients for one."

"We are going to *make* a pie crust?"

I smile and rub Laurie's shoulder. "It will all be okay, friend. Just take a deep breath. Dinner is going to be fine."

We spend the next twenty minutes mixing, rolling and patting and by the time we put the pie in the oven, it is perfect, even though we are kind of making up the recipe for this. I've never heard of a chicken enchilada pot pie.

But I guess there is a first time for everything.

Laurie keeps checking the pie in the oven, flicking on and off the light like a little kid waiting for cookies. "Wow," she keeps saying, over and over. "We made pot pie!"

"Yes we did." I grin at her as I wipe up her counters with her kitchen sponge. She's cute. I love experiencing the wonder that comes from cooking and experimenting and creating something amazing from just ordinary ingredients.

See, if I could make money doing this, I would quit my job tomorrow.

Ryan walks in the door then and Laurie basically pounces on the poor man, dragging him over to the oven by his flannel shirt collar and talking eighty miles an hour. Meanwhile, Cannon is wrestling the man's leg while shouting, "Daddy's home!" and Corbin sees his father and starts crying to be picked up.

"Look! Look! Look!" Laurie yells at him. "We made chicken pot pie! From scratch! We were going to make enchiladas but Cannon pushed something on my computer and I started making chicken chai cupcakes but Annie swooped in and saved the day and we totally made that crust from scratch and you won't believe how easy it was and sniff! Breathe it in! Doesn't it smell amazing?"

"Daddy's home! Daddy's home!"

I walk over and pick Corbin up off the floor and get him to stop crying while Ryan tries to adjust to being home.

Poor guy. It would be quite the transition to come from a quiet car into this chaos.

"Wow," Ryan says, peering into the oven and putting a hand on Cannon's blond head. "Very cool! I'm excited to try it." He ruffles his son's hair. "Hey buddy."

"Hi Daddy! We're having cupcakes for dinner!"

"Uh yeah. Good try, kid," Laurie says, rolling her eyes.

Ryan grins at her. "You have to give the child props for trying," he says. "I mean, that is pretty genius of him."

"Stinker." Laurie tries to look sternly at her son but it ends up being a very fond, sweet expression. Cannon grins at her and she knuckles his head before sending him out of the kitchen.

"Hey Annie," Ryan says, waving over at me.

I walk into the kitchen and Corbin grins a gummy baby smile at his dad. "Hi Ryan."

Ryan takes the baby and kisses his wife, who dimples at him and then goes back to checking the oven.

I grin.

"So. We are discussing details tonight, right?" Ryan asks.

I nod. "Yes. I have some questions for you and I promise that I will make my final decision by tomorrow evening." I've been keeping a list all week of things that I have thought of that I need some clarification on as far as the job goes.

"Perfect," Ryan nods.

"Is it done?" Laurie asks, peering through the oven door.

"Is it like a golden brown on top?"

"I can't tell."

"You can open the door and check," I tell her.

"It won't make the pie deflate?"

"I sure hope not. And if it does, I'd really like to know what your oven did with the filling inside the pie." I smile at her but Laurie's serious face doesn't crack. She's still balancing on her heels, staring into the oven.

Finally, she sits back and shakes her head. "I can't do it. It's too pretty through the door. I'm worried if I look at it, it will melt or something."

"Ah, the opposite super power of Elsa," I say.

"What?"

"*Frozen?*"

"Oh." She laces her fingers together and sighs. "Okay. Okay, just do it."

Ryan is laughing at her.

"Is she always this serious about her cooking?" I ask Ryan, reaching for the oven door.

"Not but you should have seen her when our coffee maker broke and she had to decide on a new one. We bought a temporary cheap pot and then she spent about a month comparing prices and reading reviews on the actual coffee pot she wanted. Then we bought one and just stared at it in the box for the next two weeks because she wasn't one hundred percent certain she really wanted that one."

I laugh.

"Hey, people, I'm right here. I can actually hear you."

I crack open the oven door and the most delicious, spicy and homey smell escapes from the oven. Laurie immediately starts dancing around.

"It smells good! It smells good!" She's doing some weird interpretive dance that I assume is again her exploding in joy over her likely excellent pot pie results.

I grin.

The pie is perfectly golden brown and I hand Laurie the oven mitts.

She freezes, mid-dance. "Why are you giving these to me?"

"So you can take the pie out of the oven, Laur."

She's shaking her head before I even finish my sentence. "Mm-hmm. Nope. No ma'am. I am not doing that. No siree."

"Laurie, it's your oven and your pie and your oven mitts, so you should do the honors and pull the pie out."

"No way, Jose. I am not about to do that. It would be completely inconceivable."

"'You keep on using that word. I do not think it means what you think it means,'" Ryan quotes from *The Princess Bride*.

"Come on, Laurie. You can do it." I hand her the mitts again and she takes them, sliding them on while mumbling under her breath. I lean a little closer. "I'm sorry, what was that?"

"If I drop this, it's on your head."

"It's probably more likely going to land on my feet, if we want to get technical," I say, opening the oven door.

Ryan laughs.

Laurie's bottom lip is between her teeth and she carefully, in slow motion, pulls the pie out of the oven and sets it gingerly on the stove top.

Finally, she breathes.

"Look at the beautiful pie!" she hollers, fist pumping the air.

Ryan nods. "Looks great, sweetie. Ready to eat?"

Laurie sets the table, Ryan supervises Cannon's hands being washed and then buckles the baby into bouncy seat. I find a few ingredients in Laurie's fridge and throw together a super quick salad to go along with the pie.

We dish out the slices, sit at the table and Ryan leans over his plate, inhaling as we get ready to pray. Cannon reaches for one of my hands and Laurie reaches for the other.

"Lord, thanks for this day, thanks for this amazing dinner and thank you for our friends and family. We pray that you give us a good visit tonight with Annie and that you just guide us all in your purpose for our lives. Amen."

There was that word again.

I smile as Cannon attacks his pie with his plastic fork and Laurie and Ryan dive in with their own silverware.

"How is it?" I ask, picking up my fork.

Laurie's eyes are closed as she chews. "Oh. My. Gosh."

"Wow," Ryan says, already forking off another bite. "I can't believe that you guys made this. It tastes like it should be served in a restaurant."

I take a bite and it really is fantastic. We found some red and green bell peppers in Laurie's fridge and chopped those up with some onion, sautéed them for a few minutes and then tossed them into the mix with the chicken, tomatoes and green chilies and a can of pinto beans that we drained and rinsed. And I added a bunch of seasonings. It actually works.

"Forget accounting, Annie. You should become a chef."

I smile at her. "I wish I could. But I'm not sure I can actually make a living doing this."

"Quick, Ryan. Add on a line to the job description about being a personal chef for our family," Laurie says.

Ryan grins.

We finish eating, Ryan and Laurie disappear to get the kids in bed and I start cleaning the kitchen.

This feels so...normal.

It's weird to me that it feels so normal.

I mean, I haven't known these people that long.

Laurie comes back into the living room and immediately starts shaking her head at me. "Stop, stop, stop," she says. "You just cooked all of dinner. You do not need to clean it up too."

"Hey, you did dinner. I just helped."

"Please." Laurie takes the dish out of my hands and nods to the family room. "Go sit in the living room. Ryan will be right out. He just was aching to get out of his boots."

Ryan reappears bootless and childless and sits on the couch, stretching his hands up and yawning. "Oh man. I'm so ready to not have the commute. Or the upper management."

Laurie sits next to Ryan, I grab my notebook where all my questions are written down and sit in the overstuffed chair catty-corner from the couch.

"So," Laurie grins, scooting closer to her husband. "How is Zach?"

"Leave the poor girl alone," Ryan says, wrapping his arm around Laurie's legs as she snuggles up to his arm.

Laurie grins even wider.

I smile and shake my head. She makes me crazy but I really do like this couple. They are fun. And weird. And loud.

So very loud.

"Fire away, captain," Laurie says, saluting to me.

"Okay. First off, I'm not sure that we've actually clarified when this new job would start," I say, opening my notebook and clicking my pen.

"When is the earliest you could start?" Ryan asks me.

With my firm, I am usually contracted to be at the new job for six months and if it looks like it will take longer, the contract is renewed for another six months. So, technically, I was contracted to be here for six months but there's no way it's going to take me as long as they thought it would at the pace I'm keeping up. "I could probably start the first of January," I say. I see the joy in Laurie's eyes and I hold up both hands. "*If* I took the job. If, Laurie. Big if."

"Oh sure, I know."

"January works perfect," Ryan nods. "I am planning on officially launching the company in February, so it would be great if you could start before that to help me get the necessary paperwork done and hiring and all that fun stuff."

"Which leads me to my next question," I say. "Would I be the only other person working for you? Or will you hire a secretary as well? Because I noticed that a lot of the job description included items that typically a secretary would handle."

Ryan nods. "For now, you would be the only one. But the goal is that eventually, Laurie will take over the job as secretary."

"I'm sorry, what did you say?" Laurie says, her head whipping around to her husband.

"You said you would do it!" Ryan says.

"I said no such thing!"

"Sure you did! I remember it perfectly. I said, 'Well, I will need to get a secretary, want to apply?' And you said, 'Yeah, I'll be your secretary in between changing diapers.' And I said, 'You can do it when the boys get a little older.' And you said, 'Yeah sure.'"

"No, no," Laurie says, straightening and scooting away a few inches so she can see her husband better. "I remember this too. And I said, 'Yeah, sure,'" she says, her voice dripping in sarcasm. "I did not mean that I would actually be your secretary someday."

"How come?" Ryan says.

"Because, babe, surely you can see that it would just be like the worst thing ever for our marriage if we worked together."

"You worked with Hannah for a long time and you guys are still friends."

"But we aren't married. Ask her how much fun it was to be married to your boss." She looks at me. "Brandon owns the photography studio and met Hannah when he hired her to be the new secretary."

"Oh," I say.

Ryan shrugs. "I think it could work. And I think it would be fun to work with my favorite girl."

"You only say that because we haven't worked together. I don't want to stop being your favorite girl."

"Honey, if I can stick it out through two labors and

324

deliveries, a house remodel where you changed your mind nineteen times about which countertops you wanted, a singing Elvis-gram sent to my work on our anniversary and innumerable burned pancakes, surely I can stick it out through you answering the phones at our business."

Laurie just looks at him. "We can discuss this later," she says finally. She looks at me. "Back to you, Annie."

I have no idea what the answer is to my question. "So yes on the secretary job requirements then?" I ask slowly.

They both look at each other and just start laughing.

This couple is just weird.

Chapter **Nineteen**

Saturday morning, I wake to my alarm clock.

Purpose is calling my name and it's time to start today. I reach over, smash the snooze button and then immediately sit up, rubbing my crazy sleep-mangled hair and push myself off the bed.

If I don't make myself, I will never start changing.

Nick keeps talking about how life is too short to never make the first move of change.

Well, today we are making the first move.

I pull on a pair of workout leggings, my thick socks and running shoes and top it off with my fleece zip up jacket and a thick hat. I pull my hair into two braids that poke out the bottom of the hat all weird but at least they will be off my neck.

I open the door and an arctic blast gets me right in the face.

Maybe I don't want to walk.

Purpose, Annie. Today is going to be one of purpose.

I take a deep breath and step outside.

I do a few stretches on the landing right outside my door and then start on a fast walk to the same trail that Zach showed me last week.

While I walk, I pray.

Here's the thing: I have no idea what to do.

I left Ryan and Laurie's even more confused last night. Mostly because it sounds like the perfect job. I get to hang out with them all day, I know that Ryan's a hard worker so I won't have to be making any more ridiculous slideshows about wasting time and I think I could honestly help him get his business off the ground.

He's done a ton of research on benefits packages, salaries and he's even got a pretty good health insurance plan. And dental.

But, it would mean a big change. It would mean putting down roots and staying in one place and deciding that this was going to be my home, at least for the foreseeable future.

I've never stayed in one place for more than two years.

I've never *wanted* to stay in one place for more than two years.

So, now I have to decide. Do I want to stay here? Am I

willing to give up what I have right now?

And really, what do I have, Lord?

A good 401K, a fairly good chunk in my savings and an empty apartment. Up until I came here, I really didn't even have any friends who have stuck it out across the miles. Not that I know that the friends I've made here will, but there's something different about this group.

I sort of feel like once they get a hold of you, they don't let go.

I mean, I visited Hannah in the hospital after having a baby, for goodness' sakes. The woman still looked beautiful. And just handed me her child without even asking if I wanted to hold him.

I'd never held a baby so little, so brand new before.

And then there's Zach.

Unconsciously, my feet start moving faster.

What do I do about Zach, Lord?

All my life, I've thought about the day when I might potentially meet the guy who would be "The One". And then when the years kept going by and I kept moving around and I was often reminded of my parents' lack of happiness in marriage, I got less and less convinced that there was any "One" for me.

But Zach...

Zach is different.

I smile, thinking of some of his weird jokes and quick comebacks. Zach is one of the stranger people I've ever met, but he's also one of the most genuinely sold-out-for-Jesus men I've ever talked to. You can't talk to him for more than a few minutes without knowing exactly where he stands on things.

I like that.

I like him.

I huff my breath out as I walk faster and faster. I'm basically jogging now.

Where does that leave me with this decision?

My heart is pounding double time and I can't decide if it's because of the jog or the job offer or all this thinking about Zach.

I've never been in this place of vulnerability before.

Being in a relationship with someone is more than just eating dinners out at nice places, it's being real with them.

I'm not usually ever that real with anyone.

Lord, you know my past.

And really, He's pretty much the only one who knows it in

it's entirety.

I think about my dad. I don't know where he is right now, true, but the bigger thing is that I don't *want* to know where he is right now. In fact, I've gone to great lengths to make sure I don't find out where he is and that he doesn't find out my permanent address.

Which isn't hard when I've never really had a permanent address.

And then there's my mom. She never yelled or got physically violent like my dad, but the years of abuse had it's toll on our relationship as well. And now she has Randy and Randy's little kids to take care of and I always just felt like an outsider intruding on their perfect family when I would go visit after they got married. It's one of those things where she would always say, "You're welcome to come for Christmas," but her tone and the *way* she would say it had completely opposite implications.

Too little for too long and now, it was too late.

And it's not that I haven't forgiven my parents. I have no animosity towards them at all. We are beyond that, me and Jesus.

It's the after-effects that still get me, though.

Like, at one point, I assume my parents were happily

married. Or at least happily engaged. I saw their wedding album. They looked happy enough. They were knee-deep in the 1980s and Mom had bangs that probably prevented her from walking through some doorways, but they were happy. Or seemed happy.

So, then it becomes a question of *when*. When did things go south? When did Dad start the violent outbursts, when did he stop being able to control the anger? When did Mom start just putting up with it and turning a blind eye toward everything? Before my birth? After my birth?

And if could happen to them, what's to stop it from happening again to me?

Lord, I don't know what to do.

I've kept a wall around my heart so high for so long that I don't know how to get over it anymore.

I get back home forty-five minutes later and start some coffee brewing while I quickly go take a shower. I eat breakfast while reading my Bible and then blow dry my hair and hurriedly pull on a pair of skinny jeans, my Ugg boots and a long tunic-style shirt with a cardigan.

Zach had texted yesterday and asked if we could get lunch together today. I figured if nothing else, he could give me some good opinions on this job thing.

My doorbell rings at exactly eleven o'clock and I trip over to the door while trying to shove my earrings in my ears.

Zach is standing there grinning, holding a huge bouquet of flowers.

"Oh!" I say, completely shocked.

"Happy Saturday!" he says, handing me the flowers and grinning even wider, if that's even possible.

I take the flowers and stick my face right into them, inhaling. They are beautiful. Oranges, reds, whites. They look like fall in lily-form. Fall is my absolute favorite season.

Too bad Colorado thinks it's already winter.

"Wow, Zach. Thank you! You really didn't have to do this," I say, going into the kitchen.

I don't think I even have a vase.

I love flowers but it seems a little weird to buy them for yourself. Especially if you are never home to see them.

I find a big glass and fill it with water.

Zach follows me in and leans his arms on the high counter, watching me fill the glass. "I know I didn't have to, I wanted to." He grins. "Next time, though, I'll get you an actual vase to put them in."

I smile. "You don't have to do that."

"Will you stop with the have-tos? I want to. Let me do what I want to do."

"Sorry. You can do whatever you want."

"That's better." He smacks his hands on the countertop. "Let's go. I'm starving."

"Did you not eat breakfast?"

"Just a small breakfast."

"Lucky Charms?"

He grins. "No, I actually ate fairly healthy today."

"Why? Are you out of Lucky Charms?"

He laughs. "You know too much. Let's go. I really am hungry."

I set the flowers in their glass on the table. "Where are we going?"

"Get your coat. You'll see."

I pull my coat out of the closet, follow him outside and

lock my door behind us. It is frigid and the clouds are hanging low over the town today like someone did a sloppy job tacking some dryer lint from a load of grays and whites up in the sky.

"Holy cow, it's cold." It's even colder now than it was when I went on my walk.

"The forecast calls for snow tonight," Zach says all cheerfully.

"How can the temperature change so much so quickly?" I grouse, quickly pulling my coat on and buttoning it all the way up.

I wish I had opted for a coat that was more functional than cute several years ago when I bought this one. It's wool and it's warm but at the moment, I want a parka with one of those fur-lined hoods.

Or maybe a Michelin Man bodysuit.

Zach smiles at me. "You get used to it."

"How about the fact that it's suddenly so dry here that I can hear my skin crack every time I bend my fingers?"

He nods. "You get used to that too."

"I just don't believe it's possible."

"Doubting Thomas."

"Insufferable Enthusiast."

"Well, now that the name-calling is out of the way, maybe we can just relax and have a good time," Zach says opening the passenger door for me.

I grin.

He's got the car all warm and toasty inside and I rub my hands together in front of the vent, letting the hot air thaw them out a little bit. Zach smiles at me as he climbs in the car.

"Here, let me help," he says, reaching over and taking both of my hands in his. He cups them together inside his and then holds them up to the vent, trapping the heat in with his hands.

Four little lightning bugs jump into my stomach and start flickering around, making it super hard to focus on anything other than Zach's warm hands holding mine.

I quickly try to think of something else — anything else — that will take my mind off of this so maybe the blush that I can feel rising up from my toes won't quite make it to my cheeks. I'm not one of those women who is a pretty blusher where they only get slightly pink on the apples of their cheeks. I go from being sort of a sickly pale to a bright lobster red faster than most people can blink.

It would be impressive if it wasn't so frustrating.

Think of something else!

Peanut butter.

Nerf guns.

Overweight walruses with tooth decay.

I sneak a deep breath and look over at Zach and he's smiling at me. But it's not his typical grin, this is something sweeter, gentler.

"You are very beautiful," he says quietly.

Oh dear goodness. And here I thought the walrus idea was going to save me.

My cheeks flame in their classic Insta-Red setting.

Lovely.

Zach squeezes my hands once and then let's them go, pulling on his seatbelt and shifting the car into reverse. "So. How was it last night at the Palmers'?"

I'm very much appreciating the change of subject, though it still takes a good sixty-nine seconds for my brain to transition from his compliment to remembering last night since my immediate reaction to his question was to think *who are the Palmers?*

"It was good," I say finally.

"Just good?" Zach asks, glancing at me as he shifts into drive and makes his way through the parking lot.

I shrug. "I mean, yeah. We had a good time."

"I thought you went over there to discuss the potential new job."

"I did. We ate dinner first though."

"That's always interesting at Laurie's." He looks at me and shakes his head. "Laurie is possibly one of the nicest, funniest, weirdest people I've ever met and she's an excellent mom and seems to be a great wife, but good night, the woman can't cook to save her life."

"I wonder if she was always like that," I say. "Or if it's just a cause-and-effect thing happening with the two kids now."

"I don't know but I've had some of the most interesting dinners of my life at her house."

I grin. "Well, last night would have been no exception. We sort of made up a recipe for chicken enchilada pot pie."

"Now that sounds good."

I nod. "It actually was pretty tasty. Kind of a different combination, but it worked."

"I'm thinking that Chef Annie over here might have had more to do with that than Laurie suddenly finding her cooking thumb."

I grin. "A cooking thumb?"

"Sure, you know, like a green thumb?" He frowns at the windshield. "Or would it be called a gravy thumb?"

I laugh. "So where are we going for lunch?"

"Questions, questions. I'm sensing some doubt in my ability to pick a good restaurant."

"No doubt, just curiosity."

"Well, you will have to wait. I'm not giving any hints, either." He's obviously excited for whatever he has planned and it makes me smile.

He's sweet.

I try to glance all surreptitiously at him as we drive. He's wearing jeans and square-toed work boots, a white T-shirt under a flannel long-sleeved shirt and a thick brown coat with a hood. He obviously didn't shave this morning and he's got a light coating of brown whiskers all over his cheeks and chin. He looks rugged and handsome and like he belongs out here in the Colorado mountains.

And I guess he does.

He's driving in the direction out of town and I look at the clock. It's getting close to noon.

"Are we eating lunch in town?" I ask.

"Nosy, nosy, nosy. No trust at all. No, 'hey, Zach's a nice guy and I bet he's got a great lunch planned so I'm just going to sit back, relax and enjoy the beauty of God's creation while I don't have to drive.'"

I shake my head. "So sorry."

"Wait, what did you say?"

"Hey, Zach's a great guy and I bet he has a great lunch planned, so I'm just going to sit here and not drive."

"And enjoy God's creation."

"Right."

He grins. "Patience, oh impatient one."

"No wonder you wanted to leave right away if it's going to take several hours to get to our lunch spot."

"The problem is that you've only been exposed to the lunches offered in town," he says. "You need the full experience of this area of Colorado to make an informed decision on whether or not you are going to stay."

"Is there a restaurant all the way out here?"

"Patience," he sings.

I laugh.

We drive for another fifteen minutes outside of town and up into the mountains. Every so often, I can see a stream running through the thick, thick trees. My ears are popping as we go higher and higher in elevation.

Finally, he pulls off on this little dirt road I would have completely missed and we start bouncing along on the gravel. I've got one hand bracing myself on the ceiling, the other hand clutching the door and Zach is only going about fifteen miles an hour.

"WHERE ARE YOU TAKING ME?" I yell over the sound of the car shaking to bits and pieces as we drive down the road.

"PATIENCE!" he replies, grinning over at me and gripping the steering wheel with both hands.

Apparently, it's his plan to take me into the mountains and murder me. Which, when you think about it, is a much better plan than that little walking path by my apartment.

Way fewer witnesses.

I squeeze my eyes tight and just pray that we get wherever

he is taking me with enough car leftover to make it back home.

Finally, he pulls to a stop and I squint open my eyes and unpeel my hands off the ceiling and the door.

And gasp.

"Wow!"

"See? Wasn't it worth the patience?" Zach says, grinning at me.

We are almost at the top of the mountain very close to the town. I can see tons of hills, trees, valleys and the stream that I kept seeing through the trees has become a rushing river with short waterfalls all around us.

"Oh this is beautiful!"

"Great! Glad you liked it." Zach shifts into reverse.

"Wait, what are you — ?"

"Didn't you hear me saying I was starving earlier? There's no restaurant here." He backs up and I just sit there, open-mouthed.

"What?" I finally say.

He backs into a big circle and then stops and puts the car in park. "Okay. Now we are here."

Now we are just staring at the dirt road that led us here.

"Honestly, I liked the view better the other way," I tell him.

He grins, unclicks his seatbelt, hops out and comes around to my side of the car. He opens the door and the air is frigid. It's even more freezing cold than it was in town at my apartment.

"Surely we are not getting out," I say, wrapping my coat even more tightly around me and scooting farther into the car.

"Surely we are. Come on. Hop out. You won't be disappointed."

I sigh and climb out, if only to make him happy so we can leave and find someplace heated.

"Come, come," Zach says, waving me to the back of the car.

Zach drives an older Toyota 4Runner and we walk to the back of it in the freezing cold and he pops the back hatch.

"Oh!" I gasp as I look in the back cargo area.

He's piled blankets and pillows of all shapes and sizes in the back. Underneath everything is a huge, old quilt and there's a big cooler and a paper grocery sack off to the side.

"Welcome to Chez Zach," he grins. "I've got food, drinks and plates. Though, to be honest, I way underestimated how cold it was going to be up here."

I grin. "This is so great!" And romantic. Holy cow. I've never had anyone do anything like this for me before.

I don't even know what to say.

Zach is grinning all cutely and helps me up into the back of the car and then plops in the back himself. He hands me about four blankets and then points to a little white plastic box next to me. "That's a battery powered heater."

"No way."

"Yep. Fire it up." He opens the cooler and pulls out sub sandwiches, grapes, bottles of water and what looks like takeout dessert boxes from Merson's.

"Holy cow, Zach!"

"Do you like it?" Suddenly the cool, together, romantic Zach disappears and I see just this sweet, shy boy behind everything.

I smile. "It's perfect."

"You aren't too cold?"

I pile two blankets on my legs and feet that I have "crisscross applesauce" like my kindergarten teacher would have said. I wrap one blanket around my shoulders over my coat and lay the fourth one over my lap. Then I turn on the little heater and tuck it under the balnkets so it's blowing on my feet.

"Not at all," I say and I mean it. It's actually a little toasty under everything.

"Good." He hands me a sub sandwich and nods out to the incredible view. "So, this used to be my spot," he says.

"Your spot?"

"Yeah. You know, where you come just you by yourself. I used to drive out here and bring my Bible and my guitar and watch the sunset and pray."

"You don't do that anymore?"

He shrugs. "Every so often. I more came out here when I first moved to town and I was living with two other single guys at church. I didn't have a place at my house that I could really just get away from everyone, so I just started driving one day and found this place. And then I just kept coming back."

"That sounds nice." I'm eating my turkey on a wheat roll and wondering if I've ever had a spot like that in any of the cities I've ever lived in.

"There's really nothing like it," Zach says. "I need to come up here more often again. Especially once it starts snowing and everything just has this white, peaceful, perfectly still feeling." He smiles at me. "So. Let's finish our conversation."

I'm drawing a blank. "Which one?"

"The one about Ryan and Laurie and his job offer and the chicken enchilada pot pie. Which really does sound pretty good. You might have to make it again." He grins.

"I'll have to remember the recipe first," I say, smiling back at him. "It sort of came about as a rescue to a half chicken casserole, half chai cupcake mix that Laurie was unknowingly preparing."

Zach laughs. "Now that would have been interesting. Chicken stuffed cupcakes."

"With frosting."

"Gross."

"Yeah. It would have been really bad."

"So." Zach elbows me lightly. "Have you figured out what you are going to do about the job?"

I can tell he really wants me to have an answer.

I really want me to have an answer.

"No," I say, with a sigh.

He nods. "I'm sorry."

"It's hard. I mean, I don't want it to sound like I don't enjoy being here or anything," I say quickly so he doesn't get the wrong idea.

Though, honestly, I'm not sure what the right idea is.

Why is it so hard to figure this out?

Zach nods. "It's a big decision."

"It doesn't seem like it should be though."

"You mentioned that you moved around a lot when you were a kid though, right?" Zach says.

I nod. "All the time. I don't remember being in one place more than a couple of years."

"Wow. That takes a lot out of you."

Like the ability to stay put somewhere?

"Yeah," I say because I'm not sure what else to say. Zach opens the dessert boxes and I see some sort of caramel chocolate goodness pie that he brought from Merson's.

I'm sitting here, eating delicious sandwiches and about to have a fantastic dessert overlooking the most beautiful landscape with quite possibly the sweetest guy I've ever met and I *still* can't decide if I want to stay here.

What is wrong with me?

"You okay?" Zach asks, handing me a dessert box and a plastic fork.

"Yes." I sigh. "No. I don't know."

He nods to the dessert box in front of him. "Sounds like a good time for dessert then."

"What is this?"

"Shawn's Caramel Chocolate Pie-radise." He grins. "Rumor has it that he let Laurie name this one."

I laugh. "She's fun."

"She's crazy. I'm amazed she's not working you over right now trying to get you to stay."

"Oh," I say, shaking my head. "She's working me. She's been sending me a list of reasons of why this town is the best for the past two days."

Right before Zach came over, I got a text from her that just said *cheap mayonnaise.*

I think she might be reaching at this point.

Even so, I owe them a decision by this evening.

It could be a long afternoon.

"Can I use you as a sounding board?" I ask Zach.

"Go for it." He forks off a big bite of pie and just looks at me with a gentle, kind expression.

"So, here's my dilemma." I take a deep breath. "If I go, I will be incredibly sad to leave everyone I've gotten to know here. I know I haven't been here long but I already feel like I know more people here than I ever knew at any other place I've ever been."

"Laurie and the gang tend to be like that," Zach grins.

"But if I stay, then I'm worried that..." Oh, I wish I hadn't even started that sentence.

"Worried that what?" Zach asks. He looks at me and I quickly look out to the gorgeous mountains, gnawing on my bottom lip between my teeth.

Finally, I huff my breath out. "I'm worried that you guys might get to know me more."

"That's a bad thing?"

"It might be."

Zach shakes his head. "I know as a sounding board it's my job to not offer suggestions or advice, but trust me. It isn't. A bad thing, that is."

"You don't know that."

"I do know that. Do you love Jesus, Annie?"

I nod and tears prick the back of my eyes.

No, Annie, do not cry! No crying allowed!

"Then it isn't a bad thing." Zach shrugs. "I don't care what you did or what happened to you in the past. You belong to Jesus and He makes new creations every day."

He says it so matter-of-factly. Not pastorally, not over-the-top in a real deep spiritual voice, just normal. Like he was telling me that we were expecting snow this week.

I can't even look at him. I just look out at the scenery. "Mm-hmm," I finally hum since I can't really trust my voice.

He eats his dessert and I gather myself for a minute or two in silence.

"So," he says finally. "What else?"

"What else what?"

"What else are you thinking about as far as the job goes? And you've barely touched your pie. I'm beginning to doubt that caramel desserts are your favorite."

He remembered from our date at Merson's. I smile, touched.

I fork off a bit that is dripping in caramel and close my eyes as I eat it. "Holy cow," I mutter when I'm done chewing.

"Good, huh? That is a dessert that you can get nowhere

else." He grins unrepentantly and elbows me in the side again.

I laugh.

"So. Go on. What else are you thinking?"

I nod. "So, if I go, I'll be staying with the same company I've been with. I'll have the same benefits, same retirement plan, get to see more of the country." I shrug. "If I stay, I'll be taking a chance that Ryan's business won't succeed, that he won't be able to keep me on long term."

Zach nods. "Good points. I think I know Ryan fairly well though. He's not going to take this step unless he has a good ten year plan already in place."

"Which he does," I tell Ryan. "But it's just not as secure."

"True."

I take another couple of bites. Zach drains a bottle of water. He twists the cap back on and puts it in the paper grocery sack. "So. What do you *want* to do?" he says finally.

"Stop thinking about it."

"And done. Let's talk about something else."

I smile. "Like what?" It's hard to talk about something else when there's this huge looming thing in the car with us. The thing labeled *will Annie still be here in three months?*

"I don't know. What's the weirdest story that you've never told anyone about something that has happened at work?"

I laugh. "Okay. I have one for this. So I was at a huge office in San Antonio a few years back and there was this lady who worked there who was a little eccentric. Okay, really eccentric. Like she would show up to work with only one side of her hair done and tell me that she just got tired of curling, so she just stopped."

Zach grins. "Okay, that's funny."

"Well, one day she came in and she was all flustered and freaked out and told me that she could swear that something was living in her car because she felt something hit her skirt while she was driving. She wore these big, billowy skirts that always used to remind me of a story I heard as a kid of a midget who hid under some lady's skirt way back when and he actually murdered some other lady at this dance —"

"Wait, who was murdered?"

I wave a hand. "No one. Well, I mean, someone was but it wasn't part of my story. Not that this is my story." I sigh and drop my face into my hands and I hear Zach start laughing.

"Annie McKay?"

"Yeah?"

"You are a terrible storyteller."

I sigh but smile. "Thanks."

Chapter **Twenty**

I pick up my cell phone that night and unlock the screen, pushing the buttons to get to my contacts and pause, my finger hovering over the name.

Ryan Palmer.

I take a deep breath and push the button.

"Hey Annie," he answers after the second ring.

"Hi Ryan. How was your weekend?" I never know what to say to men in a non-business setting on the phone. Not that I call too many men for non-business purposes, but still. It always feels a little awkward.

"It was good so far, thanks. How about yours?"

"Good."

After lunch, we drove back down the mountain and Zach ended up staying for a little bit and we just talked about everything that didn't involve the job.

It was nice. He reached for my hand and squeezed it

353

lightly when he left and then completely without warning leaned down and kissed my cheek.

I blushed deeper than I've blushed in years. Maybe in my whole life. He grinned at me sweetly and then hurried down the porch steps.

Then I spent the rest of the day cleaning the apartment, trying to stop obsessing over the kiss, messing around in the kitchen and trying my hand at baking some sea salt caramel chocolate bars.

They actually turned out great.

The whole time, I just kept praying that verse that I couldn't remember the reference for but said, "Whatever you do, do your work heartily, as for the Lord rather than for men."

What do You want me to do, Lord?

"So, Annie, have you made up your mind about the job?" Ryan asks and I blink back to the conversation.

I take another deep breath. "Yes, I have." I pause and squeeze my eyes closed.

Jesus, please let this be the right decision!

"I'm saying no."

I can almost hear Ryan nodding. "Okay, Annie."

I have a feeling that Laurie is standing right beside him and he doesn't want to have her start flipping out while I'm on the phone with him.

"I'm really thankful and grateful for the opportunity, Ryan. You have to know that. Especially since you barely know me. It means a lot that you would offer it to me. But I just can't take it."

"That's fine, Annie."

Laurie is definitely standing right next to him.

"Thank you, though."

"You are welcome. I'll see you tomorrow at church."

"Bye Ryan."

"Talk to you soon, Annie." He hangs up and I click the end button and grip my both with both hands.

I always have a horrible sense of buyer's remorse after any major decision I make but for some weird reason, I don't have it today.

If anything, I just feel quiet.

Tonight is a good night to just eat a quiet dinner by myself, watch a TV show while eating my caramel bars and go to bed early.

I have all day tomorrow to hash over my decision.

I wake up on Sunday and I spend the first few minutes of being awake blinking at the ceiling.

Well, Lord, I did it.

I don't know why I did it, but I did it. I told Ryan no.

Somehow, I doubt I will be met with fanfare and balloons and happiness at church this morning.

Word spread quickly, though, because I got a text from Zach about eight last night.

Praying for you, Annie. I know that even though this job isn't the one for you, God has a great plan for your life. See you tomorrow.

He's just the nicest man.

I take a shower, pull on a pair of skinny jeans, tall brown boots, a long white shirt and a gray cardigan sweater. It's cold, cold, cold outside today and I inhale as I open my front door and I can definitely smell the unmistakable smell of incoming snow.

Looking at the sky, I'd bet we get some this afternoon or

tonight.

Well, that settles my evening plans. I'm staying home and watching *Frosty*. And eating more of those caramel bars. I swear. If I could make a living baking, I would do it in a heartbeat.

I get to church and I'm not three steps in the door before I hear her.

"Annie!"

Laurie is right beside me within seconds and puts her arms around my shoulders in a hug. "Oh, Annie, please tell me you aren't moving away!"

I hug her and pat her back. "I don't know, Laurie."

"When will you know? And I hope you know we were kidding about the personal chef being a part of the job. I really hope you didn't think we expected you to cook for us every day," Laurie says, pulling away and looking at me, her gray eyes big and serious.

I smile. "No, of course I knew you were kidding." I lift a shoulder. "I just never had any peace about the job, you know?"

"I know, I know." Laurie sighs. "I just thought it was going to work out perfect, you know? We need a finance guy, you're a finance girl. You need to stay in town for Zach and we had a way for you to do that."

I laugh. Ever the matchmaker. "You are funny, Laurie."

"I'm just being honest. He likes you, you know."

I nod. "I like him too."

"See? I knew you did!" She looks at me. "So why aren't you going to stay?"

"I never said I wasn't going to stay. I just can't be the finance person for Ryan."

She immediately perks up. "So you are going to stay?"

I laugh and give her a light hug. "Church is starting, Laurie."

"This isn't the end of our conversation," she threatens, walking toward the sanctuary with me.

"Oh, I know it."

We are led in music by Zach who smiles at me from the stage briefly in between songs. Pastor Louis is back today and he climbs the stage and sets his Bible on the pulpit, looking out at all of us under his gray eyebrows.

"Today, we are taking a break in our sermon series and I'm going to teach on Colossians 3:23."

I flip to the verse in my Bible and immediately just start

shaking my head.

"Whatever you do, do your work heartily, as for the Lord rather than for men."

Figures.

I sincerely hope that I am not the only person this happens to, but it never fails that when I'm in the middle of a huge decision, that very topic is discussed at church that week. It doesn't matter what city, county or state I'm in, it always happens.

I'm sitting next to Hallie and she lightly elbows me in the side. "You okay?" she whispers and I realize that I'm still sitting here shaking my head like a hula dancing doll in an off-roading Jeep.

"I'm fine," I whisper, stilling my head. "I'll tell you later."

"Okay."

Pastor Louis sets both hands on his Bible on the pulpit and looks out at everyone again. "Friends," he says. "We live in a society that has two attitudes about work. We either idolize it or we vilify it. Today, I want to offer to you that neither of those options are what the Apostle Paul is trying to get at here. This chapter is all about practical advice for households. Live in peace, be thankful, be respectful, children listen to your parents. And finally, he begins to speak to slaves and in our days, I believe we can apply this to the employee and boss relationship."

Pastor Louis talks for the next thirty minutes about that one verse and I'm now having trouble fitting in my notes in the margins of my Bible.

I should have sprung for the wide margin Bible.

"So, in closing, let me just say this. Work was made to glorify God and to provide for your family. Are you glorifying God with your work? Are you lazy or do you give your best at the office? Are you constantly thinking about work, constantly putting other things on hold for work, constantly missing out on what is happening in your home because you are working? Or are you creating healthy boundaries that allow you to work to the glory of God and serve your family to the glory of God?"

Pastor Louis stops and then looks at us again. "I often get asked whether or not you should enjoy your work. And here is my answer to them: Not necessarily. If you are single, you have no responsibilities toward a spouse or children, then I say yes, find a career that you love that you feel called to and work there with all your might as to the Lord. But if you are married and you have children and a spouse that need your provision, while I encourage you to find a career that you enjoy, at the end of the day, you need to provide. So if that means working somewhere that isn't your favorite thing to do, it doesn't matter. Work hard, work well, work unto the Lord. Let's pray."

He says "amen" and the church erupts with sounds of Bibles closing, people laughing and talking and contemporary Christian music starts playing in the background over the speakers.

Five pairs of eyes are suddenly on me and I can feel them boring into my back as I put my Bible down on top of my purse. I look up, wincing.

Laurie, Ryan, Hallie, Shawn and Zach are all standing there, looking at me.

"Hi," I say, standing as well because I feel very weird sitting with all of them looking down on me.

"Well." Hallie speaks first. "I think I can speak for everyone here. We all want to know what you are going to do now. Are you moving again?"

I sigh and shrug. "I don't know," I say, honestly.

"But you're for sure not taking the job with Ryan," Shawn says.

I nod. I look at Ryan and offer a sad smile. "I'm so sorry. It really is a great job and I feel a little ridiculous turning it down but it just doesn't…" I purse my lips. "It just doesn't feel right."

Ryan nods. "I'm fine with that, Annie. I really am."

"Well. How do you feel about recycling?" Laurie asks me, looking at her phone.

"Um. I mean, I don't know that I have any strong feelings one way or the other," I say slowly, a little confused on the change of subject. "I mean, I think recycling is probably a good thing…"

"Okay. I'd call that enthusiastic about recycling. Wouldn't you, Hallie?"

Hallie shrugs. "Well, I mean, she wasn't booing it or anything."

"See? Exactly. Great. Annie, I just found you a job at the local recycling plant. We apparently are in need of someone to run the media and marketing department and you're pretty good with Facebook, right?"

"I don't actually even have a Facebook page," I tell them.

"Well. You're a quick learner. Pay is good and the benefits look great. Oh wait, hang on." Laurie stops and scrolls her finger on her phone. "Hey, here's another want ad. What are your feelings about lawn furniture?"

Zach laughs a short, tight laugh. "Laurie, let her figure out her own future," he says. He smiles once at me, but it's the same quick, if somewhat distant smile that he gave me from the stage.

Oh boy.

"You wouldn't happen to have your plumber's license, would you?"

I smile. "Sorry. I let it lapse six months ago and just haven't had a chance to renew it."

Laurie nods. "That's okay, they are willing to hire someone in the process of getting their license."

"Laurie," I say.

"Or perhaps you are great at writing greeting cards."

"Laurie."

"Or there's a night nurse position at the hospital. I'm just speaking for myself here, but I honestly think you would look pretty adorable in scrubs — "

"Laurie!"

She looks up from her phone. "What?"

I sigh. "I'll find something. If I'm even looking." I still haven't decided.

There was an email in my inbox last night from Steve, the guy who is my real boss. He was talking about two new assignments that had come up and one was in Hawaii for a year.

I've never been to Hawaii. But I've always wanted to go.

Plus, it just seemed too weird that the day that I decide not to take Ryan's offer is the day I get the email about Hawaii.

Was it God's sign that I was supposed to go? Maybe that this little town with all these eclectic people wasn't supposed to be a big part of my future but just a small blip where I learned what it's like to have true friends and be a part of a group of people who honestly love each other?

I look at everyone and at their sad faces at the thought of me leaving and realize that for the first time in my life, I'm going to be missed if I go.

Missed.

I've never been missed before. I'm pretty sure that the people I left behind in Tampa threw a party when I finally moved here, thanks to all the layoffs I had to oversee.

It's a good and horrible feeling.

"Well," Laurie says finally and the group all start nodding their heads.

"I've got to get to the store," Shawn says. "Inventory and baking day."

"And it's officially naptime," Hallie says.

Laurie and Ryan both nod. "Naptime for our boys too," Ryan says. "Let's go pick them up."

"I need to clear the stage," Zach says.

And just like that, everyone scatters. Laurie looks at me as everyone takes off and then looks sadly over at Zach and sighs.

"Well. Are you at least going to come over to our house tonight?" Laurie asks. "Hannah and Brandon are bringing little Declan."

I smile. "I wouldn't miss it."

"Okay." She looks again at Zach and just shakes her head before walking out of the sanctuary.

I look over at him too as I get ready to leave but he's very focused on getting all of his guitars in their cases. A little too focused.

Maybe it's all for the best.

Especially if my future involves beach sunsets here pretty soon.

I nod to his back and head out the door. I stop by the

grocery store and pick up the necessities. Milk, bread, eggs, cheese. I'm pushing my cart past the breakfast meats when I decide that quiche sounds good for dinner this week, so I grab some bacon and go back for some spinach and onions.

Quiche is easy. And it gives me the excuse to make pie crust.

I love making pie crust. There's just something very satisfying about rolling the dough out and making something so buttery and delicious from such humble ingredients.

I get home, put the groceries away and then just sit down on my couch.

Well.

I have about four hours until I'm going to head to Laurie's. My apartment is clean, my lunch for tomorrow is already made and I'm considering making a batch of brownies if for no other reason than just for something to do. I'm all caught up on work and in my meeting with Mr. Phillips this week, I will give him my recommendations as to how they can cut costs and increase productivity.

Some of it involves a few layoffs. Most of it involves working when you are supposed to be working instead of taking random days off or random afternoons off or making long personal calls in the office.

Just amazing what people try to do at work these days.

I pick up my phone and click over to my messages.

Nothing new.

I've always heard it's poor form to text a guy before he initiates, but maybe it's okay if you've already had a short history together.

I take a deep breath, type it out quickly and hit send before I can chicken out.

Hey! What are you up to this afternoon? Want to hang out before Laurie's thing?

I stare at my phone waiting for a reply for like three whole minutes before I finally just set it down and go in the kitchen.

Time for brownies.

I pull out the flour, white sugar, brown sugar, cocoa powder, baking powder and salt and check my phone and he still hasn't responded.

No worries. He just might not be by his phone right now.

I melt a stick of butter, add some eggs and the dry ingredients and mix until everything is perfectly gooey and chocolately. I check my phone again and then decide that these brownies are just a little too boring so far.

So I mix up a quick caramel sauce on the stove, stirring as I check my phone.

Nothing.

I spread a thin layer of half the brownie batter on the bottom of a glass Pyrex pan, slide it into the oven and set the timer for ten minutes.

It might be time to acknowledge that Zach is likely ignoring my text.

I stick a spoon in the brownie batter and lick it off, trying to swallow back the tears that are pricking the back of my eyes.

I don't blame him at all. I really don't. It doesn't make sense to keep spending time with someone when the odds of them moving very far away in likely less than a month are so high.

It's fine. It's good, really. Now I can just focus on finishing up everything at the power company and stop getting distracted with walks in the woods and romantic picnics on the tops of mountains and a sweet kiss on the cheek from a very attractive man.

And really, it was just on the cheek. It's not like it was a real kiss. I mean, I've known people at different churches who kiss people on the cheek just in a friendly greeting.

It always seemed a little weird to me. And germy.

Even though, when I think about it, it's probably more germy to shake someone's hand than to kiss their cheek.

My hands are suddenly gross feeling.

I immediately go wash my hands with soap and lots of hot water. Sometimes it's better if you don't think too deeply about different cultural norms, I feel like.

The timer on the oven dings and I pull out the thin layer of brownie and then top it with the caramel sauce, throw a few chopped toasted pecans on there for good measure, and then spoon the rest of the brownie batter on top.

I'm a firm believer that caramel makes almost anything taste that much better.

I slide the brownies back in the oven and set the oven timer again. Then I hop up on the counter and grab the bowl and mixing spoon.

Might as well.

I hear the knock right as I'm licking the last bit of batter off the spoon. I squint at the clock. It's almost two.

I'm not expecting anyone. I still haven't heard from Zach.

I go to the door and open it.

Laurie is standing there in a black wool coat, brown Ugg boots and a very bright cranberry-colored knit hat and gloves. She's rubbing her gloves together, forehead creased in a frown.

"Hi," she says and comes inside, forcing me to open the door a little wider.

"Hey. Won't you come in?" I say, closing the door behind her.

"Funny." She stands in my living room and starts sniffing the air. "Brownies?"

"Yeah."

She sniffs some more. "With caramel?"

"Yeah, I added a layer in the middle. With pecans."

Her eyebrows go up. "Now that's a good idea. I bet it would be good served with vanilla bean ice cream with more of the caramel sauce and pecans on top."

I nod. "I was thinking chocolate sauce on top too."

"Great, great," she's nodding. Then she freezes. "No!" she shouts.

I jump. "What?" I gasp. "You don't like the chocolate

sauce idea?"

"No, I am not here to discuss dessert. Though, honestly, Annie, that sounds amazing. I hope you were planning on bringing it tonight."

I hadn't thought about it but I am now. "Sure," I nod. "Of course."

"No, Annie, I am here because we have a major catastrophe."

I'm tempted to salute her Major Catastrophe comment, but I keep my fingers knit tightly together. I think she would appreciate it on a normal day but she looks a little upset at the moment.

She's pacing my living room, boots stomping on my carpet, gloved hands wringing together.

"Are you okay, Laurie?"

"No! No, I am not okay."

"What happened?" I sit on my sofa and nod to the other side in an invitation to sit but she just nods back at me and keeps stomping around.

I watch her go back and forth, back and forth, mumbling under her breath the whole time. She's reminding me of this polar bear at the zoo in one of the cities I lived in who would just pace constantly until it was time for him to be fed. I questioned one of the zoo workers about it one day and they said he paced for several hours a day.

What a sad, exhausting life.

"Can I offer you something to drink?"

"Annie," Laurie says finally, stopping in the middle of the living room and just looking at me, gloved hands up. "This is serious."

"What is serious?"

She sighs. "You and Zach."

"Oh," I say, nodding. I suppose I could have guessed that was why she was here. "That."

"No, not just *that*. It's also about you. Look, I barely know you, but I've totally seen how much you've changed even in just the short time you've been here."

I frown and pull my legs up underneath me on the couch. "What do you mean?"

She rolls her eyes. "You have to admit you are different than you were when you got here. When I first met you, you could barely touch Corbin's little toe without obviously having a panic attack and now you're going over and picking him up without anyone even asking you to. You were so weirded out by coming over for dinners or people wanting to hang out with you and now, it's like just assumed that you are coming over every week."

I blink.

"And most of all," she says, her voice and gaze gentling. "You totally like Zach. Maybe more than just like." She smiles sweetly at me. "Don't you?"

I try to keep my face neutral as I pull my sleeves down over my hands. "Laurie."

"It's just a question, Annie. And it will totally stay between us, whatever your answer is."

I sigh. "Okay. Yes."

"Yes what?"

She's insufferable. "Yes, I like him."

She squints at me for a minute. "And you're willing to give that up?"

"Give what up?"

"This!" She waves a hand around. "This town, this group of friends, Zach, a potential marriage, babies, you name it!"

My mouth drops open. "Laurie! We are barely even

dating! Not even dating, we're just hanging out as friends! And yeah, I like him, but I think it's a little soon to begin planning the wedding."

"I'm not planning anything," Laurie protests.

I give her a look and she holds her hands up again.

"I promise," she insists. "Just because I think you would be a beautiful fall bride does not mean that you need to get married then."

I start laughing and cover my face with my hands. "Laurie!"

I can hear her giggling and I look up. She's grinning and pulling at her huge, knit hat.

It's really a very bright hat. I didn't even know cranberry could be in a hue that bright. There are yellow threads woven through it, which doesn't help with the ability to look at it without squinting.

"Is that so Ryan doesn't lose you in a crowd?" I ask her.

She rubs at it again. "Hey! This hat has character."

"Yes. Yes, it does." It takes a strong character just to wear something like that.

Laurie sits on the other end of the couch and takes a deep

breath. "Look. I just don't want you to miss the opportunity that you've been given here."

I look at her and then down at my socks, gathering my thoughts. "Laurie…About Zach…"

Right then the oven timer goes off.

Laurie follows me into the kitchen. "Yes? What about Zach?"

I put an oven mitt on and pull the pan out of the oven. The brownies smell amazing. I inhale next to the pan and then reach for a toothpick to check and make sure they are done. Laurie is leaning over my shoulder, watching me stab the brownies.

Small chocolate crumbs and soft swirls of caramel stick to the toothpick as I pull it out and I smile.

"Perfect."

"Holy cow, Annie, those look amazing. And they smell even better."

"Thanks," I nod. "Hopefully they taste good. I kind of just made up the recipe."

"You made those from scratch?"

There is pure, unadulterated admiration in Laurie's tone.

I smile. "It's not hard, Laurie. It's just flour, sugar, butter —

"

She stops me. "It does no good to tell me," she says. "The only thing I can cook really well is brownies from a box. I've even been known to add candy bars in the middle of them."

"That's a good idea."

She smiles proudly. "I've matched at least two couples using that method."

"What method?"

"The brownie method. It's a potent drug, all this chocolate mixed with some attraction."

I shake my head. "You need to find a new hobby, my friend."

She grins. "I had found some new hobbies before you came into town."

"Great."

"Seriously, Annie, I knew the second I saw you that you would be the perfect match for Zach."

I sigh and peel the oven mitt off. I might as well just hash this out so she'll leave me alone. "Why?" I ask her.

"Why what?"

"Why do you think we are the perfect match? And how in

the world could you tell that as soon as you met me?"

Laurie shrugs. "It's a gift. I've known every time. Well, except for once. Or maybe twice. But even then, those were more of a guess and not a real calling. I totally knew with Lexi and Nate, definitely knew with Ruby and Nick. And Brandon and Hannah and Shawn and Hallie were just too easy."

My brain is spinning. I lean back against the countertop. "You arranged everyone? The whole group?"

She shrugs. "We weren't really a group back then. In the beginning, it was just me and Brandon. Then Hannah came along. Then Ruby changed and I introduced her to Nick. Then..." she shrugs again. "I don't know, it just kind of happened."

I just blink at her.

She nods and pats my arm. "Don't worry, Annie. We'll figure this out. But in order to see if Zach has potential, you've got to stay here."

I finally shake my head slightly and straighten. "I don't know, Laurie. My boss just sent the next assignment."

"Where is it?"

"Hawaii."

She nods after a minute. "Okay. That's a good

assignment."

"Yeah."

"Have you ever been there?"

I shake my head. "No. I've always wanted to go though. It's one of the few states I've never been to. Have you?"

"No. But I've always wanted to go, too. Ryan and I try to squirrel away all the cash we get so that we can go to a resort there for a long vacation someday. Without the kids."

I smile. "You don't want them to experience Hawaii?"

"You don't call traveling with children a vacation."

"What do you call it?"

"I call it torture. Ryan just says it's like ten times harder than just staying home. So we stay home."

I grin.

Laurie sighs at the brownies and then looks at the clock on my microwave. "Okay. I need to go get stuff ready for tonight. And Corbin will probably be up from nap in a few minutes and ready to eat. But I just wanted to tell you to think about it."

"Okay." Then I frown, following her to the door. "Wait, think about what?"

She smiles at me. "See you in a few hours, Annie."

"Think about what, Laurie?"

She waves and disappears down the steps.

I close the door and shake my head.

Weird.

Chapter **Twenty-One**

I still have a few hours to kill before dinner at Laurie's house, so I sit down on the couch and turn the TV to the Hallmark channel. The brownies need to cool for a few more minutes before I put the frosting on them.

All brownies should be frosted. It's just a good rule to follow.

I'm figuring out the plot line of the movie that it's in the middle of, which doesn't take too long, when there's another knock at the door.

Ten bucks says it's Laurie back for another pep talk about why Zach is the one for me.

I open the door and Hannah is standing there, a blanket-covered baby car seat next to her feet.

"Hannah?" I ask, a little surprised. I didn't even know she was driving again since having little Declan, much less climbing my ridiculous steep and slippery stairs while holding the baby in his car seat.

I've picked one of those car seats up once since I moved to town. Even empty, those things weigh a ton.

"Come in, come in," I stutter, grabbing up the baby and getting both of them out of the cold, closing the door behind them. "What are you doing here?"

Hannah smiles at me and pulls her coat a little tighter around her. "Oh, Dex and I were just feeling the need for a little drive, so we just sort of found ourselves over here."

I pull the blanket off the car seat and the baby is sound asleep. He's so tiny, especially compared to all the other babies I've been around lately. His little cheeks are soft and sweet and his peach-fuzzed hair is just about the cutest thing I've ever seen.

I rub my finger on his head and then tuck the blanket back around him.

Hannah is watching my TV. "Oh, hey, I saw this one!" she says. "I didn't like the ending."

"She doesn't end up with the blond guy?"

"No. Isn't that weird? He was totally perfect for her."

"That is weird." We both just stare at the TV for a few

minutes and then I look back at her. "Do you want something to drink?"

She follows me into the kitchen and pauses at the brownies. "Wow, Annie, these look great!"

I'm really getting a déjà vu thing here.

"So. Hannah," I say, handing her a glass of water. "What are you really doing here?"

She looks at me and blinks innocently. "I told you, Annie. Declan and I decided to go on a little drive."

"I didn't know you were cleared to drive."

"Oh please. The doctor cleared me at the hospital. It's Brandon who has been having a cow every time I stand up."

"Well, you look great." I've never seen Hannah not pregnant so I'm a little shocked at how skinny the girl is compared to how gigantic she was before she had Declan.

"Thanks. I feel better every day. So. Are you coming to Laurie's tonight?" She asks it all offhandedly but I can tell she's not just making small talk.

"Planning on it." I narrow my eyes at her. "Why?"

"Oh, no reason. Just curious. We're all pretty upset that you didn't take the job with Ryan. I mean, Hawaii is pretty tempting though. I can see why you didn't take it. I've actually been to Hawaii though and I'll just say, it's not all the motivational posters make it out to be."

And apparently, Laurie has been in contact with Hannah.

I smile. "No?" I ask.

"Oh no. First off, there isn't really a waterfall or a lush rainforest type of place everywhere and there's only so many beaches. And most people live in a city and it feels a lot like every other city, actually. And I've only been to one luau but the pig they killed for it still had it's head on when they served it and he just stared at all of us while we ate him." She shivers. "It was hands down the closest thing that made me almost go vegan for the rest of my life."

"What made you stay carnivorous?"

"I still really like bacon."

I laugh. "Well, that would be a problem."

She smiles. "Anyway. Just research what living in Hawaii would really be like before you move. I just would hate for you to leave everyone and Zach and end up hating the islands."

I nod. "Will do. Thanks for the warning."

"No problem." She takes a drink of water and then looks

at the clock and then at her sleeping son. "Well. I'd better go. I need to get a few things done before we head over to Laurie's."

"Okay."

"See you tonight!" She hefts the baby seat up on her arm and leaves, pulling the door closed behind her.

Well. That was weird.

I pull out my little hand mixer, soften some butter in the microwave and then cream it with powdered sugar, a dash of milk, vanilla, a smidge of instant coffee and cocoa powder. I've heard of some people adding cinnamon and all sorts of other spices and flavors to it, but when it comes to frosting, the simpler the better in my opinion.

I'm beating the frosting when I hear another knock and it's sort of a miracle I hear it because my hand mixer is super loud.

I turn it off, go to the door and I know who it is before I even open it.

"Hallie. What a surprise," I say, rolling my eyes as I open the door for her to come in.

"Hey Annie," she smiles and her eyes squinch up all cute. "I was just in the neighborhood and thought I would stop by."

"Mm-hmm. You must be the Ghost of Christmas Future,

seeing as how you are the third one."

She ignores my comment. "Wow, it smells amazing in here!"

I've already got a glass of water ready for her when she comes into the kitchen. She takes it with another smile.

"So," she says, sipping her water. "How are you?"

"Feeling a little ambushed. How are you?"

She grins. "It's nice to be on this side of things for once. I hated being in your shoes."

I sigh. "You all could have at least spread out your visits a little farther apart."

"Nah. Laurie is all about the go big or go home mentality. I have this suspicion that the main reason why she is the youngest is because her parents had her and then realized there was no way they could ever handle another child after her."

I smile and return to beating my frosting. "So," I yell over the mixer. "What advice do you have for me?"

"What?"

"WHAT ADVICE—"

Hallie holds up her hands and motions to just wait to tell her. I finish beating the frosting, stick a spoon in it to test it and then hand another spoonful of frosting to Hallie.

"Oh wow. Thanks!" She licks it and closes her eyes. "Oh, friend, this is so good!"

"Thanks."

"No, I mean, seriously." She looks at me, green eyes serious. "This is beyond good. Like, I'm married to a professional chef who spends a lot of time making desserts and I've never tasted frosting this good. What did you put in it?"

I shrug. "Frosting ingredients?"

"Wow." She squints at me. "Are you bringing these brownies tonight?"

"That was Laurie's request, yes."

"Great." She nods, a thoughtful look on her face. "Well. Thanks for letting me stop by. I guess I'd better head out. I've got to do a couple of things before heading over to Laurie's in a bit."

I look at her as I go get a pastry knife out of one of my kitchen drawers. "Wait, that's it?"

"What's it?"

"No bashing on Hawaii? No threats about me blowing my chance for romance and future babies? No giving me a guilt trip about turning Ryan's job offer down?"

Hallie grins. "Nope. I'm good. I'll see you tonight, Annie. Be sure to bring those brownies. I'm excited to try the final product."

She waves and lets herself out.

I look at my frosting, look at the TV where the heroine is now kissing the dark-haired guy who I didn't like as much out of the two choices while snow falls and "Sleigh Bells" plays in the background, look at the front door and finally at my kitchen sink where three water glasses have been carefully set.

Lord. If this is what care feels like, I'm not sure I'm ready for it.

I still haven't heard from Zach by the time I'm buttoning up my coat and pulling on my boots over my thickest pair of socks. According to the weather guy on the news just now, a big storm is heading our way and the temperatures are going to fall fifteen degrees in the next two hours.

I would stay home but I'm scared that everyone would just come relocate here and I have nothing for the kids to do at my house other than watch what are likely inappropriate for toddlers

Christmas movies on TV.

I smash a trapper-style hat on my head that I last wore when I lived in Wyoming, pull on my super thick mittens and look at myself in the mirror before I go to get the brownies.

I look like I'm hoping to play a part as an extra in *The Day After Tomorrow*. My hair pokes out from under my ear flaps and I can barely grip the brownies with my monstrous gloves.

But I will be warm.

Hopefully.

I open the door and an arctic blast blows straight through my coat, straight through my gloves, straight through my hat and takes my breath and all my resolve to go to this party with it.

"Nope, nope, nope," I say, slamming the door shut. You do not move from a two year stint in Tampa to the North Pole without needing some adjustment period and I have definitely not adjusted.

Then I look at my clean living room, my toy-less house and my kitchen table that seats four and pull my hat down lower on my head.

They would seriously all come here. I know them too well to think they wouldn't. Especially with how many times I was asked this afternoon if I was coming tonight.

I take a deep breath, shut my eyes and open the door again, willing my feet to step onto the balcony and making my arm pull the door closed behind me. I am shivering uncontrollably by the time I reach my car.

I am moving to Hawaii. No questions.

I crank the heater all the way up, turn on my seat warmer and huddle in my car like a parka-covered blob until it finally heats up enough for my hands to work the gear shift. I can barely grip it with my gloves but there is no way I'm taking them off.

I drive the couple of miles to Laurie's house and I am just finally warm when I get to her house and have to face going outdoors again. It's almost dark out now and the windows in Laurie's house are all lit up and welcoming in the midst of the cold, dark atmosphere that has fallen over this whole town.

I gather my purse, the brownies and the plastic tubs of extra caramel sauce and toasted pecans in my arms before I shove open the door and run for the house, mashing the key ring to lock the car as I jump onto Laurie's front porch and hurry through her front door. I slam the door shut behind me and shiver on their front mat.

"Chilly?" Brandon asks, grinning. He's walking past, holding a Coke can in one hand and his newborn son in the other. I can tell he hasn't been at work recently too – he's sporting quite the five o'clock shadow.

As a general rule, I'm not a big fan of beards, but Brandon actually looks halfway decent with some facial hair.

"We aren't eating outside tonight, right?" I gasp.

"Sure. Ryan's got the kerosene heater all cranked up and Laurie's dragged out some hot coals and filled up some of those rubbery bottles with hot water and I'm kidding, Annie, stop hyperventilating."

I realize I am close to breaking the Pyrex dish with my bare hands, the idea makes me so tense.

Brandon grins wider. "You should wait until January. Then you'll know what cold is. This is just a little pre-Thanksgiving snap."

"Brandon!" Laurie hurries over and quickly hip checks Brandon out of the way. "Annie! How wonderful to see you. Don't believe anything that Brandon says ever but especially with how it relates to the weather. Okay? Okay. Oh, those brownies just look wonderful. And I bet I have some ice cream to go with them." She forces me to let go of the pan and plastic tubs and hurries me into the kitchen and away from Brandon who is just shaking his head, a smirk on his bearded face.

"Come in, come in. Of course we are not eating outside. It is way too cold. And it really doesn't get that much colder here than it is right now. Those are some heavy duty mittens, Annie. Do you want to leave them on or take them off?"

Laurie doesn't stop chattering until I'm in the kitchen, plopped on a barstool and staring at a big mug of hot apple cider with a cinnamon stick poking out of the top.

"There's cranberry juice in it too," Laurie says, proudly. "See? I can kind of cook."

"Is it really cooking if it's something to drink?" Hannah asks from the barstool next to me. She's stirring her cider with the cinnamon stick.

Laurie shrugs. "Sure."

My skin is finally warming up but I keep my gloves, hat and coat on because I can still feel the chill deep in my bones. Maybe I'm getting old.

There's a merry thought.

"So, Annie. How was your afternoon?" Laurie asks,

leaning against her kitchen counter, holding her own mug of cider.

"Crowded," I say but I smile.

She grins. "Well, that's weird."

Hallie comes into the kitchen then bringing the cold and a bundled up daughter with her. "Zach just got here too," she says, shivering. "Holy cow. I cannot remember the last time it was this cold outside!"

"You're talking to the person who just moved from Tampa," I say.

"Oh that's right," Laurie says. "Man. No wonder you look like an Eskimo."

"Who looks like an Eskimo?" Zach asks, walking into the kitchen. He's wearing dark, straight jeans, a cranberry, white and blue colored flannel shirt under a navy blue puffer vest and his heavy work boots. And he's got a fair sprinkling of whiskers over his chin as well that I did not notice at church.

Maybe these guys take part in No Shave November.

For someone who doesn't really like beards, it's a long month.

Zach actually looks cute with the whiskers, though.

He never wrote me back today. I cup my cider mug with

both gloved hands and sneak a deep breath. My heart is suddenly pounding like I've just been in a Black Friday shopping stampede and despite my bones still being cold, my hands are instantly sweating.

Great.

Now I don't know if it's because I actually really like Zach or if I've somehow contracted some strain of the flu.

I knew I shouldn't have ignored all those "GET YOUR FLU VACCINE HERE" signs all over town.

"Annie does," Laurie says and I am totally lost because I can't remember anything about what we were just talking about.

I look up and Zach is smiling a sweet, warm smile at me that is nothing like the distant, quick ones he was giving me at church. "You do sort of look like an Eskimo," he says.

Oh yes. Eskimo. That's right.

I am having a hard time looking away from Zach's blue eyes that look even more blue with that vest on and his whiskered chin.

Why have I never liked facial hair? It's the most adorable thing ever.

"Hey." Zach sits on the barstool on the other side of me

and his eyes are crinkling in the corners with his smile. "Hey, sorry I never wrote you back today. I actually didn't get your text until about twenty minutes before I came here, so I just decided to apologize in person."

I shrug like I hadn't been waiting for him to write back all day and had since decided he hated me and never wanted to see me again. "Oh, no worries," I say off-handedly.

"What did you end up doing this afternoon?" he asks.

I finally look away back to my cider and somehow, we are the only people in the kitchen.

I straighten and then look at him and then around. "Hey. Where is everyone?"

He looks around as well and grins. "I feel like she's lost some subtlety over the years."

I shake my head.

He looks at me like he's waiting for me to answer and I jump. "Oh! This afternoon? Oh. Not much. I made brownies."

He grins. "What kind this time?"

"Caramel turtle."

He nods, eyebrows raised. "Sounds amazing."

"They look pretty good anyway. What did you do today?"

He immediately looks away and stands, going to the stove and putting his face over the cider, inhaling. "What is this? Why is it pinkish? Did she cut herself making this drink somehow?"

"It's cider. With cranberry juice apparently."

"Is it good?"

I take a sip. "It's different."

"Does that mean no?"

"It means I'm not sure this is actually cranberry juice."

He makes a face, rubbing his chin. "And I will be passing on the cider."

I grin.

"Nice hat, by the way."

"Thanks." I would take it off because I'm finally warm but now I'm worried that I have major hat hair. One of the things I like least about being a woman and having longer hair.

He's never actually answered my question, so now I'm even more curious. "So what did you do this afternoon?" I ask again, trying to sound all casual about it.

Zach leans back against Laurie's sink and looks at me, shoving his fingers into the front pockets on his jeans. "I just went for a drive."

"Zach. It's like the setting for a sled dog movie out there."

He laughs. "It's not that bad. There isn't even any snow yet!" He shakes his head. "Former Floridian."

"Hey. I liked going to the beach on Christmas."

"That's just weird."

I concede and pull my hat off, doing my best to finger comb my hair to at least halfway decent. "So where did you drive to?"

"Just up the mountain."

"Again?"

He shrugs and looks away from me. "I had some thinking and praying to do."

I'm getting the feeling that he doesn't want to talk about it anymore so it ends up being good timing that Laurie nonchalantly walks back in, followed by Ryan, who is holding baby Corbin. "Want some cider, honey?"

Ryan peers into the pot on the stove. "Mm. I'm good. You didn't cut yourself, did you?"

I cover my grin with my glove. Zach and Ryan are apparently on the same page.

"I put cranberry juice in it."

"For what purpose?" Ryan asks, making a face.

"To be festive, weirdo. It's the flavor of the holiday season."

"Says who?"

"Says everyone."

"I don't say it."

"Well, what flavor would you say?"

"I don't know. Turkey."

"Turkey?" Laurie gags. "I can't make turkey flavored cider. That would be disgusting. It would be like drinking gravy."

"I like gravy. I like it better than cranberry."

"Actually, I don't think this is cranberry juice," I say.

Laurie frowns. "The bottle said cranberry."

I take another small sip. "Maybe it was mixed with something else?"

"I don't know. I just saw the word *cranberry* and thought, 'hey, that's a festive flavor.'"

I grin.

All of a sudden, the kitchen is full of people and kids are running everywhere. I'm not sure where everyone was, but here they are. Laurie is shouting orders for everyone to grab paper plates and line up for the barbecue that she's pulling out of the oven.

Somehow, everyone gets their food despite all the chaos. Sooner rather than later, all the kids are seated at a little kids table in the kitchen and all the adults are crammed around the dining room table and on the sofas, balancing plates heaping with barbecue sandwiches, potato salad, some sort of pinto bean thing and coleslaw.

It's a very summertime meal for a freezing winter day.

But it tastes amazing. Everyone is laughing and visiting and chowing down. I'm sitting at the table in between Zach and Hallie and I look over at Laurie, who is holding Corbin in one arm and attempting to eat her sandwich with her other hand.

"This is great, Laurie!"

"Thanks. It's an old family recipe," she says, pulling her drink away from Corbin who has suddenly morphed from a baby who just laid there and didn't do anything to one who is grabbing for everything in reach.

"See? You can cook just fine."

"Sure can. I can cook up a phone and order from Smith Valley Barbecue faster than most people can even decide what they want for dinner." She grins.

I smile and shake my head.

Hallie nudges me. "Did you bring the brownies?"

I nod. "Yeah. I think Laurie got ice cream for them too."

"Shawn," Hallie says, excitedly. "She brought the brownies I was telling you about!"

"Brownies?" Zach perks up from beside me.

Everyone looks like they are pretty much done, so I go back into the kitchen and bring the pan of brownies to the table, along with the caramel sauce and the pecans. Laurie hands Corbin off to Ryan and then comes into the dining room with the container of ice cream and some paper bowls.

"So. What is this?" Shawn asks, peering over at the Pyrex dish.

"Just some brownies."

"That she made from *scratch*." Laurie says this like I grew the wheat and ground it to flour myself before making it into brownies.

I cut the brownies into squares and start dishing them into bowls. Long ribbons of caramel trail the squares from the pan to the bowl and Laurie starts scooping ice cream for the top. Then I drizzle more caramel over the ice cream and sprinkle the pecans over everything.

It seriously looks like it should be in some sort of county fair for the best sundae award.

We pass out the bowls and everyone stops talking and just makes chewing and *mm*-ing sounds as they eat.

Shawn takes a bite, chews and frowns at me. "What's in this?"

"Flour, baking powder, salt—"

"No, no," he interrupts. "I mean, is this a recipe you have?"

I shrug. "I mean, it's just ratios."

"You made these without a recipe?" He licks his spoon. "What did you put in the icing?"

I tell him the ingredients and he just shakes his head but doesn't say anything else.

Zach is scraping his bowl. "Holy cow, Annie. Those were hands down the best brownies I've ever had. No offense, Shawn."

"None taken." Shawn is looking at me in this weird mix of a thoughtful smile and a frown.

Hannah and Brandon make the move to leave first,

putting the kids in about forty layers of coats and blankets before attempting to trek to their house down the street. Hallie and Shawn leave soon after, Shawn still has that same expression on his face every time he looks over at me. Finally, right as he's pulling a thick snow hat on and walking for the door, he turns back and looks at me.

"Can I give you a call later tonight or tomorrow?" he asks me, pausing by the door.

"Uh. Sure," I say, pulling my own hat back on.

"Great. Talk to you soon." He leaves and even though he slips through the door as quickly as possible, he still lets in a huge blast of ice-covered air that smells just like snow.

Well, great. I bite my lip. Now I'm worried that he's going to be all hurt that I made brownies and brought them to the dinner when he's clearly the king of desserts in this group.

I pull my gloves on and rub my cheek. *Oh boy.* Way to not think about someone else's feelings.

Laurie comes running back in the house from outside, wrapping her coat around herself and shivering uncontrollably. "I'm... not... walking... anyone... else... out..." she says through chattering teeth.

I grin and give her a hug. "Thanks for dinner, Laurie."

She hugs me back. "Have a good night, Annie."

I wave at Zach, who is getting his coat on as well and head outside into what is probably the same temperatures as set was during the filming of *Eight Below*. I run for my car, dive into the driver's seat, slam the door and turn the key in the ignition.

Nothing.

I frown and turn the key again. Still nothing.

I take the key out, make sure I'm putting the right one in there since my hands are shaking like crazy, and try again.

It doesn't even have the courtesy to even try and turn over. There isn't even a click.

Oh no.

I've never had car trouble before. I'm a single girl constantly living in new cities. I buy a brand new car with a full warranty and roadside assistance every two years because I can afford to and my car breaking down on me in the middle of a deserted parking garage with a chainsaw murderer roaming the building is like number three on my list of Things I Am Completely Terrified Of.

So, I take necessary precautions.

What the heck is going on?

I try again and again and again and I'm pretty sure I'm wearing the ignition lock out before I hear a tap on my window and I jump about eighty feet since I'm now envisioning a chainsaw murderer at every window.

It's Zach.

I open my door.

"Car trouble?" he asks, frowning. He's stamping his feet, trying to stay warm.

"It won't do anything," I say and I show him how I'm trying.

He nods to the car. "Pop the hood, I'll look at it."

I pop the hood and climb out of the car, following him to the front of it.

"Hey!" Laurie yells from the porch. "What's going on?"

"Annie's car won't start! I'm going to take a look under the hood!"

I can barely hear Laurie mumbling something from the porch. Then she yells, "This is crazy! It's like ten degrees out here! And dark! Zach, just take her home and I'll get someone to look at it in the morning when it's a little warmer!"

Zach looks at me and then back at Laurie. "There's a ninety percent chance of snow!"

"So?"

"So won't she need her car?"

"I don't know about Annie, but I hate driving in snow," Laurie yells.

Zach looks at me again and I hold up my hands. "Tampa," is all I say.

He grins.

"I'll just see if it's something easily fixed," Zach says and pulls his phone out, turning on the flashlight app.

We are both shivering like crazy and I hear Laurie's frustrated *humph*. "Look, seriously! Zach! Just take her home and I'll have Ryan look at it tomorrow! If it snows, he's not even going into work, he could drive her car over for her."

Zach looks at me. "What do you want to do?"

By this point, I am so cold that I don't even care anymore. "Get warm," I say, teeth chattering.

He sighs and turns off the flashlight, pocketing his phone. "I'll take you home," he says, nodding to his car.

"Are you taking her?" Laurie yells from the porch.

"Yes, Laurie!" He unlocks his car and ushers me into the passenger seat. I wave at Laurie through the windshield.

"Good! Have a good night, guys!" She turns and runs for her front door. And I swear I see a self-satisfied smirk on her face by the light from inside her house as she closes the door behind herself.

I narrow my eyes.

Wait a minute.

Zach climbs in the driver's side and starts the car, turning the dial for the heater as far hot as it will go before looking over at me. "What?" he asks as I squint out the windshield.

"You don't think..." I start and stop.

He shrugs. "I mean, occasionally I don't. I try to think before I do most things though just because it makes it easier to remember what I was going to try to do. But yeah, sometimes I don't think. Sometimes it's good to take a break from thinking."

I laugh. "No, I mean, Laurie."

"Laurie doesn't think?"

"Laurie thinks too much."

He nods. "I won't argue with that."

"You don't think..."

"Didn't we already cover this?"

"You don't think that she maybe did something to my car, do you?" I finish my thought.

It sounds awful saying it out loud especially since the woman just fed me a very nice and likely expensive dinner. "Oh goodness, I didn't mean that the way it sounded." I'm waving my hands, looking at Zach apologetically, worried that he now thinks I'm the most ungrateful person on the planet.

He's now staring out the window, eyes narrowed.

"Hey..." he says slowly.

"Right? Am I just being overly paranoid now?"

He looks over at me again. "I mean, she was awfully insistent that I just take you home."

"She even stood outside to tell us that. This is like prime weather for Elsa and no one else."

"Who is Elsa?"

I wave a hand because there's really no use explaining an animated kid's Disney movie to a single man in his thirties.

Zach shrugs and shifts into reverse. "Well. If she did do something to your car, she is sneaky. I'll give her that."

We ride in silence for a few minutes and then I finally sigh and look over at him. "I'm so sorry, Zach."

"Sorry about what?"

"You having to take me home. In this awful weather."

"It's just cold, Annie. It's not like we're running from a tornado or a blizzard or anything."

Right as he says the word *blizzard*, I see the first snowflake I've seen in years.

"Hey!" I yell.

Zach laughs. "And maybe I stand corrected."

By the time we get to my apartment, it's coming down steadily. Thick, fluffy white snowflakes float peacefully down from the heavens like they are being gently shaken over the earth.

I love soft snow like this.

Zach parks in a space near my apartment and we both just sit there, not making any move to take off our seatbelts.

"Wow," I say looking out the windshield. "It's so beautiful!"

"It really is."

I watch the snow gather on the sidewalk and blink. "Zach!" I yell and he jumps.

"What?"

"You need to go! You're going to be driving on black ice! You can hit a patch of that and before you even know it, you could be crashed on the side of the road. Dead."

He laughs. "You worry too much. And I doubt the roads are cold enough for that yet. *And* you forget that I've lived here for years. I know how to drive in snow."

"Still. You need to go." I undo my seatbelt and grab my purse and the pans from the brownies and caramel sauce that had basically been licked clean.

Zach grins and turns the car off.

"What are you doing?"

"Walking you to your door."

"Zach, didn't you hear me? Black ice? Imminent death?"

"Well, luckily, along with teaching me how to drive in the snow, my parents also taught me to be a gentleman. If there is black ice all around, it would not be very gentlemanly for me to let you slip all over it and fall, would it?"

"Zach, I'm fine."

"You can hit a patch of that and before you even know it, you could whack your head. Dead."

He grins at his mimic of my warning and I shake my head.

"No really."

"You no really. I'm walking you to your apartment and that's the end of this discussion."

"Fine."

"Fine."

I climb out of his car with a huff. It's not even so much that I'm worried about the black ice but now I'm completely alone with Zach and there's still just this weird thing between us.

The snow falls softly from the sky and sticks to my coat, my gloves, my eyelashes. I stomp through the parking lot to the sidewalk and Zach pulls his navy blue hat over his ears. "Be careful," he says.

"These boots are supposed to be one hundred percent guaranteed against slipping in the snow," I tell him.

"Oh yeah?"

"Yeah. I saw them on one of those QVC channels one time when I was living in California."

"Wait, you bought your snow boots off a home shopping channel?"

"One hundred percent guarantee against slipping in the snow," I nod, clomping up the metal stairs to my apartment.

Zach is right behind me as I take the last few steps to the landing by my front door. "I don't see how they can guarantee that."

"Maybe the workmanship is so great that they—"

I'm screaming before I fully know what's happening as my feet slip out from under me. Zach catches me under my arms right before my butt hits the landing.

He bends at the waist laughing as he holds me in the air.

"Stop laughing."

"I can't," he gasps. "That was like the best timing ever."

"I'm never buying boots on QVC again."

He laughs even harder and helps me up, turning me around and brushing the snow off my coat and hat.

The snow is falling softly, the only lights are the street lights and the occasional strand or two of Christmas lights that people already have up on their porches and Zach's hands still on my shoulders as his eyes meet mine.

I can't catch my breath.

He bends down and gently kisses my cheek, his whiskers lightly tickling my face, his hands cupping my cheeks now.

"Annie?" he whispers. "Please don't go."

And just like that, he's gone, stomping down the steps and waving before disappearing into the parking lot.

I just stand there, snow continuing to stick all over me, staring at my front door, my hands still full of the pans. My heart is beating uncontrollably in my chest like I need to lay off the caffeine or something.

I balance everything in one hand, pull my glove off, reach for my keys in my purse and unlock my front door, hurrying inside and closing the door behind me, being careful to stay on the tile entry so I don't drip melting snow all over my carpet.

What just happened?

Lord, seriously. I need some guidance here. What am I supposed to do?

My phone is vibrating in my purse and I pull it out while setting the pans down, shaking, though I'm not sure if it's from the cold or the kiss, tucking the phone between my cheek and my shoulder and blow on my hands.

"Hello?"

"Annie? It's Shawn. I want to talk to you about those brownies."

"Shawn, listen, I'm so sorry. I was definitely not trying to encroach on your territory as the dessert guy and I promise that I'll never — "

"Annie," Shawn interrupts. "I'd like to offer you a job."

THE END

Look for the continuing story of Annie, Zach and the Lauren Holbrook gang in Bake Me A Match, *coming Summer 2015!*